The Boogeyman's Intern

The Boogeyman's Intern

Matt Betts

Published by Raw Dog Screaming Press
Bowie, MD

First Edition

Cover Image: Brad Sharp
Book Design: Kevin Kusisto

Printed in the United States of America

ISBN: 978-1-947879-04-1

Library of Congress Control Number: 2018901172

www.RawDogScreaming.com

For Mackenzie and my boys, again and again and again

1

I watched him run.

Sydney leapt over the log across the path and, after stumbling a little on the other side, kept on scurrying. His footfalls echoed through the forest as he crunched dry leaves underfoot with each step. The old blue windbreaker flapped noisily behind him like a parachute. Usually, he left it at the edge of the woods where his mother couldn't see, but today he wore it as he ran. If he dropped it out here in the woods, he'd never find it again. The sound of it rustling made it even easier for me to follow him off the trail as he slowed a bit. His footfalls became more ginger, more tentative as he moved deeper among the trees.

After a pause, he looked around and broke for a trio of pine trees that formed a triangle. I'm sure it looked like as good a spot as any to duck into. Breath coughed out of him and he dropped to his knees to crawl beneath the branches. He flinched as the needles dug into his hands but he kept going.

In the center of the trees, he looked around and smiled. There was no way to see the rest of the woods from inside the natural fort the trees made, and there certainly was no way to see in. It was a better hiding place than he'd first thought. He lay on his back, closed his eyes, and tried to catch his breath. When that failed, he covered his mouth to keep his wheezing from being heard.

I settled in for a moment on the branches above him and waited for him to get comfortable. The boy needed his moment of triumph. Before I took it away from him. I stayed perfectly still on a branch directly above him, though he couldn't see me. I wanted to laugh, but that would ruin the moment. Of course, I got to enjoy these moments every time I played a game with him, so what difference would losing one of them make to me?

"You suck at this game."

Sydney had only rested a minute or two when he heard my voice from above him. I could see him flinch, could see the look of disappointment cloud his face. He'd run his hardest from the start–beat feet for all he was worth, but he couldn't lose me. He never really understood how all this works. Sometimes you can outrun the bullies and the teachers, occasionally you can even get away from the neighbor's dog, but you can't hide from your own imagination. It stays with you like nothing else.

He opened his eyes and saw nothing at first. The trees had formed a ceiling to the woods that blotted out the sky, keeping the sunlight from illuminating the area. The forest was so thick, so dark, that there was no way he could see me immediately.

"Why do you like this game so much?" I asked. "You never win. You never get better at it and no one else but me will play with you."

He looked around, waiting for his eyes to adjust and hoping to catch a glimpse of me. "You cheat. You don't play fair."

"Play fair? I play the way you play. If that isn't fair, tough." Cheating was always his excuse when I won. I even tried to let him have a few just so I wouldn't have to hear him call me a cheater every time. But it was hard. So. Very. Hard. I knew him as well as he knew himself.

"Come on. Let's try it again." Sydney sat up, still scanning the trees. "This time I'll leave my jacket somewhere so you don't hear me so good."

The branches didn't even bend as I touched them, one to the other, making my way downward to the boy. He could see me easily at that point, surprised at how obvious I seemed. "I don't really feel like playing your games anymore. You change the rules too often and never admit when you've lost." I could only put up with so much of the annoying little trials he put me through, the stupid games, the fantasy army scenarios.

I climbed down the last few branches and dropped to the ground soundlessly, close to him.

"You *have* to do what I say. Let's go." He turned and started to push through the pine branches.

"No." I folded my arms and stood my ground. "I'm your friend, not your employee. You don't own me."

"Now!"

Some days you hate your job and some days you loathe it. I was beyond that. "How about we play my way?" I leaned close and pushed him a little. He turned around and glared at me. "What? You don't like it when someone pushes you around for a change?"

He pulled a branch out of his way. "Stop it."

I pushed him again, harder. It felt good. "Come on, let's stay here and have some fun."

"Stop; why are you doing that? Help me get out of here."

I looked around at the clearing, the bed of pine needles covering the ground, the canopy of branches. "I like it here. Let's just hang out."

"It's too dark." His jacket got stuck on a branch, and he worked to free himself. "Besides, it's late. I have to get home."

"Oh, you wuss. You just said you wanted to play." That stupid jacket. If he'd just left it up by the porch or something, he would've had a much better time of it.

"Help me get this. My mom'll kill me if I mess it up." A prickly branch had worked into the pocket and gotten twisted, making the extraction difficult while he was still wearing it. I could see dark sap on the back already.

I don't know why the jacket was suddenly such a fixation for me, but it was. "Here, let me help you with that." I reached out and focused to make myself tangible enough to affect his clothing. It wasn't something we did often, but I had learned how some time ago and was good at it.

I yanked the jacket hard, jerking him in the process.

"Hey!" he said.

I yanked again and heard a brief tear. I smiled. That sound, oh that sound. It was a millisecond long, but it was glorious.

"Oh no, stop."

The next yank changed the jacket from a solid blue to blue flecked with white as it tore again, and I could suddenly see the light-colored inside lining. This tear was longer and even more satisfying, so I did a little more and more, the whole time, the boy protesting about how his mom was going to kill him. I pulled and tore and ripped until the boy had two one-armed jackets instead of one good one. I smiled and nodded my head. "That was great! Let's do *that* again. Screw hide and seek."

Sydney was nearly crying as he looked at the two parts of his jacket, one in each of my hands. "Oh, no. I'm dead when Dad gets home." He reached out to grab them, and I pushed one in his hand and clutched the other to my chest. I'd put up with a lot of crap; it was time I had a trophy.

"Tell them it was like that when they gave it to you," I said.

His mouth was open wide as tears ran down his cheeks. "I can't tell them that." He looked down at the scrap of cloth in his hands.

"Fine. Tell them I did it. They always buy that excuse, don't they?" If I had only done all the things he blamed on me. Actually, I'd only done some of them.

"But…"

I turned on him then, the excitement of ripping something real still in my system. "Shut up." It was a calm statement, calmer than I meant it to be. "Just shut your pie hole for once."

Something he read in my voice or saw on my face made Sydney afraid, and his eyebrows raised. He stared at me for a moment before he dropped to his knees and turned to crawl under the low hanging pine branches. He scrambled as fast as he could, hands deep in the needles. I let him go a half a minute before going after him. I didn't get on my knees, though. I just waded into the branches, still partially solid, but oblivious to their points.

"Still want to play hide and seek, kid?" I asked. He didn't answer. I could see him in front of me and reached down for him. As I did, my legs became heavy. It seemed each step was harder and harder to make.

They'd caught me.

I tried to keep going, but it wasn't happening. My legs were like concrete. Very quickly, I couldn't go on. With my last step, the sleeve dropped from my hand as the fingers became too hard to move. I dropped face first like a toppled statue and came to rest face down in the needles. I could see the boy stand up and run from my vantage point, but could say nothing, do nothing to stop him.

After a moment my body felt warm, and in the darkness of the pine tree shadows I started to melt.

2

"What were you thinking?" A voice came from out of the darkness. "You are so screwed."

I tried to lift my hand, but I wasn't solid enough yet. It was too dark to see, but I could feel the familiar sticky liquid of a return tube surrounding me.

"Didn't you think the Director would notice? You've been on his list forever-ish."

I tried to reply, but no dice; the vocal chords weren't formed yet. So I waited for the whole process to be over and for someone to crank open the door. Once I was solid, I could open it myself—there was a handle on the inside—but the goons liked to open it first for dramatic effect, just to show me who's in charge. I was beginning to see the smooth gray surface of the tube a little better. My eyes were adjusting slowly, and I found I was able to groan, which was a big deal, suddenly. A small triumph.

"That was a career implosion of epic magnitude."

I was just beginning to get a tingling sensation back in my fingers when the door flew open. Two especially large goons from Personnel stood there, grinning. Both reached in and took hold, yanking me from the tube.

I caught a brief glimpse of someone large and hairy holding the door for them before I was hauled off into the humid room beyond. "Epic magnitude," he said. He reached into my shirt pocket and pulled out my assignment card. I heard him clip it to his board as he disappeared through a nearby door.

Each of the goons held an arm and a leg of mine as they carried me away. I tried to clear my mental fog enough to think of some feasible explanation I could give for my behavior, but I drew a blank.

They carried me with effortless enthusiasm down dirty corridors, up dank metal stairs, and along still more halls. When I finally managed to muster the strength to lift my head, I immediately wished I hadn't. The gigantic oak doors of the Director's office loomed ahead, and my face was on a collision course with them. I was sure the goons from Personnel were going to use me as a battering ram if the doors didn't open, so I closed my eyes to brace for the impact. Maybe one of them strong-armed it open, or perhaps there was someone on the other side that pulled it, but no part of my body made contact with them and that was a brief highlight to my day.

Light from the hallway made a yellow stripe down the middle of the room but didn't quite make it to the other side. A thin layer of water coated the floor, and the light danced in the ripples the goons made as they walked. The water appeared to get deeper as we continued into the room. When we stopped, it was high enough to cover their toes. I hung in their hands without even the strength to move my head enough to look around. From my vantage point there was nothing to see but my own reflection in the dark water below.

A red light blinked on from the other side of the room and irradiated my image on the water. I eased my head up to find its source. My eyes adjusted slowly to the severity of a lone light from the dark corner. Though it took a minute to be sure, it was hard to mistake the massive outline of the Director sitting next to the bare bulb.

The Director was the original Boogeyman. For the longest time he was it, the only one of his kind. He alone kept the youth of the world on the straight and narrow with frequent terrifying visits. Parents were speaking of him when they told their kids, "*The Boogeyman will get you if you don't watch out.*" And the children listened with proper respect.

The guards carrying me gave my body a rough heave and I was airborne in the darkness. Though I was a little upset at unexpectedly drifting through the air, and apprehensive about my impending landing, I had to admit it was one heck of a toss. It was no wonder the Personnel department had consistently placed first in the javelin toss at the Hill's annual track and field day. Had I not been paralyzed and concerned about my imminent landing, I might have complimented them on their athleticism.

Luckily, I didn't land face-first. I sort of belly-flopped, with my entire body hitting the floor flat. The inertia from their throw, combined with the wet smooth surface, made me slide when I landed. My arms and legs were still numb and couldn't slow me down as I coasted across the wide expanse of the office. Much as I hated to, I had to ride it out until something stopped me. Luckily, the office was big and gave me plenty of room to slow down. It was a mere bump into the Director's chair with my forehead that brought me to a halt, rather than a great crash.

The oversize doors I nearly opened with my face slammed closed, and my heart sunk lower knowing I was alone with him. Hard to imagine I could feel lower than being paralyzed on the floor of the boss's office, but all-time lows are meant to be topped, apparently. I was so disoriented and exhausted that I couldn't look up at him. Maybe if I didn't look up at him this whole situation would go away, like when a child covers his eyes and the whole wide world goes away until he uncovers them.

I'd had trouble with the Director before. The first time, he was mildly upset with me. We talked about the problem in a Council room, and he gave me pointers; no big deal. The second time, he was wildly upset, but we still had a constructive conversation over drinks. This time was not turning out so pleasant. He wasn't known to be a forgiving or understanding person to work for, and I wasn't endearing myself to his better nature. I was a special case, though I was sure that even special cases only got so many chances. Stern warnings were in short supply with the Director.

Minutes passed, and I began to believe that maybe my 'ignore him and he'll go away' ploy had actually worked.

The sudden hiss of air rushing into his mouth startled me. He held it a moment and then slowly let it out again. A rustling followed, and I felt myself rising up, though not through my own power.

As I moved higher in the air I could finally see the Director's dark and wrinkled head. He lifted me off the ground effortlessly with his massive right hand and held me within inches of his face. I could see the thick bags under his bloodshot eyes. At this meeting, he matched the descriptions I heard whispered from those who had yet to meet him. I used to laugh at the beastly attributes given him–after all, I had met him and he was nothing like the raging beast everyone else described—but this time was different. This time I understood what they meant.

"Why do you make me use the dramatic lighting? I hate it. It's not flattering for anyone, you know?" he mumbled. "But if I don't use the dramatic red lighting, everyone thinks I'm going soft. One time. One time, I used the crimson bulb, now I have to use it every time."

I tried to talk but only managed to push air through my mouth, which made little bubbles rise to the surface of the water, like a motor boat.

"Save it. Your excuses are pitiful. You've failed," he said, his voice filling the massive room and reverberating back. "Again."

"It wasn't my fault." My weak response was muffled by bubbles as well. It was not the answer he was looking for.

"I'm sorry, did you say it wasn't your fault?" he asked.

"Yes sir." Maybe it wasn't wise to celebrate my mouth's freedom of movement.

"By all means then, tell me. Tell me how your inability to do the simplest job we have is somehow not your fault—" His voice echoed off the walls. "I'd love to hear it."

"I—"

"Go on, how is it you can't simply be an Imaginary Friend to a little dumbass?"

I didn't have an answer. Sydney was my fourth Otherworld I.F. assignment, and I'd gradually grown tired of them. It was all about the kid, and I had no input. Kid wanted me to be short with purple hair, I was his short, purple-haired puppet. No sense of personal style, no allotting for taste. Freeze tag? I was the one frozen. Mud pies, bug smashing? That's my job. I had managed to hold it together though, until this new kid. Selfish little brat that he was, I thought I could teach him something. Fat chance.

He took a deep breath and reached down to grab me. With a meaty fist, he pulled me close to his face. "You can't explain, can you?" His breath was a mixture of onions and dirt. He looked me over and nodded. "I get it, though. I see it all the time. You're burnt out. Happens to the best of them."

I hyperventilated just a little. I was sure there would be a pummeling or serious pounding of some sort; such was the Director's reputation. If he was going to stay calm, things would be great.

"You lasted longer than most. This is what? Your fourth or fifth assignment? They usually melt down after number two. You beat the odds," he said. "Those tykes can be brutal."

He knew it was my fourth. He never forgot a number like that. I could feel more movement returning to my body and suppressed the urge to try to correct him. As good as things sounded, they could always go bad in a hurry. Still, it was always a thrill when I got back home and could feel my body coming back to the form I was meant to be.

"This is it for you. You have to find something else to do. Find a new job that you can be comfortable with, or I'll find one for you. You have a day to choose, or I'll choose for you. Got it?"

I nodded, though I didn't see the urgency. Before I realized I was no longer just thinking things, my mouth was moving and sounds were coming out. "I need to decide my future that quickly? Can't I try a few things out and see what I'm good at?" I should stop talking. "I've been at this other thing for quite a while. My skills might be rusty." My throat went dry.

"We don't have time for you to see what fits. Choose, before I move you to animal division. Find something to make yourself productive, shadow someone, learn something. You think being an Imaginary Friend is rough? Try doing it as a cat or a possum," he said. "Some sad little kid, can't get a real pet, has to dream one up? It's horrible work. Depressing as all get-out." He sighed and leaned back. "Better yet, maybe I'll even bust you to Elf division, give you some pointy shoes and have your ass making toys and singing with the fat man." He smiled. "We'll move you, forget you ever worked over here and start all over with a competent subject in your place. You understand?"

Believe me, I can say with all honesty, it would be better to be wished out of existence than have to see that belly constantly shaking like a bowlful of jelly. It's disturbing. And more than a little disgusting, considering his rumored fondness for strategy meetings in the sauna.

"Yes sir." I couldn't muster the strength to retreat graciously from him, and I'm sure he wouldn't have let go if I did.

"Good," he said. With that, it was the Director's turn to fling me, and he did so with gusto. I landed on my back and again slid across the gleaming floor, this time toward the back corner of the room. Here, where the water was deepest, was the Director's personal transporting pool. Commoners like me used the public tubes down in the Personnel Department because we weren't allowed to have our own, but it made no difference. The feelings would be the same, the process would be the same, and there was nothing I could do about it. Here, though, we had the added humiliation of having the water swirl around in a clockwise fashion, reminiscent of a whirlpool. Or a toilet. I shut my eyes and waited for the ride to end.

I didn't know when I stopped sliding. My forward motion was replaced by the cyclonic whirling and the calm sensation of floating in the warm water. I could still see the dim reflection of the red light bobbing on the water nearby, but there was no sign of the Director. It felt like the water was lightly massaging my muscles and I knew the next phase of the process was beginning. The sensation of thousands of miniscule bubbles rising to caress my back, legs and arms gradually grew more intense and vigorous. My limbs grew lighter and thinner. I looked at my arms in time to see them melt away, disintegrate in the water, as though they had become liquid themselves. Small black patches of what were my limbs drifted away from my body like little oil slicks on the ocean, each piece getting further from the rest as it went in circles toward the bottom. Piece by piece, my entire body followed suit, and all I could do was close my eyes and wait for the darkness to come over me.

In time, it did. It always did.

3

I solidified for the second time in as many hours. This time, though, I got to stay in the chamber and relax as the process ran its full course. It was like a nice hot bath that drew all the tension out bit by bit. The bubbles were always a nice touch at the end–all smooth as they ran up the back, into the crevices. The murky water started draining, and I sighed; another crappy workday was over with. Through the little porthole I could see light from the outer room. That light was blocked intermittently as someone walked or paced close to my return chamber. As the water passed my ankles, a large hairy face blotted out the glow. The thing looking in at me smiled and gave me an enthusiastic nod.

Once the water was all gone, the door hissed for a few seconds, and the thing outside stepped away long enough to pull the door open. I took a deep breath of the warm air in the room, felt it settle in my chest, and exhaled the stale taste in my mouth from the Director's chambers. The thing holding the door began talking before the last of the air was out of my mouth.

"Hey! Remember me? I was the one that told you that you were so screwed? I was right, right?" He twirled a strand of the long dark hair that covered his body and smiled. "They told me you were busted before they brought you back." His smile exposed brown teeth as thick as big toes.

"Yeah, thanks for the heads-up on that. I had no idea I was boned until you mentioned it." Despite the relaxing tube trip, I had a headache that was going from bad to catastrophic in a hurry. "You're a Bigfoot? Or do you prefer Sasquatch?"

He looked down at me and nodded. "Bigfoot's fine; thanks for asking. Most people just assume." He put out one of his long arms to me. "Name's Brady."

I tried to shake his hand, but mine was lost in the shaggy limb the instant I stuck it out. His paw was easily three times larger than mine, and everything up to my elbow disappeared. "I'm Abe," I said.

"I know." He held up a clipboard that had been hidden by the fur in his other hand. "I know all about you." He continued to shake my arm. "Everything. It is *all* right here."

His eyes lit up a little too much at that, and I started pulling on my arm a bit in hopes of extricating it. "Great, Brady. That's great. I really need to move it along. You know how those tube trips can take it out of you." I put my free hand to my head to suggest I wasn't feeling well.

He pumped the hand one last time and let it go. "Yeah, but I need to talk to you about your career choices. These jobs go quick, and I'd hate for you to get stuck with something crappy because I let you go."

Bigfoot wanted to be my career counselor. *Happy day.*

I walked toward the nearest exit. "Yeah. About the whole career thing, maybe we can pick that up in the morning?" I could hear his bare feet slapping against the floor as he followed me. "Say we meet at Happenstance, first thing? I'll get the first round of whatever?" I stepped out of the chamber and into the hall, looking for a door that went outside.

"Really? That sounds like so much fun, but…but I don't know if I'm supposed to take your file out of the office. That's not..."

I turned and looked at him questioningly. "Is there something I could sign that would absolve you of any responsibility? Do you have a pen or something? I'll sign whatever."

He stopped walking and looked down at the folder. "They don't give me pens. I just read the charts and stuff. I'm not supposed to mark on them."

"And that's okay with you?"

"Sure." He shrugged. "What would I write on them anyway?"

I had no idea. It must've been nice to have no responsibility other than reading things and talking. I wondered if his job was available. "I don't know, Brady. But you should have the option."

I found a small wooden door around the next corner and pushed it open. It led outside to a main path. Brady grabbed me by the shoulder as I stepped out. "Where are you going? You haven't checked out yet. You need to check out with the front desk before you leave."

It was protocol. "I really need to go." I grabbed at my head again to demonstrate my pain.

"But you checked in. You can't check in and not check out. That would ruin the whole system."

I patted him on the arm and he released me slowly. "That would be something you could write on my chart, isn't it?"

His eyes narrowed. "But…"

"Hey, you check out for me, okay? That'd be a big help. You probably have to return the clipboard anyway, right?" I quickly stepped outside and made my way across the grass to the path. I looked back and saw Brady staring out the glass of the door. When he saw me look, he held up the clipboard again. I shrugged and kept going.

The wide trail let away from the secluded Personnel building toward our little patchwork town.

The average Imaginary didn't have the slightest creative ability whatsoever. Only the three special entities on the Council could make something new here. Even when they made something, it was an imitation of another thing they'd seen on the Otherworld. This affected a myriad of elements, not the least of which was the environment we lived in. There were old stone buildings with thatched roofs on one street, and stone abodes with turrets and towers that resembled things right out of medieval times. Some of the structures were a little more modern–two-story buildings with bricks and slate roofs. There were even several larger buildings that were used as apartments placed at the far end of Loathing Avenue. Our Personnel offices looked almost like a factory: high windows and a brick exterior with black smokestacks reaching into the mists above. The castle was always an impressive sight at the far west end of the Hill, with a drawbridge, moat, courtyard, and guard towers. If something on the Otherworld caught a council member's fancy, you could be sure some imitation of it would end up here.

The town hadn't changed in some time, no new structures to speak of. There haven't been that many new Imaginaries, so there's no need for more living space. If it ever arose, though, I wondered if they would try a skyscraper sometime, or if that would be too much of a culture shock for all the Imaginaries that had become so set in their ways.

It was the middle of the Hill that drew my attention. Dead center, in a wide courtyard with a rolling green lawn and shrubs planted along the walkway, stood a tall white brick lighthouse with a white brick sidewalk encircling it. Its light slowly turned around and around. The beam illuminated one small section of the Hill at a time. No one I knew had ever been inside the lighthouse or knew of anyone who had. In fact, there was no door. Just another useless facsimile of another world.

I've heard stories about how radically the mountaintop had changed over the years. It started out as a couple of grand castles and that was pretty much it. Back then this place was called Asgard or Mount Olympus, depending on who you asked. It was the home of the Gods, every one of them from the Greeks to the Incas. As new societies developed, new deities and other Imaginaries emerged with new homes and new ideas.

Eventually, as the popularity of some of the many Gods waned, the castles and temples merged into the one giant fortress on the edge of town. The Imaginaries woke up one morning to find that much of their world had disappeared and was replaced with an amalgam that was something much more impressive, and somehow much less representative of the individual. Each group of Gods got one area of the castle to themselves, with several common areas in which to gather. No one complained very long or hard about losing their accommodations; most believed that as they fell out of favor with the people of the Otherworld, they wouldn't need the space. They believed they would simply disappear as their followers did. They learned the same lesson I did. They were not going anywhere. Somehow, there was always someone on the Otherworld left to keep them alive in their memory.

It was around the time of this major consolidation of abodes that a new concept was introduced: recycling. Not paper or plastic like on the Otherworld; here it was Imaginaries being retasked–moved into new roles and new uses. The readiness of the Gods to give up and accept their decline was noted by the Council. They saw these once-mighty beings reduced to lounging around and wanted to do something about it. So, they started reassigning Imaginaries to new duties, introduced a rotation for some jobs. On their authority and power, fewer new Imaginaries were created while more were just shifted around. If a little girl in Sheboygan decided she wanted an imaginary elephant, the Norse God of the forest or some such crap was moved into the role instead of making a whole new entity. There was even a job-sharing thing going on with some positions. This all happened before my time, of course, but I heard it was tricky for them at first and they're still working out the kinks.

A funny thing happened with the program, though. The whole reason they started it was out of pity; they wanted to give the Gods something to do. Once the Council worked it all out and presented it, few of the deities wanted to participate. It was beneath them, they said. The common response went like this: *The former ruler of the sea, return to the Otherworld to play hopscotch with the wee runts of the human race? And wearing a face that appeared as whatever that child wanted? Never!* The Council was not pleased. They got a better response from the general populace. There were abundantly more regular working stiffs on the Hill than there were Gods. There were Imaginary Friends who wanted to go back and do it again because they enjoyed it, but some transferred elsewhere just to break up the monotony. Rejecting the program created some bad blood between the Gods and the Council, but that was ancient history. Still, as far as I know, no God has been offered a transfer since.

I wanted to drink. The path I was walking soon turned into a sidewalk, and that sidewalk would take me directly to my favorite watering hole on all of the Hill.

Truth be told, we technically had no actual use for places like this. None of us had to eat. None of us had to drink. None of us even had to breathe. We were Imaginary. We couldn't die without the wish of those who created us, so why would we worry about all of these messy and boring bodily habits? Simple: we saw the people on that other place doing them and we imitated them. The imitation became a habit; others saw the imitation, and the practice spread. Eventually it became a social thing. Very civilized.

4

From blocks away, I saw the multicolored flashes of neon bathing the street from the sign over the bar's entrance. The steam generators gave a minimal amount of power to the Hill. Lights could be flicked on with the ease of a switch in our apartments, dining halls and bars. But this sign was the only giant electrified advertisement on the Hill. The other establishments had colorful little signs in their windows, or plain wooden ones hanging out front. I guess it was favoritism; the owners knew someone important somewhere down the line.

While the Hill had power to make signs and lights work, it had no phones like the Otherworld. I envied the ease with which those people communicated. I mentioned it a few times to my fellow Imaginaries, and they scoffed at my laziness. *Why use some contraption when you can just walk a bit and see anyone you want?* There were, in some instances within a structure, tubes that formed a sort of intercom system whereby people could talk, but nothing community-wide.

As usual, there were people milling around out front, either lingering as they left, or preparing to go in. At one time or another, the ten-foot-high flashing letters had tempted everyone on the Hill. Red letters spelling out 'T-H-E.' Blue-green 'W' and 'E' next to a flickering yellow 'T' that was supposed be fixed decades ago, all over alternating white, green and blue "D-R-E-A-M."

Ah, the Wet Dream.

It was the answer to every working thing's problems. Camaraderie, libation and a place to hide out for a little while. If there was a crazier place on the Hill, the Otherworld or anywhere in between, I hadn't found it. It was easy to forget your troubles there because you could easily find someone who had it worse than you. Have a bad day at work? There's a God over there who used to be adored by millions and now only has a plaque drilled in stone where his followers used to pray to him. He's got it rough.

At the doorway, my heart sank just a little. There was a table on the left-hand side where someone appeared to be checking IDs. This struck me as strange because technically, no one here is underage, and we had no laws regulating drinking.

Things became clearer when I saw who it was working the door; Thor, Norse God of storms, thunder and the like. Thor was a problem case on the Hill because he was one of those who had trouble adapting to the slow crawl of time. He was bitter, selfish and a bore. Thor had an envy problem. Someone probably guessed that giving him a menial job was a good step toward getting him out of their hair. Maybe my career counselor.

It may have worked for that bureaucrat, but it sucked for everyone else.

"Greetings, Abe, my friend. It is glorious to see you on this fine evening!" Thor said in his usual booming baritone. He had the sort of voice that caused people to stop and turn towards him even if the Norse God wasn't talking to them.

He wore the leather apron and thick leather gloves of a blacksmith, and I wondered if he'd just come from making horse shoes somewhere. His long red hair was receding slightly, and I immediately realized why he always wore the helmet around town. Thick black goggles were pulled up onto his forehead, which only drew my attention to his retreating hair. "Hey. Thor." I had little inclination for small talk with him. "Good to see you too. I've got to talk to Zane, have you seen him?" I didn't *need* to talk to Zane, but I really didn't need to get stuck yapping with Thor all night either.

"I've not seen him in days."

"Oh well, I guess I'll just wait for him at the bar." I broke towards the other side of the room.

"Hold it a moment, Abe," he said. "I must check thine identification."

"Thor, you know it's me."

"Aye."

"You know anyone on the Hill can drink anything they want."

"Aye."

"Then why do you really need identification?"

"'Tis my job, friend. No one passes without ID," he said, looking down at the table in front of him. A crudely fashioned sign confirmed it. *PLEASE HAVE ID READY*, it said.

"Who's going to sneak in, Thor? Hmmm? No one gets on the Hill unless they're an Imaginary," I said. "So who's going to sneak past you?"

"Did you see any television ads while you were on the Otherworld?" he asked.

"Huh?"

His hair fell forward, almost concealing his face entirely. His hard-set square jaw and pursed lips managed to peek out. "The new TV ads, are there any new cars or anything?" he said, still looking down.

Exactly what I'd tried to avoid. I braced myself for what was coming. "Yes, *Thor*, I've seen some of the latest television commercials," I said. "And no, they haven't come out with a Ford *Thor* yet." I had to be firm or he'd never stop asking me. "No, *Thor*, there is no recently discovered planet *Thor*." My voice rose a little. "Or an element that they've just named *Thor*ellium. And they still haven't named a *Thor* space shuttle."

"It's not fair," he said. "I mean, they named all of those planets after other Gods, Hercules got a comic book, a huge plane AND a bunch of cool movies, and all I got was a comic book and a couple of big rocks somewhere in Africa or something."

Thor's Scandinavian accent tended to fade as he got mad.

"Plus," he said, looking up and tilting his head to the side.

Here it comes, I thought, knowing what he was going to say.

"Look at Mercury. Why does he get all of the glory?" he asked. "He had an entire line of cars named after him, a planet, and some kind of liquid stuff that gets put into every thermometer in the world!"

Fucking Mercury. Always bitching about Mercury. "Well, not any more. I think they replaced that stuff with some other junk now," I said. "And I don't think they make Mercury cars anymore. That's something, right?"

"Still. He has that sweet deal with the flower people," he said, his right arm raised with a fist. "They use his picture and everything. They even used Merlin Olsen in their commercials!"

"Yes, Thor, I know. The FTD people are bastards, but I'm pretty sure Hermes is the guy in the FTD seal."

"No matter. All I ask is for proper recognition. When does Thor get his due?"

"I don't know, man. I really need to go," I said. "I'll talk to you later."

"Hold!" he said as he grabbed my arm.

"Thine hand doth need stamped," he said, rolling something in ink. Taking my hand, he pressed the stamp to it. "There. Enjoy your evening, friend."

"Yeah. Thanks," I said. The fresh ink formed a lightning bolt on my wrist. "Chin up, man. It is a pretty good comic book about you. And they're making movies with that character now." I think he smiled, but I didn't hang around to see it.

There were others like Thor on the Hill—Imaginaries who had faded from their former glory, scared that they might disappear if no one remembered them. They scrounged for news of their names in the headlines. Science is always a favorite place to look into. It's good for keeping names and memories alive. Astronomers name planets and stars after Gods, physicians name diseases and body parts for them, and cartographers christen places on the map after both the familiar and the obscure citizens of the Hill. Imaginaries root for new discoveries and cross their fingers when it comes time to name them. They are all big fans of science, and oddly, it comes down to the same reason some people on the Otherworld love science: they see it as a means to help them live longer. Life-saving medical advances, medicines, and technology keep those other beings alive, just like using Mercury, Mars, or fucking Thor to name something keeps us moving. Science has been a love-hate relationship for some of us, though. It came up with motion-sensitive lights, baby monitors, and other things that make it so much harder for all of us to do our jobs. Still, if the Gods didn't want to be sidelined, they shouldn't have pissed off the Council all those years ago.

I walked toward a cluster of empty barstools, taking the place in as I went. It was asses to elbows as usual. Most of the tables were taken, and it was hard to walk without bumping into someone, or something. One table had a card game going. A good-sized crowd had gathered to watch, making it hard to identify all of the contestants. One short gray Alien wearing a blue visor on his huge head seemed to be winning by the large piles of chips in front of him. A couple of Imaginary Friends also seemed to be doing all right for themselves, while an Elf dressed in a green hat and tunic was begging onlookers to stake him some money to stay in the game.

I wiped off a stool and sat down, making note of some of the other barflies. It was the usual crowd. There was a disheveled Pixie, a number of Elves, and one of the Greek Gods whose name always escaped me. He was a minor God at best. God of earthworms? That's a thing, right? At the end of the bar I could see one of many giant rabbits who filled in for the Easter Bunny one day a year and drank himself stupid the other 364 days. Osiris, an Egyptian, was standing in the far corner engaged in a game of darts with Medusa, whose slithering hair made her easy to identify. She didn't turn us to stone, though. You know? She's supposed to turn men to stone when they look at her? It's bullshit. At least here on the Hill. It's all bullshit on the Hill. We can't hurt each other with those silly superstitions. Be interesting if we could, though.

"What can I get you, Abe?" the old bartender asked.

"The usual."

"One Weather Balloon, coming up."

As the chubby drink slinger wandered off, I got a chill. Looking to my left, I noticed the ghost of a Civil War soldier walking away from me. "Hey, pal! Watch where you're going! You just walked right through me here."

"Hey, bite me buddy. It's pretty crowded in here tonight."

I let him go without another comment. The bar was notorious for its brawls, and starting something with a ghost was a losing bet from the start. You can't hit them, right? You can't break a chair over their heads. Everything just goes *through* them. Their best offense is levitating small objects like pens and mugs and then hurling them at you. Their only other weapon is giving you the chills. Do you have any idea how humiliating it is to have to put on a sweater in the middle of a bar brawl? "*Brrrr. I'm cold. You win.*" Fucking embarrassing. Best to avoid the situation and hold on to your dignity as long as you can in this world.

The gray-hair behind the bar returned with my drink, set it on a napkin in front of me, and was on his way to the next customer. I nodded my thanks, removed the umbrella from the saucer-shaped glass, and dropped the wooden trinket near the napkin.

There were other lounges and bars in town. They were considered a little more upscale than the Wet Dream. There was the Dark Logger, which was frequented by Wood Fairies, Nymphs, and other forest dwellers. Bottom Feeder Lounge was used mostly by sea-faring Imaginaries, and the head guys like Zeus and Mother Nature dined and drank at the Throne Room. Trendy places like T.G.I. Eternity's drew a little bit of everything. None of those came close to the mix of culture, ideas and oddities you found at the Wet Dream.

I noticed a trio of Boogeymen in the corner farthest from the door. They sat in a soft darkness, lit only by a small candle in the middle of their table. They'd been called a lot of things in their day, but they were Ray and Thad to their friends. Sitting between them was Ira, one of the original dozen or so Boogeymen. He had been in the division pretty much from the beginning. He was there when the fearless Vikings needed to keep their children in line with monster stories, and he was there when the Pilgrims jumped at a twig snapping in the night. He was there long before they had to change the name from *Boogiemen* to *Boogeymen* when the Otherworlders came along and stole the word "Boogie" for their music and dancing.

Ira had experienced everything a Boogeyman could, and it showed. He always looked like he'd just left one bad-ass party: sunken eyes with heavy bags under them, sleepy smile that was just on the wrong side of the creepy line, and an inability to pay attention to anything anyone else said. Instead of the new, modern sleek black garb with crisp lines his brethren wore, he stayed in a traditional baggy Boogeyman uniform at all times, with button-up pockets and a v-neck collar. Occasionally he accented it with a long black cape draped with a gold chain around his neck. It had probably been snazzy at one point.

When I first came to the Hill, I heard snippets of parts of bits of whispered tales of Ira. He was a legend among legends. A myth among myths. It was said that he went to the Otherworld and did his job with ruthless efficiency, the speed and guile of a stalking jungle cat, and an intuition unlike any other Boogeyman. His excursions to the Otherworld were analyzed by his peers like football players studying films of the opposing team in the weeks before the big game. His shit was that tight. He was that good. Everyone from the tiniest fairy to the largest Giant knew his name. He was a big man on our little Hill.

Sitting in the bar that night, I saw none of that. He was clumsy, nearly knocking over his drink twice, and actually spilling a full bowl of pretzels into his lap. When he moved he bumped into his companions and hit his elbows on his chair. From where I sat it looked like he barely joined in the conversation with Thad and Ray. The times when he did, it looked like he gave short answers with such little importance that the conversation continued without acknowledgment. Mostly he stared at the dying candle on the table. Ira never acknowledged my presence, but Ray tipped his head at me and scowled.

"Ever wonder what they're talking about?" A voice rose over the din behind me and I turned. It was Zane, the only Boogeyman I really knew well. "They're like some clique of cheerleaders in a high school somewhere, aren't they?"

"Yeah. They're a mysterious little trio, all right," I said. It was good to see Zane after the long day. He had a way of talking that put me at ease. "How's it going?" I half rose and shook his hand.

"Better than it's going for you, I hear." He raised his eyebrows a bit and took a seat next to me. "Rough day?"

Who knows how things get around on the Hill, but they do. Quickly. "Yeah, apparently I need to decide very quickly what I want to be when I grow up."

"Eh. It'll all blow over. They know you're a good worker; they'll cut you some slack." He held up a finger to indicate I should wait a second and turned toward someone standing nearby.

As Zane turned away, I noticed Ira stand up at his table. I tried to remember whether I had ever had an actual conversation with him before, or if I had always been on the edge of a discussion he was having with someone else. He smiled weakly, straightened his shirt, nodded to Ray and Thad, and walked away. After he took a few steps I lost him in the crowd.

"Hey, I want you to meet a new friend of mine." Zane leaned back so I could see the young woman who'd stepped out of the crowd. Young-looking, I guess I should say. Looks tended to be deceiving here, and she could be ten thousand years old for all I knew. It's so hard to tell how long some Imaginaries have been around. Maybe that was young, I don't know. "This is Delia. She knows all about the old employment shuffle. She's an assistant Tooth Fairy now."

"*Associate* Tooth Fairy," Delia said and stuck her hand in front of Zane's face so I could shake it. "*Assistant* Tooth Fairies just do the cataloging. Associates actually go out in the field."

I shook her hand and tried not to stare at her. She had a beauty about her that I hadn't expected from a Tooth Fairy. They usually have a bit of an image, don't they? I suppose handling teeth can give somebody a bad reputation. But something about the smoothness of her face, the way her jet-black hair flowed about her shoulders, struck me as decidedly un-Tooth-Fairy-like. I think I expected blonde hair and a tiara, though on reflection that was also my image of a Fairy Godmother. And some Sprites. "Nice to meet you." The handshake lingered and I thought for someone who worked with her hands, her skin was incredibly soft.

"We met a few weeks ago at the other end of the bar. She's a regular here, too." Zane turned so Delia couldn't see his smile get big as he introduced her; this also precluded him from seeing her own smile drop just a little. "She's had tons of jobs, and nobody gives her a hassle about a career path or anything."

"Did somebody say jobs?" The Bigfoot from the chamber butted in between Zane and me. "Hey, Delia. How've you been?"

"Hey, Brady. Did you use that ribbon I gave you?" She touched his arm, and I watched him melt down an inch or so in height. "This is the guy that keeps me working," she said.

Brady laughed and grabbed one of his ponytails to show where he had woven a red piece of cloth into his hair.

Zane watched the exchange and rolled his eyes at me before grabbing Brady's arm. "Hey, buddy. Let's see if there's any dartboards open."

Puzzled, Brady stood his ground. "But I hate darts. They're so small and sharp. *Ow*!" Brady looked at his arm. "That hurt. What're you doing?"

"Walk with me, hairball." Zane was obviously tugging on the big Imaginary's arm, though trying to be covert. Brady's eyes got narrow and he stared at Zane suspiciously, but followed. They disappeared after Zane called, "We'll be right back. Excuse us." He nodded to Delia, with no word to me.

"Think there's going to be a fight, or just a quick, stern talking-to?" Delia asked.

"Probably just a talk, though I don't think it'll be quick. Zane tends to use big words."

"Ah, boys. They're always trying to claim territory." She shook her head a little as she finished off her drink. She obviously knew what they were going to discuss and didn't show the least concern or interest for either of them. I thought to ask her how she felt about Zane, but it seemed like an embarrassing question for someone I had just met. I didn't know Brady from a hole in the ground, but it was obvious he had some degree of crush on her. I wondered how many times she got into this situation, how many times she came into this bar, or others, made a friend and found herself on the receiving end of a sudden crush. The bartender refilled her glass, and we sat without talking for nearly a minute.

"So. A Tooth Fairy, huh?" I asked. "How's that going for you?"

She nodded her head slowly and forced a smile. "Good. It's good." She continued nodding and added as an afterthought: "Collected my three-hundredth tooth last week."

Sounded impressive. "Nice. That's a lot of molars, I guess. Do you get some sort of recognition for that? A little party or something? A certificate at the very least?"

She looked at me and her fake smile turned genuine. "A plaque."

I laughed and tried to figure out a follow-up to that, but Zane returned and wedged himself between us. "Anybody want a chip?" He plopped a snack basket on the bar and stuffed his face with some of the crunchy yellow snacks from inside. He didn't mention where Brady was, and I didn't ask.

"They're bad for my teeth," Delia said. "Besides, I'm out of here." She swallowed the last of her drink. I wanted to buy her another and another.

Zane turned with her as she climbed off her stool and stepped toward the crowd. "So soon? Come on, it's still early. Stay."

She didn't appear to be swayed in the least. "I'm on call tonight. I need to get back and sit around waiting for work. Maybe I'll collect number 301 tonight."

"Aw, come on. Stay," I said, in a much more subdued manner than Zane. I really wanted her to stay, but obviously I understood duty and how bad it could be if Personnel got on your ass.

"Gotta go," she said.

"Come on, I'll buy you a puppy." Zane's eyes went wide as if he realized what a good idea that was after he said it. "Seriously. A puppy of your choosing."

"Do you actually have, or know where to acquire, a puppy?" she asked.

"No."

She turned to leave again and Zane stood up and called after her. "I'll draw you a puppy."

Without turning Delia yelled: "Do you have a pencil?"

"No."

"Paper?"

"No."

"I'll see you next time." She waved over her shoulder and was lost in the crowd almost immediately. I was left staring at the packed area of people where she disappeared, wondering if it would suddenly part and present her one more time like a wave revealing a shell in the sand before the ocean reclaimed it with the next. When she didn't reappear, I turned to see Zane hadn't even watched her go, just slid her drink in front of himself and sucked out the ice.

I noticed Brady making his way back; he was hard to miss, being as tall as he was. "How did you keep him away from us?"

"Shiny object."

"Seriously?"

"You'd be amazed."

I *was* a little amazed. Brady took his place beside us with no fuss, no malice, and not even a word about being led off. He did sport some sort of tinsel or something in his hair near his ear.

"We really need to talk about a new job. The Director set a serious deadline," Brady said.

"Did you steal my file?" I asked.

"No."

"Did you sign me out at the desk?"

"Yes."

I knew he would, the little suck-up. "Let's just relax a minute and I'll think about things I'm good at and enjoy doing. After that, we'll put our heads together and figure it out."

Surprisingly, he bought it. The three of us stayed at the Wet Dream for hours. We talked about this and that, nothing of any real consequence, certainly not work. I discovered some of Delia's other work. Her temp jobs had consisted of: Cupid-in-training, personal shopper, Hellhound walker, blacksmith, and temporary stylist for Aphrodite. I wondered if that was why everyone was fascinated by her; maybe something from Cupid or Aphrodite had worn off on her and she was irresistible to everyone now and forever. I kept the idea to myself and continued to talk about everything else with my table companions. We cheered on a despondent Gremlin, who was doing shot after shot of a clear blue liquid at the bar while complaining that everything and everyone sucked. We got bored with it at about the time we ran out of new things that could possibly suck.

After that, Brady finished his drink and flipped the glass upside down on the table. He looked at me blearily. "Tomorrow morning. You. Me. Breakfast. Talk." Burping loudly at each of us, he turned and made his way to the front door and out into the night. The stench of his breath lingered long after he was gone. It was like a fish had consumed a quart of spoiled milk and then died after vomiting it up. That might be underselling it.

"Well, I guess that means the evening's over," I said.

"You heading home or you got other plans?"

"My place, I suppose."

"I'll walk with you."

We left the bar and headed for the Legendary Arms. Zane lived across the hall from me in the dorm-like accommodations that a lot of the newer Imaginaries had to set up residence in. Our places were nothing to brag about. They had a living room complete with green shag carpet, a tiny bedroom, an oddly large kitchen and a largely unnecessary bathroom. Some, like mine and Zane's, actually had windows. For Zane, the window was a nice feature; he faced the outside of the mountain and could look out into the clouds and soothing mists. My window looked out over the town, and was actually a decent view. Except for the lighthouse. Day and night, the sunlight-bright beam from the lighthouse broke through my bedroom and lingered there for nearly a full minute before moving on. Then, exactly one hour and three minutes later, it would return on its slow sweep of the Hill.

We said little as we walked through the nearly deserted streets. On the Otherworld, at least you could talk about the weather when the conversation lagged. Here, the weather was always the same: chilly, with light fog at the outermost parts of the Hill. Someone told me it rained here once; a long time ago, but it may have been a tall tale in a land of tall tales.

Walking down the hall to our rooms, Zane removed his key from his pocket. It was his only key, but he kept it on a shiny metal chain with a fake bullet on the other end. It was one of his in-jokes that I never really got. He said it was a "Magic Bullet" that he got from some guy in Dallas on the Otherworld. He did have an odd sense of humor.

"I'll see you tomorrow, Zane." I put my key in the lock and turned the handle.

"Not if I see you first," he said and shut his own door behind him.

The place was just as I'd left it. Never changed, never would. Exactly as it was the last time I returned, and the time before that. The chair was by the door, the sofa and coffee table were in the middle of the room, the drapes were pulled, and the only painting—a depiction of the sun setting in reds and yellows—hung crookedly next to my empty bookshelf in the corner. Nothing had changed.

I dropped my key on the table and stood there in the darkness.

"Abe? Is that you?" Her voice came from the bedroom.

Everything just as I'd left it.

"Yeah, Sarah, I should've been more quiet. I didn't think you'd be here."

"That's okay. I thought I'd surprise you…I waited up for a while, but…"

I walked down the hall toward the bedroom, eagerness outweighing surprise. "Yeah, sorry it's so late. The Director was all over me and sent me on a job that took forever, and then I ran into Zane and this strange guy from Personnel when I got back and lost track of time."

I stepped into the bedroom to see Sarah lying in darkness with the sheets pulled up nearly to her chin. She was beautiful there in the black, white and gray of the night. The shadows made her seem much older, emphasizing or creating wrinkles across her cheeks and forehead. Her long hair seemed darker pulled back, like one big shadow across the back of her head. I stared at her from the doorway as she looked back with her eyes half-open. "It's a nice surprise, though."

A moment later we were bathed in the intense white from the lighthouse as it began to stream in through the open window. She was as beautiful in the bright light as she was in the darkness. Instead of black and gray obscuring her features, the yellows and reds of the bright light combined with the whites to bleach out her face. It was like staring at a photograph and then looking at its negative. She was pale now, her face an almost sickly white in the harsh light. It was so bright that I thought I could see through her if I tried.

She put her hand up over her eyes. "You want to shut that shade for me?"

I untied the strings on both sides and pulled the curtains shut. There was still light in the room, but at least we no longer felt like we should be doing a duet on stage. I stood at the window and watched her drop her hand and rearrange the covers.

"Are you coming to bed anytime soon, or are you going to stare all night?"

"Oh…yeah. Just a minute." I unbuttoned my black work shirt as I walked toward the closet. "How was your day? What did you do?" I took a hanger and put my shirt on it, putting it next to the six identical black work shirts already there.

"Some of this, some of that. You know how the job is."

"Yeah." I climbed into bed and under the covers with her.

"What's with the Director? What's he on you about now?"

"Some of this, some of that. You know how the job is."

She grimaced. "Seriously. He's not still threatening to move you, is he?" she asked as she rolled over and put her hand on my chest.

"He gave me the usual 'you're a screw-up and you're making me look bad' speech," I put my hand on hers for some reassurance. She didn't need to know all the gory details of the day, not yet at least.

"He'll keep harping on you and watching everything you do and—"

"So let him watch. I'll just be more careful and make sure I don't mess up anymore," I could see her eyebrow arch. I always thought it was cute, and couldn't help smiling. "Honest."

She nodded her head sleepily. "Okay."

"Goodnight." I leaned forward and kissed her lightly on the lips.

"'Night." she rolled over and pulled the sheets higher.

I watched as the bright light spilling out from around the curtains got dimmer and dimmer. Just as it was about to disappear altogether, I could've sworn it turned completely red, but I was so close to sleep that I dismissed the thought. Soon, the sweep of the light passed and the room returned to darkness. I closed my eyes and waited there in the quiet of the night.

5

At first I thought the continuous tapping coming from the living room was something that Sarah was doing. But after getting out of bed, I realized that sometime in the night, Sarah must've gone home. I was alone in the cold apartment.

The noise turned out to be someone lightly knocking on my front door with the ferocity of a field mouse. I opened it to find Brady staring at me, with suspicious eyes like slits. "Bad time?"

"No. It's fine."

Eyes still narrow. "You sure?"

My eyes were also beginning to narrow. "Positive. What can I do for you?"

"I'm here to take to you work," he said.

"Weren't we going to meet up somewhere to discuss this? Somewhere *not* here?"

"Didn't want you to be late on your first day." He held up a half-squished muffin in his hand and a cup of something steamy in the other. Once he started talking, his face brightened up and he smiled.

"It's not my first day. I haven't picked a new career yet."

Big Bigfoot smile. He still looked thrilled to be talking to me. "Well. No. But it is your first day without a job."

First day of unemployment. Great. "Awesome."

"If it's any consolation, it should be your last day without a job."

"Thanks, but I can find my own way." I wondered if it would be rude to take the muffin and slam the door in his face. I doubted I could get it shut with his giant frame in the way.

"Yeah, but I realized after we talked that I never told you where to go. Sure you could have found it eventually, but I didn't want you to be late on your first day. That wouldn't look good." He held the drink and the muffin out closer to my face. "Ready to get going?"

Bigfoot was a morning person. *Joy.*

On the walk over to Personnel, Brady blathered on about a million things at once, none of which I caught fully. He talked quickly and his voice got high at times, unbearably so. I wondered how Sarah was and felt bad that we hadn't had a chance to talk the night before.

In the morning mist, the Hill looked desperately and densely beautiful and it occurred to me that I hadn't been up this early in some time. I'm sure I enjoyed getting up and taking a morning walk at some point in my existence. Not recently, but I did once.

We walked across the stone-lined square, Brady still yammering. The fleeting quiet was interrupted by the tromping of footfalls echoing off the buildings. As they grew louder, four Boogeymen came into view not a dozen feet away. They were jogging in unison, or maybe it was a fast march. Their feet fell in time, creating a percussive rhythm and making the mist part before them.

Brady stopped to follow them as well. And he watched me watch them. "You could be working with them soon enough," he said. He didn't sound sure, or excited about it for me; merely factual. "They could always use new people."

I grunted and kept watching as the men disappeared back into the gray morning. And when I thought about it, I wasn't so excited for me either. But my options weren't multitudinous at the time.

The Personnel Department was just as dark and dreary as we'd left it the night before. We walked through the front door, where I checked in at the desk with my best sarcastic smile for Brady. His return smile was annoyingly genuine.

"Let me show you to my desk. We can start going through my files and maybe make a profile for you." He was genuinely excited to get started and it showed. "We could complete a form B-D4 questionnaire, maybe even read over a T69 profile."

We turned and started down a hall, only to be blocked by a duo of men. In the front was a very large, very bald man with an even larger and somehow balder woman behind him. Both wore black uniforms with traces of red lining their sleeves.

Brady was flustered when they moved to block his way. "Excuse me." They moved in front of him again as he made to go around him.

"Can we help you guys?" I asked, not ready to see the comedic stylings of the three go on.

"Messenger," the man said.

"Messenger from who?"

"High Council."

"High Council has a message for me?" I asked. The High Council hadn't met in ages. Why would they be meeting now, and what could they possibly want with me?

"I don't know what they want with you," he said. "I was sent to get you and make sure you came to them immediately."

"Uhhh. We have an appointment. I need to speak with him about his career options." The disappointment in Brady's voice was obvious.

"I'm sure this won't take long," I told Brady. "Even the High Council wouldn't dare delay my quest for a meaningful path to gainful employment." I moved from Brady's side to stand between the messenger and his friend, and when they moved, I followed Bald while Balder trailed me. We left the building and followed Old Hag Avenue, then Fairy Ring Circle to the edge of town. From there, our path turned into a wide thoroughfare lined with trees and shrubbery that eventually led to the enormous castle that occupied most of the west side of the Hill.

The path crossed The Rainbow Bridge—a horribly named stretch of path that crossed over the only body of water on the Hill. We called it the River Styx, because why wouldn't we? We figured that since it was the only one we had, we might as well go big, you know? What were we going to call it, the Mississippi? *Shit.* The river flowed from a cave near one side of the castle and ended in a waterfall dropping over the edge of the Hill. In it you could find the majority of the sea creatures, at least those that didn't have their own private pools in their quarters, or a good-sized bathtub.

It was a long enough walk to allow me the luxury of wondering why would I possibly be sent for and why the Council was even meeting. The Council had never met in all of the time I had existed on the Hill. I suppose they could have met in secret, but why? They were the three Imaginaries upon which everything else was founded. The Originals, the Basics. The Beatles with Pete Best. They began meeting as a way to corral the populace when masses of Imaginaries started showing up. They came up with rules and standards and codes for everyone and everything: how replacements were selected, what they needed in order to meaningfully participate in the lives of the Otherworlders, how to acclimate new arrivals, when to recycle the old. After a while everything seemed to be covered, so they just stopped meeting. They didn't disappear, become hermits, or make some big showy announcement; they just stopped meeting together and went on with their existence. The term "the Council" became antiquated and quaint.

I didn't exactly get the grand tour. I was ushered over the bridge, through the wide, wooden front doors and into a dusty courtyard. What I saw of the place was wonderful. The area around the castle was brighter, more colorful than the rest of the Hill. There weren't the usual moody mists and dreary clouds that pervaded the common grounds. There was natural light flooding the whole area with its warmth. It felt like I was standing on the Otherworld beneath a blue summer sky with a light breeze blowing across my neck. It smelled like freshly cut grass.

The strange thing about the courtyard was nobody but me and my two guides were there. The rest of the Hill was permanently dark and chilly, gloomy and drab, yet here was prime real estate without a god damn soul to enjoy it—like a beach after a shark attack, a ski resort after a sudden thaw. It was the greatest spot on the Hill and it was going to waste.

"Let's go, let's go," Bald said. "We're in a hurry, remember?"

I was herded through an arching door and instructed to climb the stone steps just inside. The stairway opened into a hall, and Bald stopped and gestured toward a door at the end. Balder stayed at the top of the stairs. "Please," he gestured again, pointing the way.

When I was within a half a dozen steps of Bald, he gave a tug and quickly pulled the door open. He then swooped his right arm toward the room with a flourish of his hand as though he were revealing fabulous treasures. I took a deep breath, straightened my shirt, ran my hands across it to remove dust and wrinkles and took a big step through the doorway.

The room was larger than I expected, with dark recesses that weren't obvious until you really searched for them. The ceiling was so high that six Yetis standing on each other's shoulders couldn't touch the thick wooden beams running across it. Unlit torches stuck in the walls throughout the room; they were unnecessary with all of the light coming from a massive window across the room. The same sort of wonderful light I saw in the courtyard streamed through it and fell on a long colorful rug in the middle of the room. The rug showed various scenes of the moon and stars, knights and dragons, lions and horses. On either side of the room were heavy oaken tables lined with long wooden benches. A cloth covered the whole table, and several candelabra were placed at intervals along it.

Two figures, a man and a woman, sat talking at the table to the right, while another man paced at the far corner of the room, staring out the great window. The woman wore a plain white robe that ended near her ankles, and had a wreath of leaves and berries sitting crookedly on her head. She was wonderful to look at, beautiful with bright blue eyes, delicate pink lips and long chestnut hair pinned up in braids. I could make out the small signs of age creeping into her face, like little bags under her eyes, and wrinkles in her cheeks, but they only seemed to enhance her beauty. She fixed her wreath as I got closer and laughed, smacking the person next to her on the arm. Her laugh was gentle and quiet, like a breeze blowing through the room, making everything lighter, like it might take flight and blow out an open window if she laughed much harder.

The man she was talking to seemed much older. He was tall, and sat hunched over, playing with his long white beard as he talked. He wore what appeared to be a gray sweat suit with the hood pulled back.

The light also made it hard to make out details of the person by the window except that they occasionally swung their arm and shook their head.

"Oh! Hello, hello. Come in, come in," the old man said as he stood. "We've been expecting you," he smiled as he got up and came around the table to meet me. "I'm glad you could come." I met him near the table and he stuck out his hand to shake mine. "Very glad you could come."

I didn't know I had a choice. "I'm glad too, but the messenger wasn't real clear on what you wanted from…"

"Oh, I'll explain in a moment. First…I'll get you a drink? Yes?" He asked. "I understand they call you Abe. May I?"

"Sure, whatever you feel comfortable with. It doesn't matter to me. And I'm not thirsty, thanks."

"Great. Great. Great. Abe, I'm Father Time, I'm the president of the Council right now." He took me by the arm and pulled me to the far end of the table. "Abe, this is Mother Nature, she's currently the Council's VP, as they say."

Mother Nature took my hand and shook it lightly before releasing it. "A pleasure to meet you, Abe." She smiled flatly and nodded.

"It's nice to…" Before I could finish, Father Time physically turned me to face the last council member. The large figure descended the few steps from the window. He wore a long dark robe with a wide hood that obscured his entire face. He walked with his hands behind his back.

Father Time gestured toward the figure with his hands. "Abe, this is…"

"Death," I said. It wasn't a question. There was simply no way to be unsure of who the man was. The legend preceded him. He had an air about him, as if gravity itself were somehow thicker. Thicker? Sure.

"Yes. Yes. Very good. Death. The Grim Reaper. Whatever, he answers to all of them. He lets a few of us call him Morty, but I'd wait before trying it out for yourself," Father Time said. "He used to be the Council's treasurer, but he wasn't any good at it, and of course, we don't use money anyway, so it was kind of an honorary title, really. We've been trying to come up with a new title for him." The old man sighed. "He gets bored so easily."

Death came toward me and though I couldn't see his eyes under the hood I knew he was watching me. Studying me. Sizing me up. I'd never even seen Death on the streets, let alone stood face to face with him. It was good to know that we at least had something in common: poor math skills. When he got within a few feet of me I could see he was bringing his hands out from behind his back; the right one came out quickly, as if to shake my hand. It was pale and thin as it jutted out from the billowing sleeves of his dark robe. As I reached out to shake it, his left hand came around from his back, and it wasn't empty. I saw part of a wooden handle and nearly ran, afraid Death was about to smite me with his dreaded scythe.

I relaxed when it turned out to be a tennis racket in his other hand. An old, ratty wooden tennis racket.

"Sorry. Didn't mean to startle you," Death said. "A lot of people have that reaction." He grabbed my hand as though he thought I might withdraw it and pumped it a few times. "I was playing a few sets with Zeus this morning when I got the word. Getting my ass kicked, too. I think my problem is my backhand. I just can't seem to get the speed I get with the forearm."

"You ever think maybe the robe gets in the way?"

"Hmm—I hadn't considered that. Maybe I'll—"

"All right you two, let's have a seat and get to work," Father Time said. "Oh. I nearly forgot. Abe, you've met the Director already, haven't you?" He gestured behind me with a nod of his head. I turned, and the Director emerged from an alcove I hadn't noticed when I came in.

I was startled, seeing him again. "I thought you three were the only ones on the Council," I said. He was still imposing, to be sure, but in outside of his office, in the presence of these others, he seemed almost normal. His face was a map of veins and jutting bone, amplified by the lighting in the room. He wore what appeared to be a very comfortable sweater.

"We are. Yes. We are. The Director is just here in sort of an…*advisory* capacity."

Father Time, Mother Nature and Death took their seats on one side of the great wooden table. The Director patted me on the shoulder and sat opposite them at the far end of the bench, and then patted the area next to him indicating where he wanted me to sit.

6

"Ira's dead," Father Time said. "Sorry to just blurt it out like that, but I think it'll make this whole thing a lot easier on all of us if we're all just honest and straightforward about everything."

I looked at the three of them on the other side of the table for a moment, then turned to the Director to my right. "What?"

"Ira is dead," Father Time said again. I looked at the Director and he shook his head.

"I don't understand what you're saying. Dead?" I asked. "I mean…That's impossible."

"Yes, it is," Mother Nature said. "Well, that's what we thought."

"What you thought? What do you mean? I thought you guys knew everything. You guys made all the rules around here," I said. "You've been here since the beginning."

"Yes, we have. Sure, we have," Father Time said. "And in all of the time that we've been here, nothing like this has ever happened."

"I don't understand. How did he…"

"Die? We don't really know," Mother Nature said. "Mister Director? Why don't you tell him what you know?"

"Yes ma'am," the Director said. "Ira had a job today. The Personnel office notified me when he failed to show up. Since he and I are…*were* friends, I decided to see what was going on. It wasn't like him to be late or put off a job, so I was concerned. I walked from my office to his living quarters." The Director paused for a breath. "When I arrived at his door, I knocked several times and got no answer. After a while, I decided to use my master key to go in and look for him. When I opened the door, I saw him laying face down on his living room rug. It was obvious something was terribly wrong right away."

I stuttered as I tried to come up with an appropriate question. Or maybe my mind just stuttered over the idea. "What was he like? Was anything out of place in the room?" I asked.

"Everything seemed to be in order, I suppose. I can't say for sure but it all seemed pretty tidy."

"Please, go on." Mother Nature said.

"Well, ma'am, there's not much more to tell. I felt something was wrong with him, so I shouted his name a couple of times, but he didn't move. I went over and touched him on the shoulder but he didn't move," Although everyone was staring at him, the Director looked down at the table and refused to meet their eyes. "And he was…well…he seemed to be *fading.*"

I'd never known the Director to have trouble with eye contact before. "What? You mean he was dying right in front of you?" I said.

"No. I mean fading. I could touch him and he was just as solid as ever, but I could kind of see through him."

"Like when we're on the Otherworld and we're doing a job?" The people could only see us when we want them to, and even then we only appeared to be a shadow shaped like a person.

"Sort of. He wasn't *that* transparent. He seemed normal when I first approached…well, as normal as possible, I suppose. I was staring at his body for a while, and I realized that if I looked hard enough I could see the pattern of the rug beneath him." He looked up at Father Time. "That's when I came and found you. I didn't know what else to do."

Father Time looked at me. "The three of us went to Ira's apartment. All I can really say is that we confirmed the Director's account as best as we could. Nothing seems out of place or missing, and it doesn't look like anyone forced their way in." He stood and looked toward the giant window. "We also took a closer look at Ira. He was just as the Director said: transparent. Semi-opaque. A little see-through. Not solid in the least." He took a little step toward the light. "Although we did manage to roll him over. Stiff as a board, but oddly, not a mark on him. No sign of injury, no cuts, no bruises, no nothing."

"Wait a minute, what does any of that matter anyway?" I said. "You're talking about cuts and bruises, but isn't that irrelevant? If we can't be killed why would you even look for that stuff?"

Death leaned forward. "Some Imaginaries can be killed. When kids actually wish their Imaginary friends dead, that's the end."

"Who else?"

"What?"

"Who else has died on the Hill?" Death leaned back and I turned to the Director. "You were the first Boogeyman. Have you ever seen anything like this? Have you ever seen anyone else die?"

"No, I can't say that I have. Certainly not a Boogeyman."

It occurred to me who I was talking to. "Aren't you *Death*? Don't you have a big hand in who lives and who fucking dies?" I looked around at the others. "It's right there in his *name*. I think we can all agree that if anyone does the Death-ing, it would be him."

Death shook his head slightly. "Not here, I don't. Not on the Hill. I have zero control over that. And I only supervise on The Otherworld. I have underlings to claim the deceased over there these days. You know? Like the Tooth Fairy has assistants?"

"Associates." I felt good correcting him, until I realized I wasn't sure if I was right.

"What are you talking about?" Father Time asked.

"Nothing," I said. "What about the rest of you?" I looked at them in turn. Mother Nature. Death. Finally I looked at Father Time, who had moved even closer to the window. None of them said anything, or did anything for a moment. They just stared at me. "And blood? *Blood?* Have any of you ever seen an Imaginary bleed? Actually *bleed*?" They all quickly found better places to look than into my eyes.

I stood up, pushing the bench out as I did. I had no idea why they had chosen to tell me this news, and I really didn't want to know. I wanted to go home. Go home and curl up in my bed again with Sarah. Or be back in the Wet Dream with Zane and all the other weirdos, laughing and slapping each other's backs. Nothing changing, everything in its place. I started to move toward the door, nearly tripping on the bench. "Uh, look…I don't know what happened to Ira, and I think I'm better off not knowing. I don't know why you needed to tell me all this, but thanks for the consideration…really…but I need to get back to work or something."

"Do you know what the biggest thing that the Otherworld has that we don't?" Father Time said from the window. He stood with his hands clasped behind his back, looking out the window.

"I…don't know…they've got a lot of things we don't…maybe cable?" I laughed weakly and looked behind me to see how far away the door was.

"Ha! No…No…That's not the one I was thinking of, although I do enjoy that *MTV Road Rules* program." He turned his head just enough to see me. "I was referring to crime. Crime is rampant on the Otherworld, but here it is nonexistent. Why? We can't hurt each other, because we can't be killed. Sure, there is violence. Fights are a fairly common occurrence, but no one gets hurt. It's not like the stories of Valhalla and the fierce warriors of old. There's no sport in it here. The weakest Sprite can hold its own against the mightiest Giant because eventually both sides just get tired and bored. We don't steal from each other because we don't use money or anything else of value." Mother Nature and Death got up and walked toward Father Time as he continued. "Therefore, we're missing something else that the Otherworld has." His bushy white eyebrow rose questioningly as he spoke.

"I give up. I don't know what you're getting at."

"We're missing certain *securities*? Certain *protection*?" His eyebrow rose a little higher.

"What he means is: we don't have a police force," Mother Nature said.

"Yeah. No constables. Or cops, to use the vernacular," Death said, beating the racquet against his knee.

"Well, not exactly. Not exactly. While I do feel we should have some sort of policing body, our immediate need is for an investigator. Someone to delve into the matter at hand and see what they can come up with," Father Time said. The three of them looked at me.

"Please tell me you don't mean me."

"The Director suggested you. He speaks very highly of you," Death said. "Sort of. Mostly he said you were the only one who needed an assignment right now."

I looked at the Director, who was trying to keep a somber look on his face, but I could see a smile form.

"Also…do you remember Truman Keller?" Mother Nature said.

"Of course I do. I was his Imaginary Friend." Hard to forget *that* kid.

"It seems he just got promoted with his hometown police force."

"So?"

"He's a policeman." Her look intensified.

"I'm not following you."

"You two were close. Some of his intelligence and reason must have rubbed off on you. Dig around; investigate. Find out what happened and keep us informed as you go along." She got closer and patted me on the arm.

I looked at her and thought about that statement briefly. "That's all you're basing this on? A recommendation from my boss and a hope that I'm as smart as a *real* person?"

"You'll do fine." Father Time was moving for the nearest exit.

"I'll do fine? That's it? *Dig around*? I wouldn't even know where to start."

"We'll post one of our best messengers outside your apartment door for communication purposes and you can pull two other Imaginaries off their regular duties to help you out, but that's it," the Director said. "We can't afford to have everyone dragged away from their real jobs, now can we?"

"If you're looking for a place to start, I'd suggest you inspect Ira's apartment, and his body," Death said. "We'll make an announcement to the rest of the Hill and have some sort of service in a couple of hours. We'll also make sure everyone knows to cooperate with you." With that, all of them except the Director were on their feet and heading for the door.

"Wait. Wait. Wait. A couple of hours? *Hours*? What's the hurry?" I said.

"He's fading fast. I figure he'll completely disappear by the end of the day." Death swung his tennis racket slowly—a practice swing—and then followed Mother Nature and Father Time through the door.

The bench screeched across the floor as the Director stood up. I watched him walk toward me and tried desperately to think of something to say, something to convince him that I was not the one he wanted for this job. He put one of his large hands on my shoulder. "Looks like there's a new sheriff in town," he said before he walked out. I heard his laughter echo in the hallway as he went.

7

"So that's what a dead Imaginary looks like?" Brady said. "Wow." He twisted his ponytail around his fingers as he spoke. "I can see the carpet and the rug underneath him. That's so weird." He stared another moment. "Wow."

Brady and Zane were the only two I could think of to help me out. Neither of them had any special talents in this area. Neither of them seemed to have any real talent for anything that I knew of. They were just the first two names that sprang to mind, and my time was running out. Maybe they were just the last two people I'd spoken with before seeing the Council. Brady was elated. He apparently considered himself something of an intellect, though he could never convince anyone else of it. He was thrilled to do something other than hand out career advice, read paperwork and annoy the good folk of the Hill. He moved about Ira's apartment searching for clues, although I'm sure he had no idea what one would look like. As long as he took orders and stayed out of the way, I figured he could be of some use to me. Maybe.

Zane, however, started out a little shaky. Zane, the practical joker, the life of the party, Mr. Entertainment, just stood next to the door and stared at Ira's body. Never took his eyes off it. It was like he was trying to catch Ira flinching; like he could prove Ira was still alive if he just concentrated hard enough.

Everything was just as the Council said it was. There were no marks on Ira that would show that he met with some kind of violence. No holes. No wounds. No bruises. That was about the extent of my inspection of the body. I had no other ideas on where to look, or what to look for. His clothes weren't torn or burned or mangled in any way.

I remembered that he was wearing a cape at the Wet Dream last night. That seemed very important to me. He wasn't wearing one now. It was my first inkling of a clue, and I was proud of myself for noting it so quickly. Maybe I had a detective's instincts after all. I wanted to make a note of it but realized I didn't have a notepad or a writing utensil. I needed both of those things if I wanted to do this job right.

After we'd been there for nearly an hour, two workers from Personnel came through the front door and put a makeshift stretcher next to Ira. "'Scuse me. The Director says we gotta get started," one of them said as she grabbed Ira's legs and slid them over. Her partner grabbed Ira's shoulders and slid the rest of his body onto the gurney.

"Hey! We're not done here," I said.

"Sorry, Director's orders. We gotta bring him back no matter what," she said. "By the way, you see his cape? They want it for the service…" With a nod, both of them lifted their ends of the stretcher at the same time and walked with it toward the door. "Never mind, there it is." She leaned around Brady and pulled the long black cape off the coat rack behind the still-open door. In a matter of seconds they were gone with Ira's body.

As the sound of their footsteps faded down the hallway, Zane seemed to come out of his funk and grinned. "Do we get some sort of badges or something? I mean, to make it look official and everything. Something to flash at the people when they get out of line?" He looked from one of us to the other with wide, excited eyes.

"I'll look into it," I said and took one last look around.

We left the apartment and made our way through the deserted streets toward where they were to hold the service for Ira. None of us spoke. I think it was all too much. We'd just learned of his death hours ago and already they were ready to—what? Bury him? I supposed if they waited long enough he'd vanish, if things continued as they were in the apartment. It seemed, though, that they planned some grand goodbye for him, being who he was and all. And as it was entirely unprecedented, it made some sort of sense to mark the occasion publicly. I had explained as much as I could to Zane and Brady after they were dragged to the apartment at my request, but I was sure they had questions. I wasn't sure I had answers and little time to elaborate, since things were progressing so fast. There would be time for sorting that out after the service.

We heard a loud voice at the edge of town signifying they had begun without us. Brady was the first to break out into a jog to get there faster. Actually, with his long arms and legs it was more of a lope than a jog. He seemed concerned that something was going on outside of his presence. Zane followed suit, and by the time I decided it was a good idea to hurry, they were both running.

As I sped up to try and catch them, the sweep of the lighthouse hit me. I took a few more quick steps and stopped. Standing in the middle of Vine Street,

I let the light bathe over me, almost warming me in its brilliance. In the many times I had pondered the lighthouse beam, it had never appeared to be anything but white and here it was tinged in red. I put my hand up to try to shield my eyes and squinted at the source. Rather than look away, I was forced to wait for it to pass before I could move on.

8

I started my existence with the easy task of being an Imaginary Friend to a somewhat reclusive little boy in Cygnet, Iowa. He had the extreme misfortune to be born to parents with a great love and respect for the President of the United States of America. Not a problem in itself, but unfortunate because they named their boy Truman. Truman Harold Keller. Hence his reclusive nature, I suppose.

He was actually a great kid. He was smarter and funnier than most of the other seven-year-olds, honest and kind with an immense imagination. Truman was capable of inventing fantastic future worlds and historically accurate Old West gunfights in his head. His creativity knew few boundaries.

Shy, though—painfully so—and living on a hundred-acre farm did little to improve his social skills. Truman had no siblings and no neighbors his own age when I met him. His only interactions with other children came at the park, family reunions, or through the educational process. He knew a few kids from school and got along with them, but most were discovering sports like baseball, football and basketball, none of which interested Truman. He enjoyed reading, studying. Science interested him to some degree, but his poor mathematics skills hindered him.

So, one bright summer day, young Mr. Keller sat down under the old elm tree behind the house and wished he had a friend. He wished that friend was everything that he wasn't, and everything he couldn't have. He wanted a big brother, a best friend, a bodyguard and confidant. His friend had to be strong, handsome, fast, tough, and even a little mean. Truman thought of everything, right down to his friend's brown hair, eyes...and ability to work with simple fractions.

As the heat of the late July sun beat down on the great state of Iowa, I became real, if only to a single little boy on the Otherworld.

He named me George. Literally the first name of the first president of the United States. His whole family had a thing for American leaders. As I said; quite an imagination.

When he spoke of me to others, which he rarely did, he referred to me as an "older kid" and intimated I was somewhere in my mid-twenties. Few people were privy to Truman's little secret and he was content with that. His parents sometimes caught him talking to me but didn't say anything to stifle his wild imagination. They learned to smile and nod their heads as often as they could.

It was a pretty easy job for the two years I helped Truman out. He was quiet and stayed out of trouble, read a lot, and drew pictures. The two of us played games and talked or camped out in the back yard. It was mostly just us, day in and day out. Most Imaginaries would have loved it.

From the moment I showed up, there always seemed to be someone in his life trying to make him miserable. There were bullies, parents, normal kids and of course, there were teachers. He wasn't doing well in his classes. He presented himself to his compatriots at school as a prodigy, a budding genius that they should look up to with awe. Unfortunately, I had no knowledge outside what I got from Truman himself. So, when he turned to me in a pinch for help with his mathematics, I confidently gave him the wrong answer. It didn't take him long to figure out I had no idea how to do even the simplest of calculations. "Real men don't need math," I told him, and he repeated it with disastrous results to his parents and instructors.

I was a strong male role model to an impressionable child whether I meant to be or not. I liked it, don't get me wrong. I felt a little powerful. It's energizing to have someone hang on your every word. The problem was that I had little to teach him. I was blank slate when I showed up and had a tremendous learning curve to overcome.

At the time, I had no idea what exactly I was, or what was to become of me. I knew that one minute I was literally nothing, and the next, I existed just because a little boy thought me up. I knew that when he called me, I was there. When he didn't, I was nowhere. I didn't eat, sleep or think unless he gave me the will to do so. When I was gone, it wasn't even like sleeping; there were no dreams, or nightmares, I just didn't exist without him. It was certainly a confusing time for me, to say the least. I would imagine it's like learning to walk for a child. I took baby steps to get acclimated to my situation. I learned to savor each minute he thought of me just in case it was my last. It wasn't until things came to an end that I suddenly arrived at the Hill to be assigned to someone new.

Like most kids, Truman slowly outgrew his Imaginary Friend. He won over some real friends with misplaced confidence, emerging wit and developing muscles. With my coaching, he slowly began to understand when to talk, when to nod courteously, and when a well-timed shove would get his point across. I engineered my own demise by sharing these tips with him. Each time I started to disappear into nothingness, I wondered how long I would be gone. I was afraid my absences were growing longer, but had no way of keeping track of time. Every wait went by in an instant for me, but I was sure days or weeks had gone by in Iowa. One time we waited by the window looking out as a hard rain soaked everything in sight and on my next trip we sat under the tree digging in the dry, cracked earth. One visit, we ran in the fields, through row upon row of tall cornstalks, on the next the fields would be barren, the soil turned under.

I had all of the knowledge that Truman had accumulated, so I understood that everything ended, everything died. In my limited experience, I couldn't wrap those ideas around my precise situation. I had no idea whether I could or would meet my end. These were things Truman's thoughts couldn't possibly prepare me for.

One spring, a construction company finished building a forty-house development in a field just down the road from Truman's house. Within what must've been weeks, families moved in. Truman was suddenly in demand as a guide to the local terrain. He showed them the gullies and enclaves that we used as hiding places and forts. He found himself in a situation where no one knew anyone else, and the playing field was suddenly amazingly level. Come fall when school started again, a group of those kids banded together for support as they entered the halls of education.

I didn't get any real free time when I was with Truman. I mean, I had things to do. There was still climbing, seeking and running to do when he found time away from his friends. I thought about the situation, though, when I could steal a moment—climbing a tree, on the way to the playground. Here's the final kick in the pants: None of his real flesh and blood friends had an Imaginary Friends of their own. Truman didn't need me; this I knew. He had a group of living, breathing, fleshy little things to hang around with, which was all well and good for him, but where did that leave me? An invisible man that only one kid could see?

The onset of winter brought an end to that particular chapter of my life.

The ground was covered in the fine white powder of the first big snow of winter. Truman was wrapped from head to toe in his heaviest cold weather gear. A red cap over his ears, a blue scarf around his neck, and a huge coat that hinted of several more layers underneath with its bulk. We stood by the old elm tree not saying a word for several minutes. He looked at me, cocking his head slightly as he examined me from head to toe.

From the back door of the house his mom called. "Truman! Your friends are here!" she said. "Grab your sled, you don't want to keep them waiting!"

He looked toward the door. "Okay. Just a minute!" He yelled as he began to slowly walk back to the house. He picked up his sled and glanced back over his shoulder at me. He ran around the corner of the house and I followed. He smiled as he saw his friends, and at that moment he seemed the happiest I'd ever seen him. I felt the light flakes of precipitation hitting me, and though they didn't stick to me, I loved the sensation. The snow was beautiful. The world was beautiful and I felt a calm come across me.

Then, putting his sled under his arm, Truman took off at a light run around the house and was gone.

So was I.

9

A makeshift platform was erected near an edge of the Hill with a podium and four chairs on it. Sets of wooden steps were placed on either side. Father Time, Mother Nature and Death walked up the stairs on the left and sat down as the Director stepped to the podium. In front of him was a stark wooden box that was tilted slightly so the mourners could see Ira's body inside. I couldn't tell, but from my spot so far away he appeared a little easier to see than he had been moments before. I wondered if they'd put some sort of makeup on him for the funeral?

Out of everyone who showed up, I was most impressed with the other Boogeymen. Each, except Zane, who didn't have time to change, wore their black-and-red dress uniforms and gleaming boots. They lined up with military precision in seven rows, with empty spaces left where the Director and Ira would have stood.

The funeral went on without me while I tried to get it straight in my head. I had donned a dark coat I had found on the way out of Ira's building. I'd taken it off a peg by the front door without thinking, and pulled its hood over my head so no one could scrutinize my face as I pondered the situation. Ira couldn't die, yet Ira was dead. I was some kind of lawman in a land with no laws—a line judge in a tennis match where nothing is out of bounds. I spent most of the service scanning the crowd assembled to pay their respects, searching their faces for some trace of guilt, some knowing look that would make it all clear to me what happened. In the faces of the Fairies, the Elves, the Aliens and the Gods, I gleaned nothing. Nor did I gain insight from the Ghosts or the Goblins or the others. I saw sorrow and fear in those faces. I saw steely eyes and blank expressions on all of the Boogeymen as they stared forward.

I heard voices from the podium, but couldn't bring myself to glance and see who spoke them. 'Tragic' and 'bewildering' most often described his death. Words like 'hero' and 'legend' peppered the descriptions of Ira by his peers. One speaker with a deep booming voice broke down, crying as he attempted to say goodbye to his 'longtime friend.' I wanted to look up, just to see him, just to know who the person was who claimed to be so close to Ira. I found I couldn't. I felt ashamed, for myself and for him. I figured I didn't have a right to see his grief, his tears, his naked emotions.

Soon, another voice said, "It's all right. Come on. Let me help you." It was silent for a moment and then I heard someone else step up to the podium. They began much like everyone else did, trying to say how much they would miss an old friend.

In the crowd they held each other, and took solace in that contact. I realized I was alone on this terrible and strange occasion. Zane was standing in his place with the rest of the Boogeymen. Brady was at the back of the main crowd with his arm around a shorter, silvery version of himself. My Sarah was nowhere to be found. I understood then how much of an outsider I had become. I was suddenly something new. One of a kind. I hoped word hadn't gotten around yet. If no one had heard about my 'promotion' or whatever it was, maybe they wouldn't treat me any differently. In my head, I decided it was an apprenticeship of sorts, something new that I was just trying out. Had I known how harsh the penalty was for not choosing a new career more hastily, I'd have jumped on the chance to be an Elf, I suppose.

Another realization hit me as I scanned the throng of mourners; it was shocking how many of them there were. I couldn't even identify all of them by name. I suppose I knew them all, had passed them on the street, drank with them. But their names, their purposes, and their creators were a blank in my mind. Did they enjoy their jobs or even their lives? Did they wander in the mists at night because they couldn't sleep? Did they hate their existences enough to jump over the side of the Hill?

"We will now send our dearest friend Ira on to his final resting place," I heard Father Time say from the podium, prompting the Council to stand.

The Boogeymen stepped toward the platform in two perfect lines. They walked up on either side of the odd wooden coffin that held Ira. The first ones in line continued past the coffin and stopped when the last four in each line were next to it. Then, as though they had rehearsed it a thousand times, the eight neared the coffin, bent and lifted it. The whole line moved forward toward the edge of the Hill to a gap in the stone fence that seemed to have been opened just for the ceremony. Everyone stopped, and the coffin was passed forward from the back of the line to the front. Once the Boogeymen at the front of the line had it, they paused, nodded at each other, and began to tip the back end of the coffin up. The end broke away once the incline reached a certain point, and the outline of Ira's body could be seen sliding out of its resting place and into the mists below.

The crowd dispersed slowly, like an oil slick on the ocean. Tiny black globs of mourners breaking off one by one and floating toward separate shores. Some had gone to the edge to look into the mists, while other droplets of the throng stood-stone still, waiting for some direction.

I spotted Thor in the crowd, his long hair and beard flowing smoothly in the wind. He saw me and waved. He seemed disappointed when I didn't wave back.

10

Zane and Brady met me at my apartment after the service for a strategy and brainstorming session. Less like brain*storming*, really. It was a light rain, if anything. A drizzle at best.

"Okay. What do we know so far?" The two stared back momentarily before looking around the room. Each appeared to be searching the walls, the ceiling and the table between us for the answer I was looking for. After a moment, Zane looked toward Brady to see if he was going to say anything, then slowly raised his hand and waited.

I nodded at him, and he lowered his hand. "Ira's dead?"

"Good. Let's start with the basics," I said. Zane smiled, pleased. I feared how long it was going to take to get through this. "What else?" The brief celebration ended, and they resumed their examination of the décor. "Do we know how he died?" Both paused before shaking their heads no. "Okay. We know he's dead, but don't know how." I felt I should be writing things down but was sure I got the gist of it so far. "Do we know *why* he's dead?" Blank stares in return. Thankfully, there were no shiny objects in the room, or I might have lost their concentration completely. "All right. So…he's dead…No *how*…No *why*. Very little else. Am I correct?" Brady had begun to twist his ponytail between his fingers. Zane slowly began to raise his hand again, so I reached over and slapped it down. "Just talk. Quit raising your stupid hand."

He pulled his arm close to his body. "Something's been bothering me a little. Everyone has always told us that we can't kill each other. You know, we basically only die if our creators wish us dead, or everyone forgets about us, right?" He looked at both of us. "I mean, that's what you guys heard, right?"

"Yeah. More or less," I said, and Brady nodded his agreement.

"Well, what if they lied? What if we can kill each other? When's the last time someone really tried?"

"Why would they lie? I would think, if anything, telling everyone they're invincible would only encourage more violence," Brady said. "Heck, people would be at parties yelling 'Hey! Look at me! I can't die! Somebody stab me or something!' and if everything they've told us is hooey, we'd have a lot less Imaginaries clogging up Main Street."

Zane leaned back in his chair. "First of all, who do you party with? Because I want an invitation next time." Brady began to answer, but Zane continued before he could. "The second thing is, couldn't telling us we're invincible also have the opposite effect? 'Hey, you can't kill each other; don't even try'?"

"Well, I suppose it could go either way," I said "But we've heard stories about this, haven't we? About some of the Greek Gods getting into it with the Norse in bar fights and such? What about the epic Aliens versus Elves soccer riot? Everybody has heard those stories time and time again. Things used to get ugly all the time. And I never heard of anyone dying in one of those situations."

"Yes, but who told us those stories?" Zane got up and began to walk around the table. "And do you know anyone who actually saw them take place?"

I didn't like where this was going. Zane had a point. Zane rarely had a point. Chaos couldn't be far away. Cats and mice having tea parties and the like. "I heard the stories from one of the Boogeymen, who said he heard them from somebody else, and no, I don't know anyone with firsthand knowledge of any of this." Zane having a point made the whole situation creepier than it already was. "But I'm sure we can find a witness pretty easily, right? The old guys are everywhere."

The meeting really wasn't helping anything. We started with nearly nothing to go on and were ending by doubting almost all of the facts that we started with.

"I don't think we can trust anyone else to tell us the truth," Zane said as he stopped behind me on his clockwise journey around the table.

"How do you propose we prove this little theory of yours, then? If you don't want to take anyone else's word for it—" I asked.

"*Like this*!" Zane lunged at me and wrapped his right arm around my neck. His left one then covered my mouth and nose. He pulled back, trying to lift me from my seat but succeeding only in tilting the chair back on two legs.

I reached up and grabbed the arm over my mouth with both hands but I couldn't get leverage due to the chair's position. "Don't struggle," Zane said. "This is official business." I let go of his arm and tried to smack his face. "Brady, get over here and strangle him with your ponytail or something."

Brady stood up, but he didn't come over to use his ponytail as a garrote on me. He stood there on the other side of the table staring at the two of us. His head slowly tilted to the side in confusion.

Zane continued to keep a firm lock around my neck and continually twisted and tightened his other arm trying to ensure that all of my head holes were plugged to suffocate me. I swiped and swatted at his head, trying to get him to release me. My flailing was ineffectual, although it did seem to increase Zane's resolve in continuing his little experiment. I even tried to reach up and poke him in the eyes in the hope of blinding and disorienting him, but I couldn't angle my arm correctly.

I quit struggling altogether, not because I blacked out, not because I *couldn't* breathe. It was because I *didn't have to.* The drama of the situation, the sudden attack, the paranoia that had been sown in the brainstorming session had all made me feel like I were in danger. Once I relaxed and stopped struggling, I felt quite normal. Normal except for the man with his arms clenched around my neck like a vise, that is.

I folded my arms across my chest and waited for Zane to give up.

"Ummm…Zane?" Brady finally spoke up. "Maybe you're doing it wrong, 'cause it looks like you're just making him mad now."

Zane sheepishly broke his hold on me and stepped back.

After his repeated apologies, I forgave him so we could get on with our work.

"I think the best thing to do next would be to talk with the last people we know talked to Ira. That means the Boogeymen I saw him sitting with at The Wet Dream. Maybe we can find something meaningful from them," I said. "You two should see if you can find them, while I go ask some other Imaginaries a few questions."

We each left the session with assignments. I stepped outside my door and watched my new partners leave. The rest of the hall looked empty. As soon as the two of them walked out the front entrance, I started checking the hall in earnest, squinting to try to pick out any shapes I may have missed. Still nothing. The hall appeared empty. "Hello?" I asked in no direction in particular.

It was quiet for a second or two. "Yes?" The reply came from my left.

I turned to see a shape materialize at nearly my eye level, white as paper. There were a few types of Ghosts to be found roaming the Hill. There are the ones that look like a normal person, except you can see through them.

Others look like large glowing balls of light, or wisps of smoke or mist. The one before me was the typical Otherworld-Halloween-floating-sheet-with-eye-and-mouth-holes variety. She was only about three feet tall and floated about four feet off the ground. "I take it you're my messenger," I said.

"Yep. Name's Kite. At your service. Anything you need."

"Kite?"

"Yes sir. I am a rare specimen, indeed. An Imaginary Friend *and* a ghost."

"A kid wanted a ghost for a companion? Strange. Why Kite? Where did that come from?"

Kite twisted himself around so I could see behind her. Tied up in the tatters of the sheet-like mass that made up her body were three small colorful bows. "Kid used to take me out in rainstorms and play 'Ben Franklin.' Let me tell you, I learned some very valuable lessons about lightning, my friend."

"Welcome aboard. I can use all the help I can get. You out here all the time?"

"I'm around. Just call and I'll be there."

I nodded and sent my ghost messenger off to tell the Council that I needed to make a trip to the Otherworld.

11

"So he just tried to strangle you? Right there in the meeting?" Sarah asked, struggling to keep up with my long strides. She was constantly a couple of feet behind me, no matter how hard she tried.

"Yup. Wrapped his limbs around my throat and squeezed. Like he was really going to kill me."

"Well, I guess things are a little confused around here. Maybe he's just trying to do a thorough job for you. I know it's an odd way of going about it, but it could just be his way of starting at square one."

"It's not like our whole world changed overnight. There are a few things that we can still rely on."

"Well, didn't it? One of the basic truths of our existence disappeared in a matter of hours."

I stopped and turned on my heels in the middle of Rustle Avenue. The cobblestone streets were deserted except for some heavily-armored knight of some sort, lying face-down in front of the Dark Logger at the end of the street. "We don't know if anything's changed, do we? Maybe what happened to Ira was entirely natural. Maybe it just happens and we'd never seen it happen before. Maybe the last time it happened, no one was around to see it."

She wrinkled her eyebrows in consternation. "You don't really believe that, do you? How could you possibly believe that? You haven't suggested that theory to anyone else yet, have you?"

It's true that I held absolutely no hope that the solution would be as simple as that. I hadn't floated the theory to the others because I had absolutely no reason to believe it was true. I had absolutely no evidence to support the idea. "I'm working on some correlation to the idea and don't want to tip my hand just yet."

"Right." She continued walking in the direction of the Personnel building.

"What? I am."

"Oh, please."

"How would you know?" I walked fast to catch up.

"Abe, don't be an idiot. I know you. You don't have the slightest idea what you're talking about." She tilted her head at me just a little as she walked. "It's still early, though. I'm sure you have some surprises in you."

"What do you mean by that?"

She took my hand in hers and swung it back and forth like we were carefree children on the first day of school. "Nothing, exactly. I just think you're going to really do well with this new thing." She turned toward Creak Lane. "Good luck out there."

"You're not going to walk me to work?"

She kissed me and let go of my hand. "I think you can find your own way. You've been going there for the transport tubes for quite some time now."

She started to leave, but I took her hand again. "Maybe I can't. Maybe I need your help."

"You're a grown Imaginary. You're quite capable of finding your own way." I was amazed at how easily she slipped her hand from mine. "Besides, it's right behind you. Just turn around." She made a grand gesture toward the building not more than two hundred yards from where I stood and skipped down the road as I turned to look at it.

"I know where I work, thank you. That wasn't the point."

12

It was dark when I opened my eyes. The cramped quarters I felt my body trying to conform to told me I was in a small closet. You just get a feeling for these things, I guess. When I was solid enough, I reached up and could feel a couple of winter jackets and sweaters hanging above me. A crack of light shone near the floor. I was laying on something very uncomfortable and as I reached around I found a hiking boot sticking in my back.

Nearby, a TV was blaring the sounds of sirens and gunfire. The light at the bottom of the door changed color and intensity with the sounds as the scene shifted on the television. Occasionally, I could hear the shuffling of papers. I could smell the acrid scent of cigarette smoke floating through the air and embedded in the jackets. The floor creaked once or twice in the next room. I think the other smell was bacon grease.

I waited.

Somewhere on the other side of the door was Truman Keller. Policeman.

I was anxious to see what his time on this world had done for him. To him. There were questions. *Answers*. Shit I could glean from him. For years I appeared at his bidding and disappeared to that limbo when he was through with me. I wondered how he would react to me showing myself to him at *my* leisure. I wondered if he would even be able recognize me. Surely the one who created me would know me no matter how old either of us had become, or whatever changes we'd gone through. I began to feel an excitement at seeing him again. Like a lost cousin home for the holidays. A loner at the class reunion.

I fumbled for the doorknob and turned it slowly and carefully. More light shone into the closet, and the sounds got louder as I pushed the door open a little.

Created me. My Creator.

I stopped pushing the door.

Truman created me. The only person who could kill me is my creator. Least, that was the wisdom. I was slow, but I managed to ask myself a question or two: what if Truman reacted badly to his imaginary childhood friend-turned-ghoulish-specter just showing up in his living room decades after his youth? Not everyone can handle that just right. What if he thought he was going crazy or something and in an effort to clear his mind, wished I were dead? Would that end it? End me? I suddenly felt like I should have planned this trip better—maybe asked a few appropriate questions of the appropriate people. Asked anyone anything, really. In the near-dark I listened to the television and stared at the crack of light between the floor and the bottom of the door.

Seriously. What if the he wished me *dead*? Whether it killed me or not, that kind of thing can cause damage. Serious damage.

I could've gone home.

I *wanted* to go home.

Zane and Brady probably hadn't come up with anything, so I wouldn't be the only one coming home empty-handed. We would all be washouts together. And Sarah. I could be nice and comfortable in bed with Sarah right about now. All I had to do was think about it, and I could be back home under three layers of covers with her. No fuss. No life-altering decisions. No potential for the end of my existence. Obliteration would be the last thing on my mind. Nothing nearly as serious as this. Just a quiet end to the day with the girl of my dreams.

"You can come out." A gruff rumble came from outside the closet. "I've been waiting for you." At first I ignored it as more of the blare of the television, but I noticed the light under the door growing dimmer, blocked by something. Then a click, and the din of the television was silenced in mid-tire squeal. "It's okay. I know you're there." The voice was a near whisper, but it obviously came from just the other side of the door. "At least I hope that's you, George."

I sat back on the boots, dumbfounded. He knew I was there. Called me by name—well, his name for me, anyway. The urge to run rose as a tightening of my spine, a hardening of my limbs.

I expected...

Nothing.

Any expectations I had come to that world with were gone. I imagined each possible reaction he might have to my presence: fear, joy. I never even imagined having to react to *him*.

"Am I going to have to stand here all night?"

It seemed logical to join him. I was hiding; he found me. Game over. '*All-the-all-the-outs-in-free!*' Or whatever it was Truman used to yell when we played his ridiculous games together in the woods. Sitting in the closet felt a bit ridiculous, childish, even. Any second, I expected a voice to leap from the television set, shouting 'Come on out, we've got the place surrounded' in some sort of cop-show synchronicity, but it didn't.

"No. No reason to stand around alone out there, I suppose." I surrendered my concealment.

The closet door swung slowly outward revealing Truman to me. He was still very much the boy of his youth. Taller, naturally. Most kids get taller after thirty-some years, though he hadn't grown unusually large or freakishly short. His face was wider, though not fat. If it were possible, his face was more muscular, as though it had built itself up by carrying heavy loads repeatedly for years. His hair was still slight and unruly, though the brown had faded and become washed-out. He wore blue jeans and a dark polo shirt. His feet were bare on the kitchen's rusty orange-ish tile floor. Based on the very few adults that I had dealt with on the Otherworld up to that point, I guessed Truman to be the very fucking epitome of average.

"Hi." Truman looked at me as I emerged from the closet. "There. George." At first, he looked at me indirectly, out of the corner of his eye, as if I were the sun and he knew it was a bad idea to stare at me. He had a huge smile, which faded to a guilty smirk. There have been so few actual people who have seen me, or any of the other Imaginaries for that matter, for a real length of time that there is no real precedent. What I was doing was tantamount to telling the world, starting with one person, that everything is true.

It's all real.

You were all right.

It wasn't childhood silliness.

There is something under your bed.

There is something going bump in the night.

Something is following you.

And if you ask it nicely, it might come into your kitchen and watch reruns of *CSI: Miami* with you.

"You've changed a bit," I said, trying to muster some dignity. Truman's smile had become much more natural as the initial shock wore off. "Taller… bigger." I made motions with my arms, trying to show how tall I remembered him to be the last time I saw him.

"That'll happen to just about everybody." He laughed. "You changed some, too. Still you, though. Still you. You look good." He went to pat me on the shoulder, but stopped short. He seemed unsure of whether he could touch me, and I honestly didn't know either.

"I'd like to say it's clean living that makes me look this way, but nothing I do is all that clean and I'm not really living." I thought it was a fair joke, worth a chuckle at least, but it made him stare a little closer at me. He began to walk around me, close enough that I could feel his breath move over my neck. He stopped and put his arm around me as if to hug me, but he didn't make contact. He squinted and moved his fingers. I decided he was trying to see through me, but couldn't.

I was solid.

Finally, he came back around in front of me. His wide smile was back and he slowly opened his arms to enfold me. He hugged me as men embrace on special occasions: weddings, births, graduations, important sports victories. It was strong and violent with a lot of backslapping. I stood with my arms partially apart, just enough for him to encircle me. It was the kind of greeting I would expect to get from Brady. I let him do it and didn't move away. The slapping went on for some time, and I thought that the crack of his open hand on my back served to reinforce the fact that I was there. "I never thought you'd come back." he said. "Never." He stopped and walked to the kitchen sink with his back to me. "Can I get you something? Water?" There was a catch in his voice that I didn't understand.

"I really can't drink anything in this world, you know?" I looked around the kitchen and discovered that it connected closely to the living room where the big television sat only recently blaring its sound and multi-colored fury. In the center of the kitchen, a dark table was overrun with folders and other papers. A marker and some pens sat on top of a stack of newspaper clippings. An ashtray full of cigarette butts smoldered near the only chair pushed out from the table.

I was suddenly and overwhelmingly parental. I wondered when he took up smoking. How long had he smoked? What was his brand? Why did he start? I wanted to know everything else I missed. First kiss. Love. Hate. Work. Favorite foods. I was proud that I had a hand in what he was and ashamed that I missed the parts where he became it. I wanted the chance back to hug him and slap his back loudly. I wanted to make sure I couldn't see through him each and every day.

"Oh. Of course." He grabbed a bottle of beer from his fridge while I continued to inspect his home. "I used to try to set a place for you at the dinner table when I was a kid, but Dad always flew off the handle. 'We're not settin' an extra damn place for your little invisible man,' he used to say." He took a long, noisy drink of his beer to wash the dust off the old words. "Well, the joke was on him; you didn't even *need* to eat."

I looked back at the table and noticed something that made my spirits soar. Half-hidden beneath the map and some clippings, in the opposite corner from the ashtray, near a stray pen, were two notebooks. *Two notebooks*! It seemed to vindicate my earlier instincts. I knew I needed something to write on, and here was proof. Real people took notes to work things out. Maybe I was right about other ideas I had. It instilled in me some confidence that I could do the job just fine.

Truman saw me staring. "What's wrong? What are you looking at?"

"It's kind of a long story, but someone back home got killed and it's my job to look into it." I felt something rise in my chest that I hadn't had the opportunity to feel before. "Since I understand you have some expertise in these things, I thought we could talk about it." Pride and satisfaction mixed in ways I hadn't experienced.

"Expertise?"

I nodded toward a pressed blue uniform shirt and pants hanging off of a chair back. "They told me all about what you were doing with your life."

"Kinda tough to hide things from the likes of you guys, I suppose." Truman drank deeply and walked toward the table. "Whatever you need. You want to talk out here or in the living room? Probably quieter out here." Truman grabbed a towel off the counter and used it to wipe off a chair he pulled out. "I hope you don't mind if I leave the TV on. I like the background noise."

"Not a problem."

"Look, George." Truman gathered his papers off of the table and scrunched them into somewhat of a pile, all the while smiling just a little. "I've been thinking about things that you told me when I was a kid. I forgot them for a while, but I remembered them recently. I want you to know I appreciate everything you did."

It was enough to make me lose sight of my questions for a time.

13

I left the return tubes and waved at the workers behind the assignment counters as I made my way for the exit. They didn't seem too busy; just a half a dozen Imaginaries waiting to check in or check out or whatever the fuck they were standing around for, which was unusual for them at that time of the night. This is when things start hopping around here. I thought about stopping, asking what was going on, but figured I should get back to my own job.

A gray Alien with a big head was having trouble getting in through the door as I tried to leave. He was small, with thin arms that couldn't keep two enormous beaded seat covers pressed to his body. I held the door for him and admired his craftsmanship. "This is nice; you make this yourself?" I spun some colored beads with my fingers.

"Yeah. Those UFO seats are murder. Not built for comfort in the least." He managed to find a firm grip on both covers and walked toward the lobby. "Besides, what else do I have to do in my free time, right?" He waved over his shoulder. "Thanks for the help...and watch your head as you go out!"

The door was still open as I watched him walk away with his comfortable seat cushions. "Huh? What was that?"

"Duck." He nearly dropped his seat cover, but caught it before it hit the floor.

The lines at the counter had disappeared, and he went straight to an assignment agent. She put a piece of paper in his mouth and he mumbled something to her.

I looked back at the open door. Crazy. That's what he must be. The door was tall enough for me to fit through with plenty of room to spare. What was the risk? I started to walk through at my full height, but thought again.

Duck?

I hunched over. Not a lot. Just some. Just a foot or so. Just enough that I could feign a logical reason for doing so, if someone happened to see me and question my behavior. I didn't have a logical reason prepared, but I was sure something would come to me.

I proceeded slowly out the door, partially stooped over.

As soon as I stepped out, I felt a slight breeze over my head and heard a dull thud above me. I looked up to see Zane holding the handle of a large axe with both hands. The head of the axe was buried two inches deep in the door behind me. I was all in favor of my friends helping me, but we had already established that trying to kill me wasn't going to get us anywhere.

Zane smiled a sheepish smile. "I borrowed the battle axe from one of the Gods of war—Tyr, I think. Nice, huh? Heavy, though." He tugged lightly at the handle, but his blow had buried it deep in the wood. "The lousy alien ratted me out, didn't he?"

14

I felt stupid standing there holding the flag on the ninth hole.

Death glanced at me with a smile. "You didn't just go to him. You weren't just casually going to the Otherworld to ask him a thing or two." He calmly sank the putt he had lined up.

"Sure I was. We all had assignments. They were supposed to ask questions here. I went to talk to the policeman." I stepped in front of him as he went to retrieve his ball. "You guys suggested it, remember?"

He looked down at me and casually leaned on his putter like a cane. "Trust me. Truman summoned you. He's been dealing with some things."

"Yeah. He didn't say much about it, though. Mostly listened to me. I imagine police work can be hard." Actually, I never worried about Truman's mental health until the words came out of my mouth. I hadn't given a thought to how that kind of a job would impact him. When I looked at him, he seemed fit on the outside and happy enough.

"Right. Lot of dying in that line of work. I'm aware of how hard it is to deal with. Kinda my job to keep up on these things. Ya know?" He pointed to himself in a grand manner. "Death, Grim Reaper, all that? Anyway, I thought it best to spare the ladies any gory details. Not polite." He stepped around me and waved to the women who had moved ahead. "You were summoned. He's working on this thing—It brought up issues of his own childhood. He regressed more and more into his own past, dredging up long-forgotten things." Death turned after he picked up the golf ball and pointed the club at my chest. "Like you, my boy. He remembered you. Whether you could help him or not, he remembered and called out to you. Just for old time's sake. It isn't really the way things are normally done. You resisted for a time, but you made it there eventually. You're only supposed to work with kids, after all. How would you know what to look for when an adult reaches out to you?" He walked briskly to catch up with the ladies. The greens of the course shone with the refection of morning dew. Sunshine. A golf course. I wondered how many other wonders the Council effectively kept hidden from the general populace.

"He never asked me for help. What could I do for him?" I said. I replaced the flag and wondered why I came to him for answers. "And he never mentioned anything about a case he was working on." There was so much that I forgot to ask, or didn't notice, I suppose. I went to the Otherworld to learn to be a better detective, not practice being one to an old friend. My guard was down. Did I even ask him *any* questions?

"You never gave him the chance. Once you asked for *his* help, there was no way he was going to ask for yours. It's just the way he is."

"Why would he think I could help him? He was supposed to be helping me! He owes me, right? I mean, I was the best part of his childhood."

"Were you?" Death called over his shoulder without turning around.

"Yes. I was his buddy…a pal. I kept him company, played with him, saved him from harm when I could. Other than some of the usual childhood crap, he had it pretty good growing up."

"Did he?"

Death caught up with the women and put his arms around the Muse's waist. She giggled and they fell in step together.

I cupped my hands around my mouth and shouted. "Hey!" The group didn't stop or turn around, but I shouted anyway. "I need a notebook!"

Despite the obtuse conversation with Death and the unusual manner in which Truman and I got together, I felt buoyant, held up by the thrill of seeing an old friend make good. I felt like I had a hand in him becoming and adult and being a man. I thought I could see little things in him that I could take credit for: mannerisms, verbalizations, I guess. I couldn't put a name to it, but I was proud nonetheless. On top of the reunion excitement, Truman had also given me some ideas—a solid foundation to base my investigation on. He seemed to know so much about everything. It was a long way from the boy who walked away from me that winter day, sled in hand. It made the parental pride swell in me again.

I bounced back to my apartment, which served as our base of operations for the investigation. Within minutes of my arrival, my partners came in with considerably less enthusiasm than I did.

I took my time recapping my day for them; I met the kid I'd been an Imaginary Friend to, and I played golf with Death. I used a little more detail, but I realized I had done and learned little more than that. Zane and Brady stared, mouths slightly agape when I finished. Neither moved for a moment or two. Their hesitation to speak at the end led me to believe that they both comprehended the gravity of the situation. I had done something no other had and managed to walk away from it. I met the kid, talked to the adult he had become, and walked away from the conversation. I didn't know of any other Imaginary Friend that had met the result of the child they'd helped shape.

"Look, let's sort that out after it has time to sink in." I said. "Why don't you guys tell me what you found out?"

"Nothing." Brady shrugged his huge shoulders as he said it. I wondered if he took the gravity of his tasks seriously. His regular job involved smelling bad and walking in the woods, so the magnitude of what we were doing could've been lost on him.

"I sent you to talk to Ray and Thad about the night Ira died. You got nothing? I was gone quite a while."

Zane joined in at that; "But that's what is so important. They don't want to talk to us. Every time we went around to their apartments and hangouts, they were never there. They weren't at the bars; they weren't anywhere. We looked, Abe, everywhere we could think of. No luck."

Brady nudged him. "Tell him about everybody else—go on."

"Yeah. That's the other thing. People are staring. It was kind of nice to be recognized at first, but now it's just ridiculous. They look at us like we're on fire or something."

"And none of them seem to want to help. They all get real quiet when we walk into a room. I don't know what the problem is," Brady said. "Didn't the Council tell them to cooperate with us?"

"That they did, Brady."

Zane started to put his hand up but stopped himself. "What was it like? Getting to see him again, I mean. Did he change much?"

"Well, you know, he grew up a lot." I tried to picture the person I recently saw wearing the snowsuit that the Truman I left behind all those years ago had on and just couldn't do it. "Got taller...stuff like that."

"Did he show you his badge?"

"What is it with you and badges? I'm sorry I couldn't get us some."

"That's okay; I just thought it would be neat to see."

Truth was, I would have liked to see it for myself, but I was too shy to ask.

15

Father Time and I sat facing each other in the gondola. Behind me, the ferryman guided the boat with practiced precision. His boney white face and hands stayed hidden from view by his gray robe and hood, but I knew they were there. I met him in the Wet Dream one night when we were both feeling pretty low. He was known by many names throughout many cultures, but he preferred to be called Chad. He had guided this boat from the earliest of days of the Hill. It was a far cry from taking souls to the other side, but giving boat tours to Imaginary Friends and Elves kept him busy. In the distance, I could see the bridge and wondered why we didn't just cross on it.

"Turning out to be a nice day, isn't it Abe?" I watched Father Time put a finger up to his mouth in a shushing motion as he nodded toward our pilot. I only assumed he wasn't looking directly at us when Time made the motion.

"It's not bad." It really wasn't. We were close enough to the castle that some undiluted sunshine made it to us and even cleared away some of the fog around the banks of the river. The water was still near black, but the sunlight dancing off of it seemed to make it less so. "The sun's kind of nice for a change. You know?"

"Yeah. I get the benefit of it all the time, but I forget most of you don't see it much." He crossed his legs and stared over toward the banks and the clearing fog.

We both were quiet until mid-way across the dark river Father Time said, "That's about right."

There was a jolt as the ferryman jerked back on the rudder, bringing us to a stop.

"Chad?" Father Time said to pilot. "Could you give us a few moments?"

The ferryman pulled back his hood revealing his bare skeleton skull. It was so shiny that I was sure he polished it on a regular basis. He looked as puzzled as anyone with no facial features could. He turned his head left toward the water and then right, presumably to illustrate that water surrounded our boat.

"I'm sorry, Chad, I really am. But do you mind?" I watched Father Time tip his head slightly to the right. Chad nodded affirmative and untied his sash. As the robe fell toward the boat bottom, it was obvious that his whole skeleton was shiny, as if he had buffed his entire skeletal self to a high sheen. Before the robe hit the floor, I caught sight of the ferryman's tiny formfitting bikini swimsuit, which left little to the imagination. I had to turn my head toward shore, either out of embarrassment or envy, I don't remember which.

With one step, he disappeared off the boat and into the water. There was a splash and nothing else. I waited, expecting him to come back up and swim toward shore or out ahead of us, but he didn't. I leaned back toward where disappeared, yet I saw nothing more than bubbles and ripples in the water.

"So. Little progress, then?" Father Time said, although he was really not addressing me. He had, in fact, turned his back to me and was facing the bow of the boat. Immediately, I thought he was looking for Chad as I was. As I looked closer, I realized he was looking up.

"Yeah. I just don't get it. Between myself, Zane and Brady, we've gone over all of the evidence we could muster. We've tried to talk to everyone we could find that could be involved. In fact, we'd planned on talking to pretty much everyone on this rock, but that's a big task." The slow steady movement of the waves put me in an extremely relaxed state. I hadn't had a chance to relax since the whole thing started. We had been chasing our tails, and there was a lot to do still.

"Yes, sounds very disheartening. We all know you're doing your best. You and your comrades are doing very professional work. And we all know you really started from scratch and ran with this idea." He turned in his bench seat, and as his head came around, I could swear that he had been smiling until he faced me. "And we are all thrilled with the progress you've made."

"Thank you. We—I was beginning to worry that we were unappreciated."

"No. No. Far from it. The Council is keeping a close eye on everything you do. The outcome of what you are doing will affect everything on the Hill for… well, for the foreseeable future."

"Oh. Well, when you put it that way—"

"And just to correct something you've said, you aren't close to talking to everyone, I'm sure."

"We've talked to most of the major groups, I think."

"Don't be naïve. There's more out there. Let me make a contribution to the effort," he said. He leaned closer and patted me on the knee before looking around the boat. "My silent effort, you understand? The rest of the Council probably wouldn't like me sticking my nose in where it doesn't belong, but—I feel like I can help."

Whatever it was, it had to be important. Why else would he take me out in the middle of nowhere to tell me? I had to respect his wishes, so I looked around the boat in the same fashion he had, and then looked over both sides of the boat. I nodded. "I get it. Off the record." If I had had a notebook I would have closed it just to prove the confidentiality of it all.

He took his hand off my leg—*finally*—and leaned back with arms folded. "There are people you have missed because you don't know you are missing them. There are still the ones we have to keep separated from the rest of you." Father Time shrugged his shoulders at me and turned away. I couldn't tell if it was indifference or arrogance. "What can I say, Abe? Some Imaginaries can't handle the reality, or lack thereof, of being an Imaginary. Some of their usefulness is so mundane or so brief that when they aren't doing the job, they're unable to function. They know nothing else. We don't advertise them or the fact they don't play well with others, so we keep them separate from the general populace."

"You're saying there is an entire community of Imaginaries that are crazy?"

"Completely batshit." I was glad we were in a boat. This was usually about the time in a conversation where someone would walk away enigmatically. I enjoyed a good entrance just as much as the next guy, but everyone hates a dramatic exit. I was sick of being walked away from, even if it was by Council members.

"No one thought it could be important to my investigation? I want to see them. Judge for myself whether they had anything to do with anything. Where are these things?"

"Where? Where else would you find bat shit?" He asked me as he touched his fingertip to the water. "In the caves, man. The caves further down the Hill." I watched the ripple that his finger caused grow outward until it was lost in a wave. "Believe me, I want this whole thing figured out as much as you do, maybe more so, but I honestly don't think what you find there will help your cause."

I didn't want to be disrespectful to one of the Council, but I was beginning to think they were constantly going to tell me half-truths and lead me around as they saw fit. "This is my job. I'm the one who decides what's important and what's a waste of time. Am I right?" I felt assertive for the first time in a while.

Father Time looked taken aback by my statement at first. His eyes were wide in surprise and his mouth hung open as if caught in mid-sentence. Then he leaned back against the bow and laughed a little. "Right you are, police man…It's your job, and I want to help in any way possible."

The conversation with Father Time settled to mush in my brain slowly. He suggested I go home to rest and promised that he would be waiting for me in the proper spot with some helpers to get us into the caves. The soft rhythm of the boat reminded me of how tense I was and how much I could use that time. I needed to regroup anyway, so I agreed.

We stared at each other for maybe a minute before I realized that there was no one to guide the boat to shore. "Is Chad coming back, then?"

When I opened my apartment door I saw her immediately. Sarah was waiting on the couch, reading. It was the best feeling I could have allowed myself. I didn't know when I was going to be able to see her again, so the little surprises meant a lot. I closed the door and rushed to the couch. "How are you? I was hoping I'd see you."

She rose and hugged me. "I'm good. I've been waiting for you. They must be working you hard," she whispered in my ear. The words were light in my head, floating above the weighty letters that spelled death and murder. I felt dizzy hearing them. Her voice producing the effect that alcohol must've had on the otherworld. I had trouble standing.

We broke our embrace and sat on the couch. I was more stable there. Sarah put her head on my shoulder and sighed. "Tell me what's going on. I get to see you so little lately. How are the boys? What is…"

"Whoa, easy there, missy. I'll ask the questions here," I said in my best cowboy impersonation.

"What's that? What are you doing?" Sarah asked.

"I was on the Otherworld. Watched some television. A bunch of police shows. Some about the seventies, some about the Old West." I wondered if she ever got to watch television when she was someone's Imaginary Friend. Probably not many cop shows, that's for sure. "Most of the cops on TV say something like that." I stood up and pointed my finger like a gun. "Ya gonna tell me where Mugsy is, or do I have to beat it out of ya?" She still looked at me with an incredibly puzzled look on her face. "'Just the facts, Ma'am'?"

"So, you got a free trip to the Otherworld and you waste it watching television? That's just wonderful." She had turned on me quicker than I could anticipate. I should have led with *Dragnet* rather than *Maverick*.

"No, no. I didn't get a free trip to the Otherworld. Nobody gets a free trip to the 'World." I sat back down and put a hand on her shoulder. "I was there on business. They sent me to learn some cop stuff, detective skills—from Truman."

She smiled. "You got to see him again? I didn't think anyone got to see their Imaginary Friends once they grew up. That is so exciting." She hugged me again, quickly this time. "Tell me all about it. How did he look? What was it like?"

"I don't know. It was very…disquieting? Is that the word I want? It was confusing and exhilarating and…and…everything. It was everything. All at once. Everything."

"I don't understand."

"I don't either. I was nervous at first, but when he called to me I felt…"

She leaned in closer and put her hand on my arm to stop me mid-sentence. "Wait. Wait a minute. You didn't say that. You didn't tell me you talked to him. That can't be. How do you get seen by and talked to by someone who Friended you as a kid, once they're an adult? You can't do that…" She shook her head and her narrowed her watery eyes. She was on the verge of tears and I had only begun to tell her the story. "Nobody does that."

It was then that I decided to lie to her. Not big lies, but ones to save her a little fear, if not give her some more sleep. I couldn't tell her everything. Couldn't explain the feeling that I was deliberately being left in the dark about something by people I had hoped would have answers. "I assumed that the Council had pulled some strings to make it happen, but none of them would own up to it. I've already talked to two of them, and they haven't said anything about assisting me." She hadn't started crying, but her eyes were still bright and shiny. I could tell tears were waiting for the right word to set them free, past the gates of the eyelids and onto the face. "Then again, they were the ones who sent me there in the first place."

"So, what else? What else happened to you? You said everything. Explain."

"Well—" I began to try to edit myself on the fly, but there were a couple of truths I wanted to blend in. "I was proud of him. You know? There he was, working hard. He was a good, healthy-looking man. Smart…boy, was he smart. Some of the things he told me…things he said." I was trying not smile. I wanted to be serious and as straightforward as possible. "It was just good to see him. That's all."

The tears in her eyes suddenly didn't seem so imminent. "No, I get it. I wonder what it will be like when I can't see the kid I'm Friends with anymore. I wonder what he'll be like after he leaves me. Where he'll go. What he'll become." She reached up and touched my cheek before standing on tiptoes to lightly kiss my lips.

"He smokes, though; that's not a good thing. Maybe I can get him to stop that pretty soon."

"It's all right...It's okay to be proud of him. Most of us don't get that chance. We don't get to go back and see the results..." She shook me a little as if the jarring would set something right in my mind. "I remember my first assignment. I loved that sweet little thing like my own. When we weren't together I'd sit there in my room and worry. 'Where was he?' 'What was he doing?' 'Was he getting picked on?' 'Would he still need me tomorrow?'" She rarely spoke of her work at all, let alone as wistfully as this. My situation stirred something in her to bring it on. I loved to listen to her voice and was soothed by the loving tone. "I spent my fair share of time standing by my door waiting to see if I was going back, or if a messenger was going to show up and give me a different assignment. I didn't want to leave him. I wanted to know what was going to happen to him. Where he was going, becoming, doing. I suppose some of that was just first time jitters. All Imaginaries get those their first time out, you know?"

I broke away then, quickly walking a few steps out of her reach. "It's just… it's just that I don't know if I can do this." I said. I was wrong earlier when I thought I needed rest and relaxation. Resting gave my mind nothing else to do but think about things rather than doing them. The events flew past my mind's eye like a train in the Old West about to get robbed by desperados. Unlike on television, there wasn't a cowboy hero aboard to stop them. "It's all so hard to put together. So many pieces and not one person to help me do it."

"You've got Zane and Brady. They wouldn't let you down. They're helping, aren't they?

I couldn't stop shaking my head, and the tears that were threatening her eyes found an unguarded escape from mine. "Yes, they're helping. They're doing their best, but really, they're idiots. I should have picked someone else to do it. They're like children...this Brady is nearly useless…stupid, just stupid. What was I thinking?"

"They're your friends, Abe. At least, the closest thing you have to them right now. I'm sure they're doing what they can. They're just as new at this as you are." She was worried about me, I could tell by her voice. I was worried about me as well. "Come on. Take it easy…did any of the cops cry on the shows you watched?" she asked.

That was a truth that was hard to argue. Even when they had heavy objects dropped on their feet, they never cried. I saw one show where a policeman got shot in the arm and he barely flinched or slowed down in his pursuit of justice. He certainly didn't cry. "No, but those were *real* cops. I'm untrained, confused, and wildly misinformed. I just can't do it."

"Sure you can do it. Everyone knows you can. They wouldn't have asked you if they didn't think so." She pulled me to her, and I stooped with my head to her shoulder. She stroked my head as she talked to me. "*I* know you can."

"You're just saying that because you have to."

"No, I'm not." She kissed my forehead and pulled me tighter, the closeness warming me. "I believe in you."

Those words formed the most incompressible sentence that I had heard in a long time.

I believe in you.

"Treat this like your first time ever. Pretend you are a completely new Imaginary again, only instead of being a Boogeyman, you're starting out as a whole new thing called an Investigator. It's a clean slate. You can be nervous. You can make mistakes. You can do whatever you have to do to get the job done right." The day was suddenly catching up with me, and I could feel myself relaxing. Sarah was fading too. We made our way into the bedroom and I collapsed, face down into my pillow.

"Imaginary Friend," I said.

"Hmmmm?"

"Imaginary Friend. You said I started out as a Boogeyman. I started as an Imaginary Friend."

"I'm tired. Been a rough day, and you never make it easier, do you?"

I fell into a deep sleep just after noticing that Sarah had covered the windows with extra blankets to stop the light from getting in, the word *believe* still hanging in the air above me.

16

I hadn't lost my mind completely. Even after my nerves had been calmed by a relaxing evening, I was still wary of meeting Father Time alone again so quickly. I sent Kite for Zane and Brady as soon as I awoke and had them meet me at the spot where I was to meet with Father Time.

I walked in the morning gloom with the hope that I wouldn't show up alone. The path I took to the meeting place was wide and lined with tall bushes. It was the proverbial scenic route—the way I went when I was in no hurry. I kept my head down for most of the walk, looking at stones in the pathway. I kicked one rock for a good long ways before it took a long hop into the bushes. The fog that encased that morning was the densest I could recall.

In the mists some distance ahead I could hear a tapping. It was a repetitive beat, a steady rhythm like a drummers' cadence that grew louder—closer. Without the benefit of a visual, I had to track its approach by sound alone. I could barely make out a shape, a black spot in the thick air. It was bouncing up and down and I realized someone, something was running toward me from way down the path. I looked around and realized there were no cross paths or buildings nearby, only shrubs. The bushes were thick and high. I considered whether I could get through them if I had to and decided I would save that as a last resort.

I was being silly. Who would be charging at me with some dark malevolent intent? Maybe it was a health-conscious group of Ghosts out for a morning jog or something.

For just the briefest of moments the fog cleared, and I could see what was coming. It was worse than I could have imagined.

Thor.

Thor was coming right at me, full force, and it didn't seem that this was a chance meeting. He had the look of a Norseman with something to say. Usually, anytime Thor had something to say, it took a long time. His red hair flowed, and his face strained with exertion. I didn't have time for this. I never had time for it, but that morning I had actually had an excuse, not that that would stop him from waylaying me. As much as was dreading where I was going, it was nothing compared to a conversation with Thor.

I realized much too late that there was another path up ahead. It came from the right and dead-ended into the path the two of us were on. Thor would reach it in a matter of steps and I had a hundred yards, easy. I wanted to turn and run back the way I came, but that would be childish—plus I was busy—and, with his momentum, he would catch me anyway.

Zane and Brady became visible as they stepped out from the side path, which was obscured by tall bushes, and they looked up and down my route. Once they saw me, they turned to walk in my direction.

Thor glanced at them but focused on me and continued to run. He seemed bent on getting to me before my friends, and they seemed completely oblivious to his presence.

Zane's smile faded as he seemed to read some distress on my face. I could see him nudge Brady in the ribs with his elbow.

Thor was running at top speed as he pulled even with Brady and Zane and showed no signs of stopping in his sudden, maniacal mission.

Brady never took his eyes off me, but still managed to stick his arm out at the right time to shove Thor into the bushes. "What's going on, boss?" he asked, not skipping a beat. Brady looked at me expectantly, waiting for praise or something for eliminating a perceived threat. I didn't react. We walked, and I looked behind us a couple of times but never saw anyone emerge from the shrubbery. There was a moment, just a brief one, where I just couldn't help but wonder what Thor wanted to say or do to me. From past experience I knew it was bad to wonder about that.

We walked together for a while in silence until the bushes cleared, and we were on the larger path that encircled the Hill. Even through the fog, we could see the area ahead where Father Time was waiting with two huge goons from Personnel and the Director.

"Look. I don't know exactly what's going on here. Father Time wants to show me something down deep in the Hill that he thinks might or might not be important to what's going on here." I wasn't sure what I wanted them to do. I was fairly convinced that someone would try to pull something on me, though honestly, I had no idea *what* they would try to pull on me. So far, we had proven, rather unscientifically, that I couldn't be killed. So what was there to be afraid of? "I just need the two of you to stay up here and keep an eye on things for me. Sort of watch my back." I turned specifically to Zane and made sure I had his attention. "This means I need you to lay off trying to fucking kill me. Am I clear? This is very important. I need to concentrate and I can't do that while I'm fending off an idiotic attack by you. You get me?"

"But it could be an important—" Zane began.

"I know. I know. It could turn into the thing we need to solve this. I doubt it, but I appreciate that, and I appreciate the work you're doing. But knock it off. Okay?"

"Yeah, all right."

I shook him a little and gave him my best smile of confidence. "That's my man. We're clear here, right?"

I could tell he had been formulating some plan of attack just by the way he hung his head. "Yeahallrightfine." I half-expected him to kick at the ground like a schoolboy, but he restrained himself well. A sniffle was his only derogatory noise.

"Brady?" I wanted things to be crystal clear to everyone. "If Zane does try anything, please tie his fingers in knots and then sit on him until I get back. Okay?" Brady nodded his head and began limbering up his fingers while leering at Zane. "And I can't emphasize enough...keep an eye on the Director and his people at all times. I just don't know where they fit into all this."

"What exactly are we supposed to do if they make some kind of move? Isn't the Director just as powerful as anyone else on the Council?"

I started walking, just to get this morning over with faster. Father Time and his group stared at us. "Yes, but I'm almost sure that even he can't kill anyone here. He can inflict punishments like transfers to other divisions, and he can make things miserable for everyone, but I don't think he can, you know...*end* us."

"Gosh. I hope you're right," Brady mumbled as he began to play with the long woven knot of hair.

"Gosh? That's all you've got in this particular situation? Gosh?" Zane said. "Gee whiz, Abe, I hope everything turns out just swell on your hike. Golly, but I wish we could go with you," Zane started to smack Brady on the back of the head, but seemed to think better of it. "Gosh, indeed."

"Quiet, you two." We were within easy hearing range of the waiting group, so I greeted them. "Morning, everyone."

"We didn't ask you to bring Curly and Moe with you," the Director said. "Sorry, but your little friends can't go down with you."

"Well then, we're all pretty surprised. I had no idea we'd be seeing you this morning, sir...and what a pleasant surprise it is." Father Time opened his mouth to say something, but I managed to cut him off. "Don't worry, I didn't think they'd be able to go with us. I just asked them along to help out with our descent if need be. I haven't had time to fill them in on what we're doing here." I raised my eyebrow, hoping Time would understand I hadn't divulged too much to anyone. That was actually easy.

It seemed he got the hint; he reached out and touched the Director's arm, patting it lightly. "I doubt they need the help, but I'm sure they'll enjoy the company." He headed toward a large device set up at the edge of the sheer face of the Hill. It sat right about where the stage for Ira's funeral had been. Ropes as big around as my waist wound though a system of pulleys and blocks leading to a large wheel with several handles. The ropes were finally attached to a scaffold that sat on the ground just inches from the edge. As I got closer, I could see that it was made out of nothing but logs and rope. It was large enough for several people, though I questioned whether such a rickety structure could hold more than the thin old man and myself. It had a floor: two high walls to the sides and shorter walls, half as high as the others on the front and back. Father Time opened a wooden gate that was tied shut on the side closest to us. With a flourish he waved his arm toward the opening. "Your chariot awaits."

I nodded to him, and as I stepped onto the wooden floor of the scaffold I became nervous. Walking up to the Director's group I was confident; I felt like I was doing my job, doing what needed to be done. Now, without Zane and Brady to back me up, I was much less sure of what was happening. Though most of what I had done up to that point had been without them, it was nice when they were at my back watching out for me. I felt bad about the things I said about them in my apartment. We were a team, and I kind of wished they were going.

I watched them both shuffling around, trying to look busy, or important. They'd do fine without me, I was sure. For the second time in recent days I felt an overwhelming sense of pride in something that I had a hand in. I didn't say anything to Truman about my feelings, so I felt I had to acknowledge my closest friends. I looked up and waved, smiling with confidence. From his position where he was sitting on Zane, Brady waved back with a broad smile of his own.

He leaned down and smacked his captive on the back of the head until he too waved and smiled. I felt conflicted.

Our transport rumbled a little as the huge ropes went taut. The Director was standing at the side, guiding us as we slowly inched toward the edge of the Hill. Beyond Zane and Brady I could see the two men from Personnel walking in circles around the wheel to which the ropes were attached. Every revolution they made brought us slightly closer to dangling over the side. Father Time leaned on one of the smooth handrails that was built into the half-walls. He looked out toward the edge and the mists beyond, while I was having trouble taking my eyes off of my crack team of law enforcement professionals wallowing on the ground.

"You'll want to hold on to something for this," Father Time said when we were almost to the drop-off.

I grabbed one of the railings and leaned toward it, bringing myself face to face with the Director, who was still on the ground pushing us. I nodded a hello/goodbye at him. "Take care down there, boy. You never know what you might find," he said, his voice a rockslide in my ears. Then he dug his feet into the ground and put his back into one last push that took us across the last few feet of solid ground.

We were flying. The ropes hadn't yet gone taut and our little craft was swinging through the mist, held aloft only by the force of a shove. Father Time held on with one hand and stared out into the mists, the clouds, and the darkness while I gripped the rail as though my existence depended on it. I stared at the land, at the Imaginaries that were standing there watching us now. I wanted to be back there at that moment, standing among them. Mostly ignorant, and without a care. I wanted to go back to what I was doing before Ira died. I wanted to be a regular working stiff.

We hit the rope's limit and our transport jerked to a stop. We hung there, suspended in the air, light, weightless. Just as I could feel movement back in the other direction, Father Time turned to me. I saw what I thought was a glimpse of sadness in his eyes. I wondered first if he was let down by me. There were thousands of things that could've made him unhappy, but I first thought of myself. Surely if he were disappointed in me he wouldn't have taken the time to go with me like this.

The scaffold quickly stabilized. We swung back toward the land but only came within ten feet or so. Then we swung back out, then to and fro a couple of times, but much less than I would have expected. We started our descent almost the moment we stopped rocking back and forth. It wasn't the jerky, stop and start, down a little...down a little...progress that I had expected. It was a smooth, steady ride, fluid like the river. I relaxed my grip on the rail and leaned against one of the side walls. Father Time had already done the same and was just staring at me.

"Couldn't we just...I don't know...appear down there? I mean, can't you pretty much do anything you want?"

"That's what everyone thinks, isn't it?" He chuckled a little and looked me in the eye with contact that made me uneasy. "I wish I could do whatever I wanted. No, I can't just make people, least of all myself, appear wherever I want. There are certain laws as to what can happen, even here." He nodded his head and looked at the rocky face of the Hill as it went slowly by. "It'd be fun, though."

I looked over the side and down in the mists below.

"You know, some Imaginaries have gone so far as to jump over the side of the Hill. I don't know if it was out of boredom, or some test to see if they could end their own lives. Yep. Leapt right over."

"And?"

"Nothing. They went so far, soaring through the air, and then they woke up in a tube. Nice and snug. Each of them. It's simple, really, the same principle as going to the Otherworld. We are all dissolved into blackness and emerge from it too. They fell past the very clouds that are below us right now. Underneath, there is nothing but darkness. Once someone hits that darkness, they are transported back to a receiving tube, where they solidify and go about their lives." He shrugged his shoulders at how mundane the process was. "Besides... this is more scenic. You get a wonderful view that not many Imaginaries ever get to see." He waved his arms grandly, first toward the sheer rocky face of the Hill, then again at the openness at the other side of the little gondola. Truthfully, there was little to distinguish them. The clouds and mists on one side were gray and white with streaks of black, while the face of the Hill only had the addition of the brown dirt and mud.

"I do have these, though," he said. From out of a pocket inside his robe he pulled a stack of blue cards that looked very similar to our assignment cards. "These are master key cards for the Hill. I can use these to go anywhere on the Hill I like. Everyone on the Council has them—the Director, too. It doesn't help me get to the Otherworld, but it simplifies things here." He fanned the cards out, and I could see the destinations hand-written on them: Castle, Wet Dream, Dark Logger. "Works quite like the cards you get for jobs, only these have the destination names right on them, as opposed to the assignment cards that are just coded. These can be taken back out of the slot instead of staying in there like yours. I put it in, take it out, then I have a couple of minutes to get in and seal the tube."

"So you can go from transport tube to transport tube?"

"I can use the regular pools too. Like the one in the Director's office."

"Nifty. How do I get a stack of those?"

"Only the four of us have them, and that's the way it's been for hundreds of years, so I don't think it likely we'll make another set soon."

If we all had them, everyone would become lazy and never walk anywhere, I supposed. There would be lines at the tubes just to go to the bars. Reminded me of those Segway scooters on the Otherworld. Stand there and get from place to place without the hassle of fucking lifting your feet. Enjoy nature without all of that pesky exercise.

Father Time steered the talk away from cards and transporting. "There are three areas I am going to show you. I will tell you what you need to know about them as you need to know it." He held up three fingers as if I might not be certain what the quantity of three looked like. "The first we will see briefly, for there is not much you could possibly glean there. Its citizens have limited knowledge of our world, or the Otherworld. We must be careful there, though, for the inhabitants of that cave are many." He shuddered and his eyes narrowed. "They are many, and they are devious."

That made me a little more nervous than I wanted to be. His warning was as ominous as it was vague. *The inhabitants of that cave are many.* What exactly did that imply? I wondered if Time would take me into some kind of danger without first warning me about it. Was he leading me to something that may have had a hand in Ira's death? Why did he need to be so secretive? "Do we really have to be down here? Couldn't you just explain this whole situation to me? It'd save a lot of time."

"You have to see this for yourself. It's not something you can just conjure in your mind. Believe me, if we had that option I'd would have presented it to you. No, no, no. It's important that you *see* it. Seeing is believing. Or so I'm told."

I was used to answers that didn't answer anything by now, so I let it go. I believed I was getting a headache, though I couldn't see it.

"Then we'll go to an area known to us as the Ward. That is where we'll find a few of the still crazy, but less hostile Imaginaries, than the cave's entities. There's actually quite a few of them." I wondered how whoever was in charge distinguished between the various stages of crazy for Imaginaries and the normal activities of most of them from day to day. There were things and then there were things.

Our primitive elevator creaked and twisted ever so slightly on our descent. I examined the floor just to make sure nothing was coming apart. I checked each floorboard lashed to the next with brittle, frayed rope—checked each log for hairline cracks. I couldn't find anything to justify any alarm; after all, what would happen to me if I fell? "You use this thing much?"

"Not really. Nobody comes down here on a regular basis. No need. Most of those down here are pretty self-sufficient, which makes us feel less guilty about having to leave them stuck down here."

I nodded my outward understanding while inwardly, I was as fucking confused as I had been all along. "Hey. Didn't you say we were going three places? There was the first one and then there was the Ward. But you didn't mention anything about the last one. What is it?"

Father Time clasped his hands behind his back and turned away from me to look out into the mist. "I'm still deciding on that one. I can't figure out if it's too much for you to handle at this point...or if your very existence depends on seeing it."

"That's quite an important distinction." I tried to force a laugh out of my throat to show how nonchalant I was, but I couldn't get anything out. Instead, I swallowed hard and set my jaw tightly shut.

"There it is," Father Time said, pointing a skinny finger at the rock face behind me. I turned to look and saw a nine-foot tall yellow arrow with the letters N-Y-B under it pointing to a large cave. "First stop," he said.

17

A wooden dock sticking out from the front of the cave made it easy for us to get out. On either side of the cave were large torches, flaming high and throwing off light to brighten the entrance. I looked around and realized how far above us the faint glow of the Hill was.

Father Time stepped into the large mouth of the dark cave and waved his arm for me to follow. "Do you want me to take one of these torches?" I asked, a little trepidatious about going into the darkness unprepared.

He didn't look back; rather, he kept his eyes on the cave ahead as he walked. "No. We want to try not to make them aware of our presence unless we have to." He made his way; it seemed, only by the feel of the walls. "Although sometimes they just know, no matter what you do." I followed at as great a distance possible without losing him. The cave snaked to the left for a while, then to the right. It sloped downward for a moment and I nearly fell. "Pay attention. I don't want to be here long," he said. The glow of the torches behind us had already faded and I could make out some light source up ahead.

The smell was the first thing that tipped me off as to what I was in for. It was the type of smell that seemed to take on a life of its own. Clawing around your nostrils and getting into your clothes, avoiding every swat of your hand like a gnat. It was light at first—an annoyance. But the more we traveled, the stronger it got; more forceful, more insistent. "What the hell is that horrid—?" I said. Father Time turned and covered my mouth with his paper-thin hand.

"Did you not hear me say I didn't want them to know we were here?" His voice dropped to a whisper. "Yes, it stinks. Deal with it and we'll get out quickly. Understand?" I nodded, and he let go of my face.

A sound came to me then. I wasn't even sure I really heard it at first. It was a melody in the back of my mind and then it was gone. The sound came back stronger as we moved forward, but it seemed like a different melody this time, and it remained just below my ability to distinguish exactly what it was.

We continued on into the light, sound and smell. Each got stronger until the tunnel was almost fully lit and I could see the floor and walls easily. Ahead was what looked like the end of the hall. Father Time got down on his hands and knees and motioned for me to do the same. I wasn't sure why we were doing it, but I wasn't about to open my mouth and ask him why—by then, what was the point? My real concern was for what had gone so wrong that these things needed to be hidden from the rest of us never to be spoken of in more than a whisper.

The music was definitely changing. It was a slow soft tune for a couple of minutes, then it changed to something more upbeat and faster, like a march or something. I knew I'd heard these songs in the Otherworld at some point; I just could not place them.

Our path ended at a drop-off leading to a well-lit cave below. Father Time made it to the edge and shook his head sadly. I could see shadows moving on the walls of the cave opposite us. They were the wavering shadows of huge-headed monsters dancing back and forth in the firelight, their small arms waving in the air. Time waved me closer.

Everything came together for me before I even looked.

The songs that were playing: Auld Lang Syne and some children's sing-along song that I'd heard blaring from a TV while scaring some child.

The light: a bonfire in the middle of the room.

The smell: diapers.

Father Time leaned close to my ear, "Welcome to the Cave of New Year's Babies."

I peered over the edge to see that we were about fifteen feet up on the wall of a large room filled with wobbling, tottering infants.

Dozens of babies.

They all seemed to be able to walk upright, although a few crawled on all fours. Some wore fancy black top hats and sashes emblazoned with a year. Some just had the hat, others just their sash. Many sat gurgling and cooing to one another on hand-stitched blankets. A group of five or six babies were huddled in a circle playing cards and laughing until one lost a hand and started crying. I could make out something on the sashes one of them was wearing. It was a group of numbers, a year: 1963.

There was a trio of them dancing around the fire in the center of the room, although they didn't seem to be quite in tempo with the song. They waved their arms deliriously and took tentative steps on fat stubby legs. One fell and sat there dumbfounded as to how he got there. His eyes began to fill with tears, but just as he appeared ready to cry, he smiled at one of his dancing friends and wobbled his way to his feet again.

The music itself issued from a record player in the far corner. Two babies with tattered sashes identifying them as 1958 and 1993, respectively, appeared to be pushing each other down for control of which song would play. Whenever one would gain the upper hand they would change the song.

Teething rings were everywhere.

There were doorways to other rooms in which I could see more babies napping on blankets and mats.

"Spooky, isn't it?" Father Time propped himself on an elbow. "Babies as far as you can see...and some of them over a hundred years old. We tried to integrate them into the society up top, but they just couldn't function."

"I...wow...that's a lot of babies." I couldn't fathom a society consisting completely of infants lasting for very long. "I don't see how they can stand it down here all the time."

"Most of them don't know anything else. They're like insects in a way. Some bugs are born to pollinate a flower or two and then die—their life's work done. The babies are similar, except they don't die. They just pollinate the flower and then buzz around and around and around. They don't have any more flowers to pollinate." He rested his head on the cold stone floor and gave me a glance. "Each of them represents a year. They're trotted out from say, Thanksgiving—early December at the latest—and by the second day of a new year, they're history. No one needs that Baby New Year any more, so into the cave. Their reason for being is brief, and their dubious purpose has just become cloudier over the years." Father Time had stopped looking at the babies altogether and was watching me instead. His stare made me cold. It looked as if he was anticipating some reaction from me or expecting a question. "Somewhere along the line people's hopes and fears for a good new year became infused in these poor infants. Despite the fact that no one actually 'believes' they exist, it seems they can't be let go."

"So if no one believes in them, why can't they just disappear like all the other Imaginaries in the same situation?" I was already afraid his earlier statement was right. Maybe this whole thing was going to just confuse me and throw me off track.

"Another part of the fluke that makes up the New Years Babies. Those people's expectations for a particular year become so attached to that particular little tyke wearing the banner of the coming year that each new baby is forced to live on with that energy. It's powerful enough to create a new baby and keep them around forever and ever. It's sad, really. They're all kind of cute."

"And there is no way to set them free?"

"Well, I suppose if every person on the Otherworld forgot a certain year, and then every history book, calendar, and scrapbook omitted that year...maybe the baby representing that year could move on and disappear. Normally, an Imaginary whose main job or duty has been fulfilled can get reassigned."

"Like me."

"Yes...like you. But these entities haven't had enough experience to grasp what we are...what we do. Their minds can't quite catch on, haven't had time to take everything in."

"Don't you appear annually as the outgoing year?"

"Yes."

"So, why is there a new baby each year, but only one of you as the past?" I was becoming more of a detective every day.

"The Council thought it would be cute. A new little infant each year? Come on! It was a great idea. Who could have anticipated the mess? And it's kind of taken on a life of its own. We've created a tradition and we seem to be stuck with it. Despite all our power, it just keeps going on without us." He pointed to the room writhing with children. "And I do it every year because I'm bored. I've been around for years with very little to do. I was around long before the baby idea. It's kind of like my cameo appearance. People look at me and think, '*Is that really...? Nah. Couldn't be.*' And only I know the truth."

It was not reassuring in the least to me that Father Time saw himself as a guest star on the Otherworld. It gave me the impression that maybe he didn't take any of this seriously. Did he see himself as a featured player in our current drama as well? Was he still just bored and looking for something to get him out of the house?

I watched the chaos below, wondering to myself what was so crazy about them. They appeared to be a herd of lost and directionless Imaginaries. Did the Council not foresee what the end result would be to sticking babies in a cave and leaving them there for centuries?

"Hey! There's that bastard Time and one of his cronies!" I looked down to see 1948 stand up and push the oversized top hat back on his head with his stubby arms. "Look everybody, Time's here!" The words were a harsh staccato against the cave walls, but the voice was high-pitched and light. Whether '48 knew it or not, he was cute. I desperately wanted to say "*Awwwwww*" but felt it would be inappropriate.

The babies all stopped what they were doing and looked up, with the exception of '81, who was looking in the opposite direction, and '92, who seemed to be looking at his own stomach.

1932 absently tossed a card on the pile and straightened his top hat. "It can't be a new year already, so what is it today, Time? Ya got some sort of new pacifiers for us? Blue ones, maybe?" The rest of his card players stood up around him, or managed to pull themselves up with furniture and stood wobbling on unsteady legs. "We're sick of it down here, old man." He reached up and grabbed at two other card players to help himself up, but only managed to pull them down to the ground with him. One of them started crying. 1932 ignored him and pushed himself to standing. The music stopped with a headache-inducing scratching noise.

They were only a couple of feet high, but I could already feel their tiny teeth sinking into my ankle and their sippie cups bouncing off of my head. The sheer numbers and pack mentality alone made me shudder. "We're coming up to the surface with you, and we're going to have a nice little talk after our nap," 1932 said. '55 and '75 grabbed flaming logs from the fire and pressed toward the area below us.

"We'd better get going, Abe. If they start stacking their high chairs they might make it up here." He stood and walked briskly in the direction we came.

I waited and watched the babies advance. With my suspicions about the Council misleading me, I wondered if it might be a good idea to stay and talk to these poor souls. Possibly glean some useful wisdom from the older ones. Play peek-a-boo. They were damn cute.

I was hit in rapid succession by three colorful blocks; H-R-T, which I was sure wasn't a coincidence, but I didn't stand there waiting for one of them to heave a U to finish spelling the word. I did notice that they had, indeed, started to pull out a stockpile of high chairs, and they were advancing with them when I ran. I kept bumping into walls and tripping, but soon the light from the front torches made it a little easier to see. I used the bare light and felt along the walls to make out what I could and prevent myself from falling. Father Time was waiting at the entrance for me and I ran to the scaffolding's open door. Father Time stayed at the entrance fiddling with something.

"What are you doing? Let's go!" I wasn't anxious to see whether the babies were really dangerous in any capacity other than mentally.

"Hang on, this stupid baby gate is stuck again...ah-ha!" He gave something a great tug, and out of the wall of the cave stretched a two foot high plastic baby gate. He latched it on to something on the other side of the cave and then casually strode toward our ride. "The gate always gets 'em. They still haven't figured it out."

I pondered the possibility that a brood of babies could engineer a ladder out of chairs, but be stymied by a plastic gate as the scaffold descended again.

18

"Some people want to be victims," Truman said. "They do everything they can to attract people that want to do harm to them." He told me they didn't mean to, it just happened. Their lives were so busy and cluttered with extraneous crap that they don't see what they're doing and are fucking floored when someone takes advantage of their situation. "Whether it's physical harm, mental, financial, whatever. There's always someone there to gladly inflict it."

The babies had shaken Father Time up a bit. The rattles, the chants, the music. They were hell on a person's nerves, and it showed in Time's face and in his eyes. The long ride down the side of the Hill with my suddenly silent companion gave me time to reflect on things and I thought first of Truman and the conversation I'd had with him not so long before.

"They stand on dark corners in parts of town that they don't know, thumbing through their phones or their tablets or their pockets for an address, a phone number—maybe checking their wallets for cab fare or a business card. They get drunk in bars and go home with strangers. They leave their cars running in the driveway, they take the same route home every day, and they never look up from their own lives to see what's happening around them. They never see it coming, and they're always shocked when their world gets turned upside down." He spoke with an authority that came with experience, someone who had seen the victims of crime, and I listened as a student, taking everything he could offer.

"There are, of course, the opposite. Those who take every precaution, think everything through, stay away from the wrong side of town and still get preyed upon. Those that don't see it coming because they are so careful and think that nothing could possibly harm them." He sat back in his recliner and smiled. "It's been my experience that they're all wrong. If someone wants to harm you, kill you, they'll find a way to do it. There's very little you can do if someone is persistent, halfway intelligent and out to accomplish something." He was very matter-of-fact, and I appreciated that. I didn't have much time to spare and preferred the short version anyway.

"I have no idea how Ira died, but that's handy information," I said.

"There are two types of assailants as well. One who is meticulous and planning and the other who is spur of the moment and spontaneous. The second is sloppy and usually found out easily. It's the first kind you have to watch out for."

"Because they cover their tracks so well, and they're harder to figure out?"

"For starters, yes. I don't know what exactly happened to your friend, and I can't speculate, but you have to ask yourself what type of person your friend was and how he fits into any or all of those basic categories."

19

At first, I thought the ride was much shakier this time. Maybe the Personnel people were having a tough time on this leg of the journey. As I tried to stabilize myself on the rail, I realized that it wasn't our transportation, but my whole body that was shaking. It was worse in my right arm than anywhere else. It was a steadier shaking—if shaking can be steady—and my will alone was not enough to stop it.

"The next one should be a little less disturbing for you," Father Time chuckled. "These particular Imaginaries just don't play well with others. They're nice enough and harmless. They somehow don't realize they're Imaginary." He leaned back and folded his arms, a sigh issuing from deep within.

"I'm fine," I said as we both looked at my shaking arm on the rail. "Well, I'll *be* fine. What do you expect? Nobody likes babies in top hats. It's just not right." He nodded his agreement then turned to look out at the mists as he had on our first leg of the journey. When I was sure he wasn't looking, I grabbed my arm with my free hand and shook it violently to try to get it to stop. It looked like I was trying to swat a fly with a cold strand of linguini. When that didn't work, I put my right hand on the railing and punched it over and over, checking to see if Time was watching after each.

I was preparing to smack it against the wall of our scaffold when I saw we were coming up on another cave. It had a wooden dock just like the last, but there were no torches. We pulled even with it and kept going down without slowing. "Who's in that cave?" I asked.

"No one." Father Time didn't turn around. "Yet."

"Yet?"

"Oh. You just never know when someone is going to go completely around the bend and you'll have to put them away, do you?"

"Yeah. I guess anybody can go a little nuts at a moment's notice." I looked down and saw my hand was no longer shaking, but I was still beating it against the rail. I stopped. "*Crazy as a cave full of fucking babies,*" I said with as much conviction as I could muster.

"There are a few others like it around here. You know...in case." I could feel his cold hand pat me on the shoulder. "Just another minute or two and we'll be there."

The further we went into the mist, the stronger this feeling of dread was deep in my body. I looked up and watched as the last bit of the dock disappeared into the mist above me. "Good. We need to speed this whole thing up a little. I've got work to do."

"Don't worry. It'll be there when you get back."

The entrance to the next cave was hard to miss. The dock was more festive, decorated with balloons and streamers. It was surrounded by hanging lanterns and tiki torches. There were actual beings standing outside this cave entrance laughing and dancing, though I heard no music. I could make out a Ghost or two talking to a large beast with bat-like wings. A female, I think female, Alien with a bulbous head flitted from conversation to conversation. Near the entrance, a well-dressed Leprechaun sat on the ground hugging his knees and rocking. "Should they be out like this?" I asked.

Father Time put his hand on my shoulder reassuringly. "Oh, they're all harmless. We let them come and go as they please in their rooms and throughout the caves." He patted me on the back as our descent slowed to a stop at the dock. "Just don't look the Leprechaun in the eyes."

Before I could ask what seemed to me to be an incredibly obvious question, he opened the door and strode forward. As I fell in behind him, I was amazed that none of the dozen or so beings acknowledged us in any way. They didn't stop what they were doing, didn't look at us, didn't move out of our way. We sidestepped nearer to the mouth of the cave where the Leprechaun was still rocking silently. He was hard to miss in his bright green tuxedo and derby hat. I watched him as we approached, careful to focus on a point on the wall above him rather than directly at his face. The allure of the forbidden pulled my eyes lower and lower to his hat. I figured one peek couldn't possibly harm me. It was police business, and maybe he had a story to tell.

It was Father Time that interrupted me. "Abe, this place is safer than the last, but you should stay as close as possible. Wouldn't want you to get left behind or lost or anything."

Before I realized it, we were in the cave and past the leprechaun without incident. I started to look back to see how far past him we had gotten, but figured I shouldn't press my luck. The 'left behind' comment really held my attention, and I followed closely on my guide's heels.

This passage was a far cry from the rough one we had recently fled. It was smoothed out and made to look like a long hallway. There were paintings hung on the walls every so often—colorful depictions of nature with fruit and flowers. There were scenes of couples lounging under trees and by waterfalls. All very soothing, very serene. The hall was level and nearly straight, turning only once, even then at a ninety-degree angle. Lamps were placed at intervals to keep it easy to navigate. There was no stumbling or sudden drops to our stomachs. The air somehow smelled of flowers, roses, maybe. "As you can see, these Imaginaries are a little more civilized. They're willing and able to keep their surroundings tidy and more...*aesthetically pleasing*." He stopped to adjust a painting of a ship at sea that was a little crooked. It seemed to be at a much more precarious angle when he was finished. It leaned too far left. For a moment I pictured all of the water spilling out of the scene and onto the floor.

"They're all acclimated to their little world down here; it's just too bad they can't rejoin the rest of us on the Hill."

"I'm still kind of hazy on why they can't do that."

"Well, they were all disruptive in one way or another. They wouldn't 'fall in line,' so to speak."

Clarity, thy name is Time. "Example?"

"Some of them consistently ignored their jobs. For example: Mari. That gray alien girl we passed on the way in? Remember?"

I nodded.

"One day she was assigned to go to the Otherworld, land in some farmer's field, wave her probe around, and then slip back home in the darkness." The hall ended at an open doorway, and I could smell the sweet scent of something freshly baked emanating from the room beyond. I could see a table and couple of chairs near a wood stove. Father Time stopped at the threshold and lowered his voice slightly to finish his story. "Her assigned time comes...no Mari. Ten minutes past time...no Mari. Finally we have to grab something to fill in for her. Not an Alien in sight. Not a one. Do you know what we had to use?" He leaned in even closer and lowered his voice just a little more. "We had to use this big-ass Yeti named Betty. Ugh! Can you imagine that poor hick's confusion when that came trotting down out of the UFO? Then again, maybe it made a good story to tell." Time smiled a wide smile and rocked back on his heels. "Gather 'round now, fellers, and I'll tell bout the day I dun seen an albino Bigfoot and a flyin' saucer all at the same time. No pushin', now." He broke out in a barking, braying laugh that certainly didn't seem to go with the hushed whisper he was using just moments ago. "Maybe that's not the best example, but basically, some of these Imaginaries just can't accept their roles—they want to be something else."

It sounded very familiar when turned around just a little. "Isn't that what happened to me? You wanted something new and changed my role? From an Imaginary Friend to a policeman?"

"That's a very different situation. You earned that promotion. You accepted the roles we gave you and excelled at them. You *are* excelling at them. These are confused, aimless flukes of the imagination."

Excelled? I didn't want to bring up the fact that I was on my third strike with the Director when I was given the 'promotion' to policeman. "The people on the Otherworld are victims of their own excesses in many aspects of their lives, but none more so than their imaginations. They just don't know when to stop."

"Victims of their imaginations?" That was a harsh way of looking at the people responsible for our very existence.

"Let's get through this so we can move on." He waved me quickly forward. "Come on, come on, I only have a couple of things I want you to see before we head further down the Hill." Father Time has holding my arm and forcing me through the large arched doorway with dark iron doors. "Down this hall is one of the great wonders of the Hill." Time was walking quickly for such an old man. "One of the greatest citizens of our fair realm." This end of the hall was wide and had closed doors on either side—more than a dozen of them, but we ignored them in our rush toward the end. The air became thick with a musty, moldy scent. I could hear faint laughter coming from a room to my right and heavy sobs from one on my left. I wondered which rooms the Imaginaries outside belonged in. "Luckily, someone along the way on the Otherworld believed there were two of his kind, which gave us a backup."

A light splashing sound made me realize I was stepping in puddles. Looking back, I had unknowingly managed to avoid similar ones scattered to the left and right of my path, but now they got larger and harder to miss as we neared the doors. In fact, it would be impossible to get through the doors without stepping in water. "Ignore the mess; it's just impossible to keep the place clean with him around." He practically bounded to the doors, splashing in the puddles like a child, kicking water as he went. It landed in great dots on the walls. His robe was soaked at the hem but he took no notice.

"With who around?"

He turned both of the handles and pushed with his shoulders, forcing the doors open. "Who? Why, Elliot, of course!" The doors finished swinging open on their own, and he threw his arms up in grand presentation.

Not fifty feet in front of him, a long gray neck ending in a slender oval head extended from an enormous pool. The thing looked at us with marble-like black eyes and then slowly sank below the surface.

"That's Elliot?"

"That's Elliot."

"Hmmm." I didn't get why he wanted me to see this so badly. I wondered what it had to do with anything. I watched the creature's dark form move slowly beneath the water, "So, he's what? The Loch Ness Monster?"

"Yes. Well, one of them." He crossed his arms and looked very pleased with himself. "The other lives in the moat around the castle on the surface, when she isn't scaring the crap out of people in Scotland. *She* is well-adjusted." He waited for a response from me, as though I should be impressed and awed. I was more uncomfortable than anything, I had no desire to be soaking wet and staring at a huge beast. I looked around for a dry place to stand.

The room was the biggest I'd seen on the Hill, or anywhere else, for that matter; it was larger than the main hall in the castle, larger than the auditorium in the Personnel Department. The high ceiling was curved and painted with primitive depictions of the sky visible from the Otherworld, though the detail was hard to make out from so far away. The pool spanned the length of the room, which must have been hundreds of yards. Statues were lined up along one side of the pool, though I couldn't make out who they were. The other side was lined with great thick columns that extended to the ceiling. Water covered the floor, making it hard to tell where it ended and where the pool began.

Father Time was still staring expectantly.

"I don't get it. Okay? Why is he down here? Was he late for a haircut one day, so you put him in a hole?"

"No, Elliot's a special case. He's the Loch Ness Monster."

"Right, we've established that. I'm a policeman, you're Father Time, he's a Loch Ness Monster."

"I don't think you're getting it. He thinks he's the Loch Ness Monster."

"And...?"

"Look, we all do our jobs on the Otherworld and then come home and have a drink. We're Imaginaries. Your friends are a Bigfoot and a Boogeyman. The three of you converse, communicate and relate easily. Everyone here speaks the same language: Norse, Irish, Greek, American and otherwise, with only subtle accents to tell one another apart. Just about everyone takes classes to learn how to do their jobs better. We work at being what we are. You with me?"

"So far, so good."

"When some poor Otherworlder sees an Alien and freaks out, that Alien chuckles and then gives himself a pat on the back for a job well done. He transports himself back here, goes to The Dark Logger or The Wet Dream, and tells his buddies. He goes to sleep at night satisfied he's done what he was made to do and is content knowing his place in the grand scheme of things, right?"

"Sure."

"This is Elliot. Elliot thinks he's a monster. He swims. He eats. He grunts and wails. He doesn't seem to understand anything anyone says to him, and vice versa. He doesn't try to socialize with anyone, doesn't seem to aspire to anything or want something more." Father Time motioned around the room at the statues and paintings and I involuntarily examined each one with him. "We've tried exposing him to the arts—music, literature. We've forced the sciences on him—Mother Nature read him theorems and formulas. He hid from her for a while, and then he swam, ate, and grunted."

"What about the other one? The female? Can't they find some common ground and get something going?"

"We got them together. The results were disastrous. Nothing but a big mess. She won't have anything whatsoever to do with him anymore...anything whatsoever."

"So you've written him off?"

"What else can we do? We've tried to send him on jobs, but for some reason, he won't dissolve like everyone else. We've tried doing everything we can think of. Turned out the lights, left him in the dark. He won't go to the Otherworld, we can't make him. We have to write him off. He's not an Imaginary. He's a beast." I watched as Time's smile got wider. "He's a beast and an animal. We've had a hard time admitting it, but sometimes a monster is just a monster and there's nothing you can do about it."

"So what's funny about it?" His mirth and nonchalance baffled me more than I could express to him. There we were, in a place that they didn't acknowledge to anyone else on the surface, looking at what was an enigma that had plagued our leaders for longer than I knew. But it made Time happy?

"It's funny because I've given up trying to figure it out. I just enjoy it now. It's something that's never happened on the Hill before or since. It's something we can't explain. Something we don't know how to deal with, nor prevent in the future. So, I stopped trying. I just let it go now. I come down here and admire him, sometimes. I bring a chair..." He pointed out a cluster of statues on our left, "...put it over there, and watch him swim around. He's kind of graceful, despite his bulk and those tiny flippers. I think he likes this little habitat. He swims, floats, does what he pleases, for the most part. I have to say, his innocence and obliviousness are refreshing. Wish I were that ignorant, that's for sure."

In a way, so did I. As an Imaginary, I did what I was created for, what I was told to do. Even though things changed, I still did what I was told and I still had someone to answer to. A choice would've been refreshing. "So there's another monster just like him that does the Loch Ness jobs in his place?"

"Yes. The other one that someone imagined. Glad for that. At least the work gets done, right?"

The stale smell was strongest here—surrounding me on all sides. I was sure that I could bat at my clothes and see the smell flow off me like a cloud. It would billow off of me like the dust off of a rain-starved field in the middle of Iowa. I felt heavier with the smell. I stood watching the wide dark form zip around in the blue, blue water and I made no move to elude or oust the smell.

There was a crash from the hall where we entered.

"*No. No. No,*" Father Time shouted toward the door. "Look. Wait here. I'll be right back." He splashed his feet angrily as he walked.

"Wait here? Where are you going?"

"Just need to calm somebody down and put him back in his room; nothing to worry about," he said through gritted teeth. "Strangers get him all riled up."

"But am I okay here? I mean, is it safe to be in here with Elliot?"

"You're fine. He's harmless." He opened the door and yelled into the hall. "Put that down. That doesn't belong to you." He smiled weakly back at me as he closed the door behind him. "Stupid leprechaun," I heard him mumble as he left.

I shuffled in place a little but couldn't decide where exactly I should stand.

Father Time talked about how relaxing it was to watch Elliot, so I moved a little closer to see if I could catch a glimpse of him. "It's just me, Elliot," I shouted. "Abe? I came with Father Time." He was so far off that I couldn't be sure if he could hear me or not. Hear me? Could he *understand* me? That was the real question. Even if the words reached his ears, why would I think he could interpret the meaning of the sounds I was making? Did he have ears? In my mind, deep down, I wanted to believe he was faking. Somehow I thought he pretended to be this wild beast just to get out of working like the rest of us. The water looked so inviting, so cool. If he was faking, I could understand why. There are certainly worse places to ride out your existence than this.

I noticed Elliot had chosen to continue swimming at the other end for a while. It was fine with me; I was curious, but I wasn't looking for a close-up. Father Time would return soon, and with this shy creature keeping its distance, what would the harm be in relaxing while I waited? My feet were tired from walking, so I took careful steps to the edge of the pool, sat down and dipped my feet in. It was cool, and a slight current ran just below the surface, lightly massaging my legs. In the gloom at the other end, I lost sight of Elliot and wondered if the underwater movement was a result of his swimming nearby, or if the water was fed from a stream that pushed the water along at a faster pace. I liked the sound of the low waves lapping at the side of the pool. It reminded me of the Styx farther up the Hill. The sound was almost identical to the way the water hit the side of the gondola Father Time and I had sat in and leisurely discussed matters.

I lounged on my back and let the water calm me. Where would all of this leave me? What came next? It was because of something Father Time said: '*Sometimes a monster is just a monster*,' that I felt a sense of home there in Elliot's lair. It popped into my head that the smell that lingered on this place was gone. I couldn't have grown acclimated to that musty stench so quickly. No one could.

I heard some splashing but didn't bother to get up. Tilting my head a little, I thought maybe I saw a dark fin off in the distance, though I couldn't be sure. The surface of the water was definitely broken, and a series of ripples issued from the far side of the pool. The surface calmed as I watched, and I rested my head on the cold stone slab again.

I could see the statues directly behind me with a clarity I couldn't where Time and I were standing before. There were three of them, each representing a member of the Council standing on a pedestal. Each of them were shown in a heroic or intellectual pose: Time stroking his beard thoughtfully; Mother Nature with arms outstretched warmly; Death swinging a croquet mallet over his head wildly. At the far end, though, was a lone crumbling pedestal. There could have been a statue of anyone there, I suppose, but I was astounded not to see one of the Director. In my head, I heard him barking about not having time to pose for a statue, but I knew that was crazy. He would make time, if it meant having his likeness around to be admired for eternity.

As I focused on the view I had of the ceiling, I heard more splashing but ignored it. It was Elliot's place; he could flop around all he wanted. I let the water soothe me.

My life was a mess that didn't look to be shaping up any time soon. I wanted things, needed things, but what? I couldn't understand how I could come all that way and not know what I wanted. In the scheme of things I was important; I had made some sort of mark on my world. Isn't that all anyone could hope for? Doesn't everyone want to be remembered? Wasn't that Thor's motivation, the Director's as well? Really, I had made an impression on two worlds. The things that I did now reverberated on the Hill as well as the Otherworld like an undampened cymbal strike. I could still hear the ringing long after the initial crash.

Lost in my thoughts, I closed my eyes and drifted toward sleep. Father Time was right; it was calm there. I decided not to fight it, sleep might do me good.

A series of water droplets landed on my chest, then neck, and finally, one or two more on my face. I ran over my checklist again, afraid to open my eyes right away.

Soothing? Check.

Calm? Most assuredly.

Safe?

Ahem. *Safe*?

I couldn't answer myself on that score and unfortunately, there was only one way to figure it out. I opened my eyes slowly, afraid that the mere action of opening my eyes would somehow startle Elliot, and it might drive him into a frenzy of some sort like a bull with a red cape.

There was no missing the fact that he was indeed, towering over me. I had seen Elliot from a distance before, and that in no way prepared me for the experience of a close-up Loch Ness Monster. His slender head was easily four times bigger than me. It was attached to his nearly twenty-five-foot-long neck, which curved out of the water toward the ceiling, then straight back down at me. He seemed to be trying to stay motionless, but he still swayed gently from side to side. A drop of water came loose in the movement and slid down the ridge between his glassy eyes, past two tiny nostrils, and fell onto my head. He smelled like pool water and pineapples.

The creature backed his head up a few feet. There was a rumble that started somewhere deep in Elliot's chest and traveled the length of his twisting trunk of a neck. He shook his head side to side but never stopped watching me. Elliot's mouth opened wide and he squeezed his eyes shut hard, but no sound came out. He did this a number of time—eyes wrenched shut, mouth snapped open—until a sound escaped from him, so slight that I initially didn't think it came from him.

"Keh." It did definitely come from him. His eyes opened and his mouth closed after the sound came out.

Keh? He wanted to communicate, I could tell. He was just looking for a kindred spirit to share his thoughts with. This was why Father Time brought me down here in the first place. He thought I could get Elliot to open up and reveal his secrets, or prove he should be working like the rest of us Imaginaries. I was sure Elliott was just looking for someone who understood.

"Keh."

"Yes, yes, 'keh'. I hear you," I said. "Go on. Say what you need to say." I wanted to stay rooted in that place until he spit out every last word that he had kept bottled up for so long.

The light sound he was producing got deeper and more throaty on the next attempt. "Khuunnh!" Same expression on his face as it was rapidly followed by another "Khuunnh!" Louder this time. He was trying, I gave him that, and I rooted for him with every sound. He just left his eyes shut and mouth open as a burst of them issued back to back. "Kuhkuhkuhkuh."

He lifted his head up and gave one last wet sound before abruptly throwing his head forward again. "Agck." I ducked and covered my head, afraid his enormous weight might come crashing down on me, but it didn't. Immediately following that violent outburst, I heard a thud somewhere behind me. I looked up at Elliot, who seemed to have recovered himself after his fit. He stared at me for a split second before sinking back into the pool. His head was last to disappear into the water, barely causing a ripple.

I turned to investigate what caused the noise behind me and discovered a small shape by the wall that hadn't been there when I first came in. I stood and allowed my legs to stop shaking before I walked over to the pale object.

It was gray and wet, covered in what I was sure was Elliot phlegm. He hadn't been trying to communicate; Elliot was choking on a large piece of the missing statue of the Director. It lay at my feet—bits of it, anyway. I could see the better part of his torso, shoulders, and nearly three-quarters of his head. The rest of the head lay in little bits nearby, apparently broken off on impact with the wall.

Father Time was right. This was very relaxing.

As I walked back to the doors, I wondered if he had really noticed me. Had he at any point considered how good it was to have someone's company even for a brief moment?

I sat on the floor with my back against the doors and waited for Father Time to return. The smell of tropical fruit and chlorine was refreshing, if not as relaxing as I'd first believed.

20

We were on our way down again when Father Time spoke up. "I'm taking you to this last cave against the wishes of the rest of the Council." He nodded at me, and I got the feeling he was convincing himself it was a good idea.

"I wasn't sure they knew about any of this. If they aren't keen on me going, why are you doing it?" To be honest, I wasn't sure it was a good idea either. Our last two stops really hadn't sunk in; did I really need to add something more to the equation? How did New Year's Babies and wayward lake dwellers fit in to what I was trying to accomplish? Time gave no explicit instructions about keeping quiet about what I saw, but I suppose it was implied. I could just tell Zane and Brady. Of course, that seemed like the craziest idea I could've had, since they were having trouble dealing with our reality already.

I didn't like Time's silence. "In that last cave, I thought we'd see more of them. You made it sound as if there'd be, I don't know, hundreds of them."

"There are. Most of them went to their rooms when they heard us coming. They don't like new visitors; perhaps they were startled by you." Father Time's habit of not looking at me when he spoke was really getting to be annoying.

"Do they have some reason to hide from us, or from you in particular? Could be you're not all that well-liked." It seemed that Father Time had received a bad reception in the first cave. Maybe it was a trend. Time was one of the people who put these things here; it only stood to reason that more than a few would be upset by that.

That got Father Time to look at me. He turned away from the fog and smacked his open palm twice on the wall. In a second, our descent stopped, and we were left hanging in the air. We swayed a little, just enough to notice. "You can be funny and it seems like a breath of fresh air to me sometimes. But you need to be careful. The others are less enthusiastic about you. Also, if I were hiding something from you, if I thought there was something you shouldn't see, you wouldn't be here seeing what you are seeing. Understand?"

"Yes, sir." I'd made the mistake of letting my new position go to my head. I was placing myself on the same level as the Council, and that was obviously a miscalculation on my part. I had to watch the way I said things.

"The reason many of them hid is because they are just as afraid as they are confused about their situations. Contact with us can be a painful reminder of the life they've lost, or lost out on. We try to keep them comfortable so as to avoid pandemonium."

It made sense to me as he said it, but it would have been more convincing if he would have mentioned it up front, rather than as part of a wrathful proclamation. He was right about respect and probably about things like dire consequences. "I see. I'm sorry."

"While I'm making things clear, understand this: There are three votes on our Council. I voted for giving you the chance to do what you are doing. I have continued to vote as such. A second member has voted likewise. The last member of the Council has voted to…*terminate* your position and has been very emphatic about ending your investigation. The Director has recommended on numerous occasions that we reevaluate your performance. All it would take is one vote to flip your world upside down." He didn't pause for a reaction of any sort; rather, he turned and slapped the wall three times. We immediately started moving again.

21

The last dock was under the mists and clouds, where the sky was pure black. The landing itself was shrouded in darkness and unadorned by lights. I could barely make out the wooden planks of the dock that was just a foot in front of me, let alone the mouth of the cave itself.

"I'll lead you up there. Just stay with me and hold onto my robe," Time said as he unlatched the door. "We keep it dark down here just to be sure no one happens onto her lair by accident."

Lair? That made me nervous. I was descending an upside-down pyramid of crazy that ended in a fucking *lair*. Of all the things I had seen since Ira's death, I assumed that this would be the worst. I was going to see a woman, that's all I knew. A crazy woman. A crazy woman with no porch light. Surely, that was the worst kind of woman. An unlit woman.

I kept a grip on Father Time's robe and he pushed on, surefooted, through the darkness. I felt the pebbles crunch beneath my feet, heard them grind into the dirt and stone below. Something sweet came to my nostrils, sweet and minty. The smell reminded me of the times I had joined Truman for Christmas. It was the smell of the candy canes in the stockings and on the tree. Truman would go around before everyone else was awake, and he would break all of the candy canes except his own. He did it with other candy, but he was ruthless and efficient with it at Christmas time. It was his own Yuletide tradition. When his family came down to open presents, they would dump out their stockings and find nothing but bits of red and white and a pile of dust. Pulverized or whole, they still had the same sweet smell of the holidays.

I breathed it deep. The thought of Truman and Christmas was something that took me out of the moment and relaxed my nerves. I closed my eyes and let Time lead me wherever he needed to. I thought back to the few Christmases that I spent with Truman and the things he got. He was especially excited to get a special toy policeman's present for the last Christmas I got to be with him. That was only days before he bid me farewell. He loved those toys: cap gun, badge, and a pair of plastic gray handcuffs. He ran out of caps by noon Christmas day and cried for an hour when his dad told him all of the stores were closed and they wouldn't be able to buy more for a number of days. He cuffed together everything that was cuffable and wore that little plastic gray badge that said 'Official Deputy' on it everywhere for days on end. I asked him why he liked the cheap plastic trinkets so much the day before I left. "Do they make you feel like a big person?" He looked at me with curiosity.

"They don't make me feel like anything. A badge keeps the bad things away," he said. "People like a man with a badge. They trust them more. A badge makes you a good person."

I'd never looked at a badge in that manner until he put it that way. I always thought of it as just a part of a uniform. A way of saying, "this is what I do." No different from a postal worker's patch or a baseball player's uniform. Following Father Time through the darkness, I remembered Zane's offhanded question about whether we got badges for this job and suddenly wished I had one. I desperately wanted something to keep the bad things away. Whatever they may be.

22

"You can open your eyes now," Father Time said. "We've almost made it." There was a curve in the tunnel ahead with light coming from it. The cave was much like the first: rough, unfinished. Although the light didn't extend to the ground, I could feel rocks and pebbles. I lost my footing a couple of times.

"All I can tell you is to take what you are about to see at face value. Don't try to read too much into it. She's just another Imaginary with her own special brand of cuckoo," Father Time called to me over his shoulder with a whisper that made the tunnel all the more creepy.

We turned the corner, and I could see a door just a few more feet ahead of us. To the right of it was a shelf with a metal device above it. Light streamed under the door and through its smoked glass panel.

I peered over Time's shoulder to see what he did next. He picked up a stack of coins from a shelf and set each on end in the metal device until four of them were in a line. Then, he looked at me dully and pushed the device until it disappeared into the wall with a loud clicking sound. He held it there until we could hear the coins falling into what sounded like a metal tray on the other side of the wall. "We don't really need to do this; she just seems to enjoy it. Kind of like paying a toll to get in or paying a washer at a laundry." He took his hand off the wall, but the device didn't return with his palm. He looked at it crossly and then smacked the wall, causing the device to pop back out. "I'd advise you to take a stack of coins for yourself."

I fumbled for a few of them, knocking a number on the floor in the process. "Thought you said it wasn't necessary." I listened to one of the coins spin to a halt on the floor.

"No, the device isn't necessary, but if she sees us, she's got to have the coins or she'll freak right out." I grabbed a few more off the shelf to make sure I was properly prepared. He didn't elaborate on what freaking out would entail, though I was sure it wasn't fucking good.

He turned the knob and swung the door wide, revealing a dimly lit room. Iron bars cut the room in half with only a couple of wooden chairs on the side of the room with Time and me. On the other side was a reasonably well-equipped bedroom. A four-poster bed sat dead center with a fluffy quilt covering it. A nightstand on one side held an old-fashioned alarm clock and a colorful lamp. A red, high-backed chair on the other side of the bed was flanked by a small reading lamp. On the back wall near the far corner was a simple wooden door. In the opposite corner was a pile of coins that would have come up to my knees had I waded into it.

A young woman sat atop the pile running her fingers through the loose change, raising fistfuls of the quarters over her head and letting them rain down into her hair. She was a lovely blonde with her long hair tied back loosely in a basic bow. Her simple sky-blue dress puffed out and surrounded her like a parachute—wide and billowy—tamped down only by all the silvery tokens raining from above. Behind her, thin wings stretched, flapping wildly every time she dropped another handful of change.

"Tooth Fairy?" I asked.

"Yup," Father Time replied as he folded his arms and sighed.

"*The* Tooth Fairy?" I wondered if she was one of those copies, or assistants, whatever. I could see one of them losing their marbles pretty easily.

"The very first. She seems a little agitated today."

"Hmm…I was expecting someone older or *uglier*, I guess. Some sort of harmlessly plump, spritely Nymph." Actually, she was cute and just a *little* spritely. "So, she's nuts, you say?"

"Absolutely."

"Shouldn't she be sitting on a huge pile of teeth instead of quarters?" Seemed logical. "What does she do with all of those teeth anyway?"

"Well. She used to bring them back and pile them up right where we're standing. She would occasionally dive into the pile and shower herself with them, as you suggested, like she's doing with the quarters now." Father Time had a stern, fatherly look about him as he leaned against the wall and folded his arms. "The whole room was starting to fill up with them, and she wouldn't give them up. We tried to come in and take them from her, but it was a real chore. Have you ever tried to subdue someone with that many teeth? Not a lot of fun, let me tell you. It's not like she could hurt anyone, but it got really unpleasant for all of us trying to take care of her."

"I would think."

"So, one day when she went to the Otherworld to make a few switcharoos, we cleaned the place out and put the bars in. She really had no choice then but to make a little deal with us. Now when she comes back from a job, she gives us the teeth and we trade the money she needs to leave for the kids. It's her new currency. We trade one thing for the other. She gets the money for the kids, and we keep the place a little less gross. It's a fair deal. Without us she'd have nothing to give to the kids. She'd just be a tooth thief, and that's not her style." Time looked slightly disgusted. "I think she secretly manages to hang on to a few, though."

"Where would she keep them?" She seemed oblivious to us and continued to sift and shuffle the coins, piling them in stacks and then knocking them down.

"Who knows? There are plenty of places to squirrel them away out of sight. It's not like we inspect the place anymore. No one has gone over there since we barred her in." It occurred to me that there was no door built into the bars. There was no way to go in and out even if someone wanted to. I couldn't imagine what it must be like to live life in a dark exile.

"How does she still do her job?"

"The closet back there in the corner. We have it rigged for her to go only to the Otherworld, and straight back to her little slice of the Hill. She can't change course and end up anywhere else, thankfully. It's a one-way round trip."

I thought about that for a moment, sure he meant something else. A one-way trip only went one way. "You still trust her to do her job?" None of the others that Time had deemed crazy were still on the job as far as I knew, but The Tooth Fairy, whom he seemed to suggest was the craziest, was still punching the clock regularly. "I would think she'd be replaced the fastest. Aren't you afraid that she'll flip out and blow her cover somehow?"

"Nah…she's crazy, but she lives for her job. She likes all the subterfuge of sneaking around, taking and giving on the Otherworld. It's the safest place for her to be. No one and nothing can really bother her there. I'm more concerned with the damage she can do to the people on our world. She can be contagious once she gets rolling." His lips curled up in a wistful smile, a grin rather than a grimace, at the thought of something. "Still…it's never a dull moment with her, I can tell you that."

Half of her dress had disappeared beneath the onslaught of coins. She stopped pouring them on herself and slowly stood up. She hadn't noticed us with her head down; looking at the change sliding off of her, I wondered if she ever would. She stood shin-deep in money before pulling each foot out and shaking off the excess. In the lamp light I could see the delicate outline of her jaw, the crimson streak of lipstick on her upper lip. I felt the cold coins in my hand and wanted to be rid of them.

No…not rid of them.

I wanted her to have them.

I didn't know whether I wanted her to have them out of pity or out of desire, but I wanted to hand them to her nonetheless. Not just give them to her. Hand them to her. I had to put them in her palm with my very own fingers. "Can we talk to her? Can she hear us?"

Any fondness or contentment on Time's face disappeared in an instant. "Yes, she can hear us, and I don't know whether anyone talking to her is a good idea. She isn't exactly good at cocktail parties. She doesn't…*play* well with others." He turned me away from the room. "We should probably just go. You've seen what you needed to see. Let's just get back to our own little world."

"She still does her job. How do we know she didn't interact with Ira on his last trip to the Otherworld?" I was stretching for a reason to stay, although it was a miniscule possibility. It could have happened. Maybe they met up by accident or by design at the same place and some unknown factor set Ira's death in motion.

"Abe...come on. We've been down in these caves long enough, haven't we?" he asked me in a low, conspiratorial tone. His arm was around my shoulder and he was guiding me in a slow shuffle back to the door. "I mean, really. You have so much to do in your investigation, don't you? And I'm pretty busy myself. I took time out from a full schedule to bring you here—"

"Yes, you did, and I'm grateful for that. But why? Why did you bring me down here if you didn't think it would help me? Why waste all this time?"

"Have you learned anything here?"

"Besides the fact that there are crazy people living under my hometown? No...I haven't."

"I think you have. You'll see." He put a finger to his mouth in an approximation of intellectual thought.

How convenient. "Yes, it's been a regular after-school special. I'm tingling. Really. I still think we...I...should talk to her for a moment." Actually, I was tingling just a little bit. The thought of her was like a stimulant under my skin; a cool breeze that raised goose bumps on my neck.

His hand was already on the doorknob and turning it. I could feel his other arm around my shoulder again—steering me. "She really does seem out of sorts. It probably wouldn't be a good time to speak with her anyway."

Man, was she pretty. I thought maybe we could talk to her for just a minute. What could the harm be in that?

Nothing was getting done topside. Brady was probably still sitting on Zane. Ira was still dead, and Truman needs my help with something.

"You have my word that you can come back anytime you want."

We walked out one after the other and as the door shut behind me, I heard a voice. Not even a voice, really; it was light and airy. It was so unexpected, so natural, it was like a part of the surroundings. I stopped walking and leaned back toward the door in hopes of hearing it again, but was without luck. My first instinct was that I had imagined it; I wanted so badly to speak to this wonderful creature that my mind had fabricated the whole thing. And the words I thought I had heard were weird enough to have convinced me of the hallucination theory.

"Your gum plaque is diseased." Or something like that.

"Did you hear that?" I asked Father Time.

"I didn't hear anything but the door shutting," he said. "Why? What did you hear?"

Silently, I waited for more words to come to us, but nothing new issued forth from the room. I stood still so I wouldn't make a noise to confuse with what I wanted to hear. After a couple of minutes I felt silly, and I thought that if I was given a message, it was just for me. "Nothing. I thought...nothing."

I followed him back outside and onto the scaffold without another word.

Your gum plaque is diseased?

23

"The Director left in a pretty big hurry after you guys disappeared from view," Brady said as we walked briskly toward my apartment. "I mean, a real hurry."

"Mother Nature stopped by for a few minutes. Stood at the side and looked down the rope." Zane was almost running to keep up, but I didn't want to slow my pace. The events of my recent voyage had started to swirl together in my mind the moment I stepped back on the Hill. I felt dizzy with the burden of new secrets, and powerful to be one of the select few allowed to know them. I had to get away from unfamiliar eyes that would judge and evaluate me. I was *someone* here now. Things had changed. Once I was home, in the safety of my living room, I could release whatever it was that was building inside me: good or bad.

"What happened down there?" Brady asked. With his long legs, he barely had to speed up his stride to keep up with me the way poor Zane did. "Why in the Hill is everyone in such a hurry?"

I couldn't even answer him. I was afraid of what might come out of my mouth once I opened it. Secrets, lies or gibberish seemed equally likely. Maybe I had unknowingly traded this knowledge for my ability to communicate, and was stuck talking in nothing but high-pitched squeals of dolphin code from now on. There was also the possibility that I might start screaming and never stop.

Something did distract me from all of my confusion. It was what Brady, of all people, had just said. Why *was* everyone in a hurry? We certainly were never a bustling society and I could see no reason why we would have suddenly become one. I knew why I wanted to get someplace fast, but what was up with the Director? And as I thought about it, I remembered how quickly Father Time disappeared once we landed topside. A pat on the back, a "*See ya later, see ya later*" and he was out of sight. It was the Council members who seemed like they needed to be somewhere fast. They hadn't had regular meetings for ages—why now? Or were they even meeting? Maybe the difference was that we all had something to hide now. We all knew something valuable, although for the life of me, I couldn't figure out what my secret was. Maybe we were all in a rush to get back into our respective corners before the next bell rang, or the next tribulation presented itself. It was also possible that we were all just a bunch of roaches that wanted to get under the stove before the lights came on.

Running down walkways and into the center of town, we began to see people. In fact, there were groups milling around. We hadn't seen much of anyone in public since Ira's funeral. Of course that was just—yesterday? Maybe? Out here now, it was like people thought whatever killed Ira would find them if they locked themselves away in their homes. They were clinging to each other like funeral clouds.

They gave us a wide berth as we neared them. Granted, most people get out of the way when a large hairy beast comes at them, but these stepped further away than they needed to. Imaginaries we had known and worked with for years turned their heads and looked away from us. Looked at their feet, their hands. Looked at each other, the sky and the nearby buildings—anywhere but at us. We witnessed a Nymph knocked to the ground by a minor love goddess. Such was the combined concentration on not looking in our direction.

We continued, spurred on by the spurn. I unlocked my door and yelled over my shoulder for Kite. "Gonna need your help in here, I think."

She materialized near the table as we all sat down.

"What's going on here?" I asked her. Zane and Brady turned toward her.

"Going on?"

"First no one wants to help these two while I'm on the Otherworld, now everyone looks somewhere else when we come around. On top of that, everyone's in a hurry. They're running around like they got somewhere to be all of the sudden."

"Well..."

"Well?"

"Something has changed. Something big."

"Big?"

"Yes, and it has people gossiping. Not long after you went down, the Director had a little conference and announced a new one."

"A new one?"

"Yeah. He said they needed someone to replace Ira and to keep up with demand. In order to do that, we need more Boogeymen—that was the gist of the grand speech, anyway."

"He made an announcement that we need more Imaginaries to scare people?"

Kite nodded.

Did Father Time just take me on that meaningless trip to get me out of the way, or did someone else plan it so both of us wouldn't be a problem? There seemed to be an awful lot of Imaginaries standing around doing nothing for the Council to suddenly need help so badly they had to move someone over to the Boogeyman division. Brady mentioned Mother Nature coming to check on us after we left. Was she checking to make sure we were still gone, or hoping we would return in time to help with something?

"So they promoted someone to Boogeyman? Who? Anyone I know?"

"I'm not sure. He wasn't real clear on that."

"The new Boogeyman wasn't there for the announcement?" Brady asked.

"Nope. The Director said he was hard at work on his first assignment. 'Doing us proud already' or something like that."

I had to know exactly who was on what team. "Were any of the Council there?" I already knew that Father Time was sidelined because he was with me, but I had to know who made it without him.

"Nope. Not a one. The Director stood up there all by himself, gave the speech, signed some kind of paperwork, and walked off just as alone as when he started."

"Signed the paperwork? Did it have all the signatures of the Council on it?"

"I don't know." Her tails twitched side to side. "He said something about the full sanctioning of the Council, though."

"He signed something? So, he had a pen?" I asked.

No one answered. The full sanctioning? It was a given on the Hill that anything done officially had to have the official okey-dokey of the Council, and that meant their signatures. Even on the smallest of decrees, they sat down and signed their names on an official document. They were, in fact, very proud of signing things. I heard that back in the old times when they first became the ruling body, they would have marathon signature sessions. Everyone on the Hill would line up and file past them as they slowly and carefully put pen to paper to fashion their official marks on hundreds of proclamations and decrees. It seems they had enough things to sign to keep them busy until each and every person got to see them that wanted to.

And suddenly they just sanction things?

"Thanks, Kite. This is all very helpful. If you don't mind, could you wait outside? We might need you again soon." I could tell she was a little let down by my not asking her to stay. Her facial features, such as they were, fell just a little. The eagerness and excitement that energized the colorful bows on Kite's tail drained and it fell still. I wasn't sure that I could trust her as fully as I would have liked. She was the only member of our little team that I hadn't hand-picked, and that made me nervous. If any or all of the information that she had just given us was true, something big was happening, and I couldn't afford to have doubts about my group. My immediate fear was that she might run to the Director and tell him what we were planning or how much we knew. That fear subsided when I realized we knew nothing and had absolutely no plans.

"Oh…right. Sure, Abe. Just give a call if you need me. I'll be…" Brady stood up and opened the door for her. Unnecessary, really, since she could go through it, but at least it felt like she was truly out in the hall rather than just invisible in the room. "…I'll be right outside the door."

"Why can't she stay?" Brady asked as he clicked the door shut.

"I don't know who's on our side now. I'm actually not sure I ever knew."

They were silent for a time. It was a lot to absorb. At least I had the benefit of being there for much of it. I'd seen it with my own eyes, felt it with my own hands and let it sink in, whether I understood it or not. These poor saps could only take my word for it.

It was Zane who finally broke the silence. "So, this new guy?"

"Yes?" I said.

"I don't like him," Brady said. He crossed his arms and huffed.

Zane nodded and pointed. "Thank you. I don't like him either, but I didn't want to be the first to say it. He seems like a real jackass."

"You don't know him. You haven't even met him yet." I didn't like him either. "Give him a chance." It was official: we were going to go ahead and hate the new guy before we even knew his name. It was good to see the mischievous look on Zane's face again. It was infectious, and Brady joined in immediately, eager for something fun. Anxious to belong with us.

"He's new. He's inexperienced. How about Baby? We could call him Baby. That's kind of mean. He could be referred to as the Baby Boogeyman, or what about Boogeyman Baby?" Brady suggested.

"Nah, that almost sounds too hip," Zane said.

I didn't have time for the game, even though it brought some much-needed levity to the situation. "Let's just call him Bob."

24

There was only one member of the Council who hadn't piped up and talked to me yet: Mother Nature. The others had come to me or at least made themselves available, but she had remained in the background. After I heard that she had come to check up on us at the scaffold, I wondered if she had something to say to me. If not, she at least had some interest in my continued existence.

I decided to stop by her office and see what she could tell me. Her Nymph receptionist, Gina, kindly asked me to take a seat in the waiting area. Mother Nature apparently had a pretty full schedule, but would be with me just as soon as she could. I nearly tripped trying to cross the thick carpet to the plastic bucket seats of the designated waiting area. Why would anyone have such wonderful, soft carpeting around such cheap, uncomfortable furniture? The room smelled of fresh cut grass and honey. I felt the urge to sneeze.

I waited politely, figuring that waiting was part of a detective's job. Plus, Mother Nature had yet to reveal whether she had any real alliance or affiliation, so it might pay to be respectful. It was boring, though. There was nothing to read anywhere in the room. No books or magazines, no pamphlets on the virtues of abstinence, not even a safety poster or evacuation chart. There were paintings, though, sharp as life, showing trees and clouds. There were bright blue skies and grassy fields bathed in sunlight. The detail was so fine, so minute that I could picture the artist laying in a lush field somewhere, staring at each individual blade of grass and each nearly tangible sunbeam, then painstakingly filling in color to the blank canvas.

I realized as I was staring at the paintings that Gina hadn't made any sort of effort to announce my presence to her boss. She just sat there, staring at me. "Don't you need to tell her I'm here?"

Her dreamy-bored expression didn't change. "She knows."

"Are you sure? You didn't say anything or leave the room or send a messenger to announce me or anything."

"Trust me. She knows." She folded her arms in front of her on the desk.

Her face went back to a blank stare, drilling into my head. She moistened her dry lips once with her tiny pink tongue and smacked them together.

"Would you mind...?"

"She knows."

"Thanks."

She was small, even for a Nymph. I figured I could force my way past her if I needed to. I wondered if she was truly meant to be any sort of deterrent for the various disgruntled personnel who might be determined to get to Mother Nature. Did she know some sort of martial arts—a form of hand-to-hand combat only revealed to Imaginary secretaries and personal assistants? Her desk was oversized and shiny, a polished oak affair buffed to a high gloss. I wondered if it was that large for a reason. It could conceal something. Anything was possible in our little world. Maybe she had a three-headed dog under it. Maybe she casually propped her legs on it day after day, just waiting for the first sign of trouble, upon which she would unleash the mongrel to cause mayhem and discord. It would leap upon the intruder with a malice unmatched by anything on the Hill and carry its prey up and down the streets of town as a trophy, occasionally shaking its head with dizzying cruelty.

I stared at the little name plate on Gina's desk. *Personal Assistant*. It reminded me of Delia, and how she was an associate Tooth Fairy. Or did we decide she was an assistant? Nonetheless, it took me down the path of thinking about the Tooth Fairy in the cave, and my gums and whatnot. I still had a few coins in my pocket that were meant for her. She was most certainly as batty as Time had made her out to be, I was sure.

"You're not as big as the other guy," Gina said in a monotone grumble.

"The other guy?"

"Yeah. The new guy. Not many people have been in here for a while. You and him, I guess." She leaned back for the first time since I arrived. Maybe the beast under her desk was shifting around to get comfortable. "He was kind of rude."

"The new Boogeyman? He was here recently?" I needed to catch up with him, if for nothing other than welcoming him aboard. I initially felt left out more than anything. But as I stared at her mouth moving, the words sunk in and I realized that if I'd played my cards right, I could have been the new Boogeyman. If I had learned of Ira's death before I'd been railroaded into this detective role, I could have checked that box on my application or my service record or whatever. When I initially met Brady, I could have said "I want to be a Boogeyman when I grow up." And that would have been the end of it. I wouldn't be in this odd fucking situation I was in.

"Yeah, left just a bit ago. Said he had stuff to do, but he didn't say it nice like that, if you know what I mean. He was all snotty about it."

"Sounds like a charmer."

"Yeah, well. I guess nice isn't his job."

"Tell me about it," I said. I hoped by talking nice and smiling I might get her on my side. "Kind of a jerk for talking poorly like that to you, though, I think."

"Yeah, but what can you do?"

Mother Nature cleared her throat behind Gina. She looked much more professional than she had when I met her the first time. Her attire was more formal, businesslike, even. It was an expensive-looking white robe that looked like it was on loan from one of the Goddesses. The hair that had been so scraggly and free was now confined to a tight bun screwed to the back of her hair. Her eyes narrowed as Gina and I stopped talking.

"Mother Nature will see you now, but you must keep it brief. She's very busy," Gina said without turning around.

"Indeed." Mother Nature turned on her heels and retreated down a hallway that curved behind the receptionist's desk. I stood up and walked quickly to catch up.

As I passed Gina's desk, I smiled and nodded. I couldn't resist a look backward at what was under her huge desk. I stumbled a bit as I thought I saw half a dozen eyes peer out of the darkness.

"Get in here," Mother Nature said coldly as she held the door to her office open for me. I was surprised by how cramped the space was. There was room for two large, well-stocked bookshelves along the back wall, a small desk and wooden chair for a visitor to sit in, and that was about it. Papers were cluttered everywhere. I was sure peppermint candies were lurking somewhere beneath the mess.

I moved toward the only seat available to me. "Don't bother. You won't be here long enough to get comfortable," she said, her voice dropping. The pleasant demeanor of our first meeting—the helpful attitude, the light laugh—was all gone. "What do you want?"

"I—It's just that I've spoken with the rest of the Council at various points during the last few days, but I haven't managed to catch up with you." I wanted the meeting to go well but hadn't expected the attitude. I loosened my body language and gave her my best smile. "I thought it would be good to check in and see if you had any suggestions or observations that might help my investigation. You know, anything you might have thought of since the initial meeting." She stared at me with an intensity that made me think she was trying to make my head explode through sheer concentration. It felt like it was working. "Maybe you noticed something in the last couple of days that might help me?"

After what seemed like one last valiant try to get at least some part of my body to burst into flames, she gave up and tried talking. "Help your investigation?" Her tone made me wish she had managed to solder my ears shut. "What investigation? What exactly have you done since we sat you down and gave you this assignment? Please, lay it out for me."

A progress report? No one had asked for a progress report before, no one said I'd have to give one. Everything I did since then? I couldn't remember everything I did. She knew I went down to the caves with Father Time, so it would be dumb to leave that out, but I really wasn't supposed to be there. Was I? "Well…first I went and looked at Ira's body and gleaned what I could from his apartment. Talked that over with my associates—" She looked impatient and wasn't likely to let me pat myself on the back. "Then the three of us discussed everything we knew about the case for a while. I went to the Otherworld and consulted with a detective over there." I was proud of that fact and felt a little like rocking on my heels as I said it, but I kept in mind that the Council actually recommended that one, so it wasn't amazing work on my part. "Then, I mulled everything over with Death and Father Time…" Was that really it? "Which sort of brings us up to date."

"Did you interview any potential witnesses?" she asked.

"Zane and Brady were supposed to interview some key people, but they couldn't find them."

"Ah, your crack team of investigators. Did any of you interview anyone at all?"

"Just Truman. He spoke at length about all kinds of things." That ugly truth again. It sucked.

"Yes. Your old friend. Did he say anything in particular that stayed with you?" She seemed doubtful even before the words got out of her mouth.

"Sure."

"All right. Give me something. Tell me anything that you felt was particularly insightful. Anything that really helped you? Anything at all."

"Well..." I couldn't help but sigh. If I'd only written things down along the way, I'd have every word at my fingertips. A notebook.

"Well?"

It came to me like a clap of thunder during a light rain. I did remember something. "He talked a lot about people being victims. About wanting to be a victim versus not wanting to be one." I remembered him saying that, but not the context it was in. Why would that be the one thing I could recall?

"Isn't that an odd topic for old friends to discuss at a reunion?" she said.

Did she forget why they sent me there? "Of course, this is a murder investigation of sorts. We had to get around to talking about a victim sooner or later, didn't we? He's had the training and the experience to help me understand some things. I mean, it's not like we sat around and played party games and looked through yearbooks or anything." We did watch TV, though.

"I guess you're right. That is why you were there." Her defiance slowly dissolved until she finally managed to uncross her arms. She even sat down at the chair behind her desk. I saw this as a sign that the hostile portion of our talk was over and that we could talk calmly about the world around us. I bent to sit. "Don't," she said, less angrily, but still forceful. "We're done here."

"But, we still have—"

"No we don't."

"I—"

"No," she said with an exasperating finality. "Try to talk to people about what they saw or what they remember." She was up and around the desk, and guiding me to the door so quickly, I wasn't sure it was really happening until I was in the reception area. As I walked out the door I heard her call after me. "Talk to them soon Abe; people tend to forget. It's easy to forget."

25

Of course there were people to interview, places to go. I knew my job better than anyone, after all. I was the first to do it, and I had the training, not them. They could only speculate as to how to do it; I had experience. Relevant experience.

I knew when to wait and how to hide. How many times had I played hide-and-seek as an Imaginary Friend? That was waiting and watching, wasn't it? That was observing.

That meant I knew how to do surveillance.

I sat down on the cold dirt and waited behind the row of high, thick bushes that lined the building on the same side as the main entrance to the Personnel Department. There was only a narrow gap between bushes and just a few inches at the bottom that allowed me to peer out from behind them. I could see everyone and everything that came and went from the door easily without being noticed unless they were really looking for me. Or they were fucking invisible or something. That's annoying.

This was what I did every day of my existence, except I usually played with kids, not Boogeymen. Who was to say it wouldn't work? Same principle, just a slightly different target. It did feel awkward to be doing it on my home territory. I figured that Thad or Ray, or both, would have to come by here soon. They both still had to work, didn't they? I didn't think they would be given the luxury of time off, no matter what they had to do with this whole situation. The Otherworld wasn't going to take a break just for them.

I leaned back against the cold bricks and hugged my knees. I was prepared for a long stretch of staring intently. I told Zane and Brady to go out and interview everyone they saw, whether they had any connection to Ira or not. Everyone. See a Rat Boy off to trundle through some city's sewers? Talk to him. A Mothman slamming himself against the neon lighting near the Wet Dream? Take him aside and have a chat. Anyone. I laid out a set of questions that they should consider asking when they had the chance: "Where were you...", "What do you know about...", etc. They readily agreed, and I told them I was going to find our two wayward brethren. They both smiled politely and wished me luck. I suppose I should have said the same for them, given their track record, but I was trying to have better expectations when it came to their involvement. Like Sarah had said, they were friends and they were doing their best. I had to have some faith in them, had to sit back and let everything just happen. There was really no changing them now.

I couldn't get comfortable, and it was distracting to the point that I couldn't stare at the walk. I moved away from the wall and stretched myself out a little. I was used to sitting and waiting, but I was out of practice or out of shape or something. Maybe it was all of the police work I was doing. It got me out of my routine and dulled my natural instincts. I tried lying on my back but found it was impossible to see the walk from that position, so I ended up on my stomach with my head propped up on my arms. That was comfortable, practical, and stealthy, as well. For years, I could sit in a closet or under a bed and wait for hours without a problem until a kid nodded off, and yet there I was, unable to get comfortable on the simplest of assignments with more room than I ever had on one of my Otherworld jobs.

I was prepared to wait for Thad and Ray for as long as it took. What else was I going to do? This was my job now, and I had nowhere else to be. I realized from the beginning that I might be hours and hours before I found them. I was hours into my vigil when I had a revelation. I wondered if it came from my position as a detective or if I would have come upon it anyway, but it didn't matter.

Not only had I not seen the two I was looking for, but I hadn't seen anyone go into or out of the Personnel building.

No one.

Not a soul.

Usually, there are crowds—a line to get in and to wait for a free tube. Sometimes the line stretches out the door. Even at the slowest, there's always a steady flow to and from the place. Where was everyone? Why weren't they working? There were people that needed us, depended on us as a part of their lives. At the very least, there should be Imaginaries taking classes. "Ring-Around-the-Rosie and Other Children's Games for Newbies" wasn't being offered just for fun, was it?

I began to think something had happened. Like, maybe there was a huge fucking meeting going on somewhere that I was supposed to be a part of but no one could find me. I hadn't even told Brady and Zane where I would be, only that I would be looking for Thad and Ray. Maybe I was hidden *too* well, and no one would even see me. Maybe someone else was dead, and they needed an investigator. Better yet, maybe Ira wasn't really dead, and they didn't need me anymore. I considered breaking cover and going into the building to see if the workers were at their stations waiting for orders to come in.

Some movement on the sidewalk stopped me. Someone was finally coming. I could see from the shape that it was probably a man. I saw him from a fair distance but couldn't tell who it was. It was a large, dark-clothed Imaginary, a good foot taller than me, I guessed. He walked quickly with long, purposeful strides and was on the steps quickly.

He was so close to me that I could have easily hit him with a dirt clod if had been so inclined, and yet I still had no idea who he was. He had long, scraggly hair that moved on his head with each long stride. It was like seaweed moving in and out with the tide. It seemed the same color and consistency, too. His face was pointed, long with a chin that nearly hit his chest. His squinted eyes were large enough to show yellow with large black pupils. From the time his facial features were discernable, his wide mouth was open in a smile that nearly reached both ears. The teeth his smile exposed were curved—half-exposed rusty scimitars buried in his gums. He was gone from my sight as he entered the building.

I had a full view of most of his body and didn't recognize him, yet he was wearing the same clothes that Boogeymen wear.

I knew every Boogeyman except one.

Bob.

Whatever the Hill his name was.

No one comes through those doors for hours until he comes trotting up the lane? Something about that didn't sound quite right.

It was time to meet the new guy.

I stood up and pushed through the line of bushes and onto the walk. In three steps I was on the front stairs of the building and nearly holding the handle to the front door already. I couldn't see him ahead of me through the glass. I tugged the door open and found the main hall empty except for two assignment agents named Heins and Helga. They were sitting at the long counter where everyone went to be told where their next job would be. I looked all around but found no one but them.

I walked quickly in their direction across the shiny marble floor. The room had a high ceiling and columns near the doors. My footsteps echoed in the cavernous room. Both Heins and Helga stood a little straighter as I approached and put on their work faces. They seemed to be grateful to have something to do. I walked directly for Heins for no other reason than that he was closest. I had gotten my assignments from him before, and we were on friendly terms. He was originally a troll under a bridge, but developed a case of claustrophobia and got transferred to the office.

"The guy that just came in here. The big one." *The only one.* "Where'd he go?" I yelled while I was still twenty feet away.

He looked surprised at my abruptness. "I can't tell you that, Abe. You know we—"

"Look. You know me. You know what I am. Didn't the Director of Personnel tell everyone to cooperate with me in any way possible?"

"Well, yes, but I don't know..." He looked over at Helga, who shrugged her shoulders and turned to read some paperwork.

I had crossed the rest of the lobby and was standing in front of her. "Look around here." Helga and I scanned the lobby in unison. "Pretty slow. Isn't it?"

"Yeah." She nodded.

"Been this way for a while?"

"Yeah." She nodded again.

"I'll bet this new guy has been in here a few times, though. Am I right?"

"Yeah." Helga looked questioningly over at Heins, who quickly turned back to his papers.

I took her hand and looked deep into her eyes. "He's kind of an ass, isn't he?"

She smiled at me. "Kind of."

"You know me, Helga. I've been here for a while. Who would you rather help out, me or some new jerk?"

"But you're both—"

"Working with the Director? Yes, I know. We're supposed to be on the same team, but I don't know the guy from a hole in the ground." I thought I could avoid the hassle if I just waited here for him to come back, but I wanted to see what it was that he was doing. What was so great that he was suddenly getting all of the business?

"No, I meant you're both...new guys, so to speak."

"So what harm could it do to have both of us in the same place? On the road together again...for the first time...come on." In the end, my best argument was "come on." *And it worked.* Helga and Heins looked at each other with identically perplexed looks on their faces, and neither could come up with a valid defense against "come on."

"All right." Helga handed me a card from under her counter. "Tube six." She pointed needlessly down the hall to where that particular tube was located. I had used the tube before. In fact, tube six was my lucky tube.

"Helga, I thank you." I took off at a sprint down the hall toward the tubes. If I hurried, I might still be able to catch up with him before he finished whatever it was he was assigned to do.

26

It was dark.

It's always dark.

There was always blackness at the beginning.

I was materializing in the cover provided by an alcove where two parts of a building came together. I waited, feeling the various parts of me come together and congeal. I felt the heat of a late summer afternoon, even in the shade that I was laying in. Unable to move yet, I stared up at the deep blue sky and watched a puff of cloud drift through my vision, and I thought of the beautiful area around the castle back on the Hill. I wished I had been tapped for an easy job filing things there. I wanted a job that was easy enough to afford me time to lay around and watch clouds. When I pictured someone to watch them with, I saw the Tooth Fairy, not Sarah. I wondered why I thought of her first when I hadn't even talked to her, couldn't even imagine the sound of her voice saying my name.

I sat up and surveyed my surroundings. The building was shaped like a "U". Everything in the middle was paved over with rough crumbling blacktop. There was a large blue dumpster overflowing with trash, mostly paper, immediately in front of me, and concrete stairs leading to a large metal door behind me.

I stood up and put my hand on the dumpster to steady myself. Once I did that, I could see around the garbage bin and found that the alcove opened out onto a lush green grassy area with several big trees and a playground area. Amid more blacktop and stones were swings and slides, tetherballs and teeter-totters. Eight children, boys and girls, played on and around the equipment. They were screaming and laughing, running to and fro haphazardly. They were eleven or twelve years old, maybe, and they smiled easy, wide smiles that children on the Otherworld could afford. Three kids sat apart from the larger group, throwing rocks into the distance and pulling grass from the ground in big handfuls.

The whole area was beautiful. There were tall, neatly trimmed trees at intervals in the freshly-cut lawn. The smell of fresh cut grass drifted to me and concealed the stench from the packed trash container. I expected to see bunnies and squirrels skipping hand in hand in the sunset. I knew animals only did things like that on the Hill.

There was a pair of wooden benches under every tree, one on either side. I saw movement under the tree closest to me and detected a familiar shape beneath it.

I could see the large shadowy figure hunched over the back of the park bench on the other side of the tree talking to someone. The bench was in the shade of a tall leafy elm and the shadow nearly came all the way to my hiding place. I hesitated, looked again at the serenity of the surrounding area, stepped closer to the tree, feeling safe in its shadow.

I could hear a conversation, low and secretive, coming from the two. I leaned against the tree and peered around it. I could see the new guy clearly talking to a child on the bench not a dozen feet away. The words were a mystery to me but the tone seemed calm enough. There was no shouting or heated gestures being exchanged. It was just the new Boogeyman kneeling in a park and talking to a child on a bench. The little boy was dressed in a nice red sweater and had his arm around a large backpack with large black straps. His hair was cut short and combed neatly down on the sides of his head.

The fact that a Boogeyman was having an open conversation with someone wasn't lost on me. They reminded me of when I was working with Truman as an Imaginary Friend. The talk was easy and light, and they were at ease with each other, like the two of us had been. I wondered if he had been this boy's Imaginary Friend before he was promoted, and he had been called back to work with him again for some reason.

I pressed myself closer to the tree and inched around it to try to hear what they were saying. The bark of the tree felt cold and rough against my cheek and I winced. I made myself a little less solid to avoid painful contact with the world.

Luckily, they had their backs to me, so I had some room to maneuver without being seen. I stayed close to the tree and moved slowly anyway, just to make sure someone else didn't happen to see me. I considered making myself like mist and drifting closer to a better vantage point, but it was hard to control my movements out of doors. A light breeze could throw me so far off course that I would be hard pressed to recover any advantage I had.

27

Ghosts can turn themselves invisible and misty whenever and wherever they feel like it. It's part of their essence. The rest of us, however, can only do it on the Otherworld. On the Hill, it just doesn't work for us. It has something to do with the fact that the whole place is surrounded by fog already—that interferes with the process. At least, that's what everyone would have us believe. I was sure it was true, but the paranoid conversation I'd had with Zane and Brady made me question things I had accepted offhand throughout my existence.

Once, Ray and I had accidentally been assigned to the same job. Clerical error, whatever. He was to really lay it on thick for a couple of little ones who were out on a camping trip with their family. They were pretty young, both still in the single digits age-wise, and were already not thrilled about the deepest, darkest woods of Michigan's Upper Peninsula. I was the girl's Imaginary Friend. She believed I was a strange-colored teddy bear named Hailey. The girl's name was Linda or Leslie or Laura. An "L" name, anyway. I think. The girl and her older brother, Paul, put on brave faces and assured their parents that they could sleep in the tent by themselves for the night. And like chumps, Mom and Dad let them try it. They left a couple of big flashlights with the kids, just on the off chance that they might need them for finding a snack or something.

Flashlights are tricky for guys like us. On one hand, they're worse than nightlights, because nightlights are stationary and you can predict the path and radius of the light they throw off. Flashlights can be moved; they can be focused on one spot and then refocused on another. On the other hand, they're still pretty useless in a big, shadow-rich place like the woods. Even if they managed to point a light right at a Boogeyman's hiding place, they probably still couldn't have seen much besides the dark form in the blackness that the woods provides. The lights also add to the dramatic effect. The calamity of a wildly waving light in the darkness is a beautiful thing to someone whose sole purpose is to seed chaos and watch it feed itself to the bursting point.

So there I was, sitting comfortably next to a sleeping bag, waiting for the children to nod off, so I could go home and look halfway normal. But, unbeknownst to me, Ray was up in the branches of a tree, high above the children's pale orange tent, waiting for the little timer in his head that let him know it was time.

I could see the flashlight that they had left on in the middle of the tent pointing upward. Once in a while the boy would startle and suddenly the second light would appear and scan the tent's zipped up flap. There was whispering and nervous giggling for long into the night, prompting gruff warnings from their parents in the larger purple tent on the other side of the dying campfire.

"*Get some sleep, you two. We've got a big day tomorrow.*"

The still-shining flashlight in the middle fell over to point at the wall of the tent eventually, and it stayed there without being righted by either of the children.

I stretched out and shook some life back into my limbs while I watched and listened. The boy was out, and I was ready to fade at any moment. While I waited, I noticed a shadow moving somewhere outside. It got larger as it approached, and I assumed one of the parents was up and coming to shut off the lights in order to save the batteries.

But rather than move for the zipper and enter the tent, the shape went to one corner and began messing with the stake that held the shelter in place. After a moment, it moved to another corner and shook the anchor there as well. It occurred to me that the whole thing would fall on the kids' heads. I watched as it loosened the next one and then moved to the final support.

I took a deep breath, bringing in the smells of the forest and the plastic of the tent, the cloth of the sleeping bags, the metal of the flashlight, and I noticed something else—something familiar. It was hard to place, but it was something from the Hill, not the Otherworld. It quickly made sense that it would be a Boogeyman, but I wondered what brought him here to the same place as me at the same time. Maybe sent to vex Leslie's brother?

I wondered if I should make contact, but I was having fun watching his technique. He was pretty stealthy, I suppose. That dark shape crept around in silence for just a couple of minutes, but he knew his job. He slipped on the dew-covered grass once and nearly fell on the tent, which would have scared the kids but ruined the artistry. His ingrained stealth enabled him to regain his balance without alerting anyone to his presence, I suppose. He took a moment to regain his composure and moved on. When he was done, he turned and crept to the rear of the structure.

I thought it was a good time to have some fun with whoever it was. I grabbed one of the kid's flashlights and slid myself through the gap in the bottom of the tent zipper. I had to make myself a mist, because it was too small of a space. I solidified on the other side and reached back through to pull the light out. I looked for the shape and waited to try to anticipate the Boogeyman's movements before he managed to pull the line and brought the whole thing down. I looked down at myself and realized I was just a little teddy bear and wondered how much I would actually surprise my fellow Imaginary, but I didn't care. It would be a great fucking gag to play on someone whose reason for being was only to startle people.

When I felt that the tent could take no more, I held the light as best I could in my paws and flipped it on, but kept the light muffled against my chest. A second later, I jumped out to show myself to the Boogeyman, planning on holding the light to my face while I gave him my best stuffed animal growl, but it went completely awry. When I jumped, the light flew from my hands and landed on the ground at my feet. And as I planted my feet to roar, they had become paws with thick claws digging into the dirt, and the rest of me had grown as well. I was no longer a tiny stuffed, imaginary bear; I was an eight foot black bear, real as life and screeching in Ray's face.

Honestly, all I wanted to do was finish the assignment and have a little fun with a fellow Imaginary—we do it all the time at home. I just wanted to give him a little jolt, just a tiny scare that we both could sit back and laugh about sometime in the coming years. At the same time we would be scaring the kid in the tent and we could go home. It went a little further.

Ray was so surprised he let out a cry of his own. It was the same high pitched squeal of fear generally reserved for little girls on the Otherworld when we made them think their dollhouses were haunted. It was a long, loud, sustained shriek that echoed back through the forest. He spun around to run a bit too quickly, and lost his footing again in the slick grass. He fell backward onto the tent with his arms flailing wildly for balance. That brought the whole tent down on the kids.

I think that was when he saw me. In the split-second before the tent gave way, his eyes were drawn toward me. Instead of a look of relief, recognition, or even anger, Ray looked even more afraid. As soon as I saw that, I stopped what I was doing. I thought maybe he hadn't recognized me or something. I figured if I stood still he could get a better look at me and then realize it was me. But really, my form was unrecognizable to anyone at that point, and the collapsing tent had already enveloped him. He disappeared into its folds.

Until that time, there was a muffled and frantic conversation coming low from the tent. As the whole thing came down with someone on top of it, the children's voices became decidedly louder. They screamed and cried all of the possible variations of the scream in just a matter of seconds. They cried out together, nearly on the same pitch, they took turns wailing while the other caught their breath, they tried to breathe while shouting for help, which led them to take even deeper halting breaths. They used high-pitched and low-pitched yells, nearly inaudible whimpers and siren-like moans of woe. They were screaming prodigies, it seemed.

It was like a symphony. The music of panic echoing the mayhem back to us and doubling it. Ray's flailing at the tent creating a percussive rhythm that drove the others to their parts. The shouts, the cries like woodwinds and brass belting out their parts to whoever would hear them. Like a conductor, I was proud when all the parts came together in perfection. I was pleased with the way my plan had created such a masterful work of art.

The parents were up and loudly fumbling to get their tent unzipped, and I knew our time was up. Ray was apparently too confused to realize that all he had to do was turn himself to mist and float free of the tangled mess, and he continued to struggle amid the metal poles, tent plastic and rope. I saw one of Ray's kicking feet sticking out of the folds of the tent, so I grabbed him with a thick, meaty paw and ran for the trees. It took a good tug to extricate him from the melee, but we made it into the woods just as the metallic zip of the tent flap announced the arrival of the parents on the scene.

Immediately after we made it to the darkness, we both began to dissolve. I was still snickering just a little, but Ray wouldn't even look at me. I honestly wasn't sure he recognized me.

When we got back to the Hill, Ray avoided me. He never said another word about what happened. Even at meetings that we all had to attend he acted as if he couldn't see or hear me. I sent him an apology when I realized that I had gone much farther than I had planned. He never responded.

It was no wonder he didn't want to talk to Brady and Zane. He'd probably found out that they were with me.

I questioned the Director about the mix-up once. He was kind of sheepish about the incident and avoided explaining exactly how it happened. "Sorry, Abe. In all the centuries we've been using this system, we've never accidentally sent two people to the same job like that."

28

I found it easier to hear them when some of the children who were running, screaming, and laughing in the distance left the playground.

The new Boogeyman was indicating the smaller group of kids sitting on the grass not far away. "Are you sure those aren't the boys?" he asked the young man next to him.

"Yes, I'm sure." The young man sounded annoyed. He didn't turn to look at the thing talking to him over his left shoulder.

Conversely, the thing over his left shoulder never took his eyes off of the boy on the bench. "Positive? They seem to be the same little bastards as the last time." He leaned forward, closer to the boy's ear, but kept staring. "You sure the one in the middle isn't one of them? He's got long hair like the one that took your stuff." Even though he was within inches of the boy's ear, I could still hear him clear as anything whispered in my own ear.

"It's not them," the boy said flatly, disappointed.

"You sure?"

"Yeah."

"Really?"

"Well, yeah."

"I thought you wanted to get even here. Wanted a little payback." The Boogeyman was louder now, his voice bigger.

"I do."

"So what are you waiting for?"

"I just want to make sure we get even with the right people. I don't want to hurt anybody that doesn't deserve it."

"Oh, that's nice. Sweet, in fact." He put his hand on the boy's shoulder and waited until the kid turned to look him in the face. "But seriously, which of them doesn't deserve it? If they're your friends, why haven't they helped you out when you were getting picked on near the buses a few weeks ago? Where were they when you were getting beat on in the hallway after class?" He stood up and walked around the bench to sit down next to him, never losing eye contact. "If they're your friends, why am I the one sitting here talking to you and not one of them?"

"I didn't say they were my friends. Just that they didn't do anything."

"Mmmmmm. Uh-huh. I see." He shook his head up and down in long, smooth motions. "I see now." He looked away as he spoke. "That makes it a lot clearer to me. Now I understand why they did nothing while these things happened to you...why they laughed at your misfortune instead of standing up for you. I wasn't aware you had to make distinctions like that."

"Stop it, Bob. They didn't do anything!" The boy was losing his patience.

Bob. That was the first time I had heard anyone use that name with him. The kid always got to pick the name he wanted to call his imaginary friend, but that name fit with what we'd decided to call him, just for fun. I wondered if he showed up and told the boy what to call him.

I'm Bob. Call me Bob.

Did we create that somehow? Or was it just a coincidence?

"Don't take an attitude with me. I thought you were serious. I thought maybe you had the balls to stand up for yourself...get the job done."

The boy put his hands over his ears and shouted toward the ground. "Shut up!"

"Look, I'm just trying to help here."

"Shutupshutupshutup!" Standing, the boy wagged his finger in Bob's face. "You're not trying to help. You're not. You're trying to get me to do something I don't want to do." In the distance, some of the other children noticed the lone little boy yelling at the park bench. They were intrigued. "I'm not going to do it, so why don't you just leave me alone?"

Bob stood up so the boy had to look up to talk to him. The Boogeyman's finger came down and pointed in the young man's face in a sterner, steadier imitation of what the boy had just done. "No." He stood there with his finger steady near the kid's nose and waited. It was an amazing transformation that came over the boy as he stood with this large digit so close to his face. He blinked a couple, maybe three times, and the frustration, the bubbles of anger that were quickly boiling to his surface were gone, replaced by an eerie calm. His brow unfurled, the down-turned grimace of his mouth became a straight line, and his narrowed eyes widened. "You are going to do this, or maybe I'll find another friend. Maybe I'll find one that listens to me," he said.

In the distance, I could see a group of some of the other kids walking toward the boy laughing and pushing each other closer.

"I'm going to leave now, but I'll come back." He took the pointing hand and patted the backpack that the young man was now holding tightly to his chest with both arms. "And when I do...I want to see some action, understand?"

The boy nodded.

Bob stepped around the bench in one great stride and nearly ran directly into me. He didn't look surprised or shocked to see me, really. He seemed delighted, in fact.

"Hey there, professor! Fancy meeting you here." He put his arm on my back and kept walking. "Spying on the new guy? You naughty bastard. Did the chief send you, or were you just doing a little spot inspection?" He pulled me along with him as he continued for the alley. I looked him up and down and couldn't make out his features, not the way I had outside the Personnel Department. Here, now, he was a void, an immeasurable darkness in which I thought I could see all of the stars in space. In the center of that night sky, I could make out white eyes and a chasm for a mouth. He didn't give me much time to stare as he moved on.

The boy took a step back when Bob started talking to me, but his face stayed stony and unmoving. He watched as the two of us walked further away from the tree. He only looked away as the other children got closer. He didn't turn to see them; rather, he watched for them out of the corner of his eye. I couldn't tell for sure, but I could have sworn a tear welled up. If it did, he refused to let it free.

"I'm sorry, if I'd have known you were there, I'd have let you in on the action. I don't know if they've ever tried letting you guys double-team the little buggers in the past, but just think of the damage we could do!"

"No. They never let two of go on the same mission," I said. I had done nothing the whole time I was there, but I was exhausted.

"Yeah. But it's a whole new ball game now, isn't it?" He patted me on the back and took off at a light jog toward the darkest corner of the alcove. His voice was calm and soothing, like when he was talking to the kid. "Who's going to stop us?" He called over his shoulder as he disappeared into the shadows.

I stood and looked back out of the darkness at the little boy standing under the tree. I intended to wait and see what happened next, wanted to make sure he was all right. When I saw him, I saw Truman and felt that same paternal twinge tug at me.

As the kids got closer, I turned and walked toward the same shadow Bob had. I wasn't his Imaginary Friend and I couldn't do anything to change that boy's life. There was nothing I could do for anyone in that stretch of green on that particular day.

I lifted my face to feel the warmth of the sun and to look at the bright blue sky. One tiny white cloud made its way across the sky before I stepped into the shadows and waited to become nothing to the Otherworld.

29

By the time I arrived back at the Personnel Department, Bob was gone. The attendants told me he went out the front door. I looked for him, but he was nowhere to be found in the mists. I ducked my head back in to thank Heins and Helga for their help. No reason not to stay on their good sides.

I went straight back to my apartment to check in with my two able-bodied assistants. In the hallway, I found Kite and sent her to the Personnel Department to wait and come and get me when Bob showed up again. She was thrilled to be back in the game again and took off down the hall dipping and soaring like her namesake. I still had trust issues with her, but my friends were few and far between. I gave her a shot out of necessity.

Inside the apartment, my team was lounging at the dinner table with good news: *things had happened.*

Both Brady and Zane looked pleased with themselves for doing their jobs so well. They smirked and clowned around as I asked them the same question again. "So, you actually stopped people and asked them for information?" I was apprehensive at first, thinking that Zane was trying to lull me into a false sense of security before lunging on me with murder in his eyes. It was comforting that he seemed way too pleased with himself to make any sudden moves to try to kill me. He generally could only focus on one thing at a time when he wasn't working in his Boogeyman capacity. "That's quite a breakthrough."

"That's right," Brady said.

"And you managed to talk to quite a few of the citizens of our fair city?"

"Yep. We asked everyone we saw if they'd killed him. And nobody did." Zane looked as if he might win some sort of prize for his answer.

"Did you ask them the other questions that I suggested?"

"Ah. No. We figured that we shouldn't confuse ourselves—"

"Or the people we were interviewing," Brady interrupted.

"*—or the people we were interviewing* by asking a lot of questions. We plan on going back out tomorrow and asking everyone we see the next question."

I was stumped. How could I have knowingly and willingly saddled myself with idiots of this caliber? I had to keep reminding myself what Sarah had said: they were my friends and they were doing their best. "Which is?" I asked.

"Which is what?" Brady leaned in and narrowed his eyes as if he suspected it were some trick question.

"What is the next question you plan to ask?"

"Huh?" Now Zane looked suspicious.

"You said you were going to go back out tomorrow and ask the next question. What is the next question you plan on asking?"

Neither moved.

I shook my head and thought about questions I needed to ask, too. And who hadn't been asked yet.

30

The boys lowered me by a rope for nearly an hour to get me to the Tooth Fairy's landing. If I had blood, it would have all rushed to my head as I dangled on that line. I would twist for a while counterclockwise, and then stop. It happened so slowly that it seemed to be an afterthought when I began to twist clockwise. It was easy and slow.

Zane, Brady and I agreed I needed to follow up on unexplored or promising leads. After I had mentioned my puzzlement at the cryptic visit to the Tooth Fairy, we decided that I should meet with her outside of Father Time's watchful eyes and ears. I played up the information-gathering angle; as far as they were concerned, I was all business. I didn't mention how badly I wanted to see her again.

We agreed I didn't have time to waste down there, so I was to keep the rope tied around me. They would bring me back when time was up. I only had a couple of hours to make it all the way down there, talk, and come back up. We were concerned that something else might happen while I was gone. We were still waiting to hear from Kite about Bob.

At the Tooth Fairy's landing, I gained my footing and I started down the tunnel. With my first step, the memory of being led in by Father Time flooded back to me. He knew the route. I didn't. I was afraid we hadn't factored in time for me to navigate the dark, winding tunnel. If I couldn't get there quickly, I wouldn't have much time with the Tooth Fairy.

I tried to run carefully, but I still managed to go face-first into the wall at the first turn.

And the second.

I picked myself up and stumbled in the new direction slowly with my arms out in front of me. After a few more minutes of blindly bumping into walls and falling down, a light presented itself dimly and helped in my navigation. A few more quick, jagged turns, and I found myself at her door. It was locked and no amount of rattling it back and forth seemed to help that fact. I looked to the right and grabbed a handful of coins, following the same procedure that I had observed Father Time demonstrate. The door opened easily after I heard the coins fall into their metal container on the other side of the wall.

The place was comfortable in its familiarity. Everything in the same place, lights just as bright, coins sparkling on the floor.

The only difference was the Tooth Fairy herself. She was laying on the bed with her feet dangling over the edge. She wasn't dressed in the poofy dress this time. Instead, she wore light blue pajamas with big round buttons on the top and little pictures of toothbrushes all over them. On anyone else, I might have thought they were comical and childish, but they were perfect for her.

"I was afraid you might not come back again," she said without turning toward me.

"I'm glad you're happy to see me." I stepped up to the bars and felt weak about being that close to her. To calm myself, I pulled on the rope and coiled some extra near my feet. It made no sense not to be prepared. I continued gathering until I thought I had enough to get about a minute's warning when they started to recall me back up the side of the Hill. I tried a little small talk, but found it only slowed my coiling efforts. "My name is—"

"Oh, Abe, stop being silly. Leave that rope alone and come closer. Did you bring me any quarters?" She seemed to take a certain pleasure in not looking at me, as if she knew I wanted to look deep into her eyes and find the meaning of everything—life, thought, movement, happiness—resting at the bottom of her soul. I thought about it for a moment and realized that I never took the quarters out of my pocket from the first time I had come.

I wasn't infatuated enough to allow her knowledge of my name slip by me. "How do you know who I am? Did someone tell you about me?" I dug into my pocket, remembering how badly I had wanted her to have that change not so long ago.

"You were just here the other day, stupid. You stood at the door with Father Time. *Very* rude of you not to say hello, by the way." Still flat on her back, she stretched her legs straight up in the air and kicked them back and forth like scissors, her colorful pants billowing with each movement.

"Sorry. So you did see us?"

"How could I not? Do you like my new pajamas? I got them just for you." She laughed a soft, feathery laugh. "Sorry I couldn't find any of those with the feet in them, but these were hard enough to come by." As she rolled off of her bed, I was struck by her grace and poise, the fluidity of each movement. She was condensation running down the side of a glass of lemonade in summertime on the Otherworld. Such grace, wasted on someone who slipped coins under children's pillows. She posed like a runway model, first hands on hips, then pointing at her top and matching bottom, and finally twirling until I was transfixed by each light step she took. She struggled to keep a serious look on her face, but I could tell she let herself laugh every time she faced away from me by the way her shoulders shook. She looked at me, a glimmer in her eye like the headlights of a car barreling at me in the night.

"Yes, they're nice," I said, following her as she walked to the far wall and back. She picked up a blanket off the bed and threw it over her shoulder casually and continued her catwalk. "Look, I'm down here to just ask you a question or two about something that happened up on the Hill." I had to ask, just so I could say I did.

She stopped and turned to me. "Ooooo! Like a policeman." She held out both of her wrists together toward me. "Do you have handcuffs?"

"I don't even have a badge." Or a notebook.

"Well, I'm already behind bars. Are you planning to interrogate me?" She was trying unsuccessfully to look serious again, but the laugh was impossible to contain. She enjoyed making me uncomfortable, and she flitted from subject to subject too quickly for me to keep up. She correctly guessed things that would distract me from my whole reason for being there with uncanny precision.

"Look, I don't have much time." I shook the loose rope at her to punctuate my need. "So please tell me whatever you can before I have to go. Please?"

"You're leaving me again?" Her coy demeanor gone, she stepped closer to the bars. It was the closest we had been since I walked in, and I could smell something that reminded me vaguely of flowers or fruit. I wondered if she had put on perfume in anticipation of me coming back, but considering she was the Tooth Fairly, I realized that it was just as likely that she had used a strong mouthwash and I was misinterpreting the smell. Still, it was pleasant. "We just got back together and you're leaving me?"

"Yeah, I'll have to. I can only stay for a few minutes. Now let's forget about the stupid investigation; how do you know me?" I had no idea how much time I had left, or how much I had wasted just staring at her.

"You really don't remember? They said you were a little batshit, but wow." We got within a few feet of each other, and I could tell through the bars that she was blushing. "You used to look down my shirt."

I was sure I'd misunderstood everything she'd said to me since I'd arrived. "I used to *what* down your *what*, now?" Had *she* just called *me* nuts? Wasn't the going theory just the opposite?

"You couldn't see anything from way up there, though. Not like you had a telescope."

"You've lost me. Can you clarify that a bit?"

"Well, you weren't always looking down my shirt. I mean, once I caught you staring, the game was pretty much up, wasn't it?" I was sure there was some sort of truth to what she was saying, but she was enjoying dragging it out so much that I had a hard time knowing what to believe. How could we have possibly known each other? "Of course, that was when the real fun began. You should have gotten my attention earlier. It would have prolonged things, wouldn't it?"

"I have no clue what you are talking about. Are you saying…?" There was a sound in the room that hadn't been there when I had arrived. It was a gravelly hiss that had started a few seconds earlier and seemed to be picking up in volume. "Are you saying that we've known each other for a while? More than just the other day?" The hiss was steady and annoying, and I started to look around for the source.

"Knew each other? Abe, my dear, why do you think they put up these bars?"

"Father Time said they were put up in order to take the teeth away from you when you came back from the Otherworld. They said they had to force you to give them up."

"Force? Ugh. What would I want with a bunch of nasty teeth from a horde of Otherworld freaks? I've always gladly put them in a box until they came to collect them." She seemed genuinely creeped out by the prospect. "By the way…?" She pointed to the ground by my feet and waggled her finger around a little. The neatly coiled rope was slowly but steadily uncoiling and retreating back toward the door. As it went, it scraped against the dirt and rock of the cave, making a steady scratchy sound that anyone who was distracted enough could mistake for a mystery hissing sound. Nearly half of the coil was gone before I realized it.

My time was almost up.

"Please. We have to hurry." Time for the Lightning Round. "Where'd I look down your shirt from?" Three loops left on the floor next to me.

"I can't believe they let you out."

"Oh, come on!"

"From *your* cave, stupid." Two loops.

There's an answer I could have done without. "So I was—"

"Just like the rest of us down here? Yep. The factory was still open. They were just making something different for a while there."

One loop.

"What did I do?" I said.

"What do you mean?"

"What did I do that was so bad that I had to be put down here?" The last slack of the rope started to run out. "Please. I have to know."

She walked up and reached through the bars with her right hand and touched my face. "I'm sorry. I don't actually know." She shrugged. "I mean, you were a Boogeyman for a while, but that's all I ever knew." Another shrug, this time with a smile. "Hey? Quick kiss until the next time?" I suddenly liked the way she changed subjects.

I wanted to at that moment and every moment before it. I leaned in quickly, dusty lips poised, when I felt the rope around my waist go taut. I grabbed the bars to try to pull myself closer in the hopes of getting our lips to at least brush but had no luck. As I held on, the lower half of my body became airborne and I could feel the weighty pull of my friends up above dragging me back. I tugged at the rope with one hand, trying desperately to untie it, but it seemed to be tangled and tied with some obscure Imaginary knot that I never took the time to learn. Or maybe it was a secret Sasquatch tie only Brady knew.

"I don't suppose you have a knife or something to cut this rope with do you?" I asked.

"No. How are your teeth? You could gnaw your way through it." She put her hands on mine where they gripped the bars like vices.

I examined the ropes a little closer. "They seem kind of thick." I wasn't strong enough to keep my grip and felt my fingers slip. I knew I had to let go. "Here." I let go with my left hand and she took the quarters that were still there. "Why did you say my gum plaque was diseased?"

"What?"

"Last time I was here."

She laughed, "I said 'Come back and see me, please.' You were way off." I took in the rosy smell of her delicate breath one more time then opened my hands and fell to the floor. I looked behind me to make sure the door was still open before I was dragged through it and into the pitch-black hall.

31

It was the timing that kept me from asking questions. Kite arrived just as I was being pulled up over the side. She was already yelling about Bob getting called in for an assignment. He was going to be reporting for the job in just a few minutes, and I needed to hurry if I was going to catch up with him. "All right, guys, let's go," I said. "I need some answers."

"But Abe, we need to clean this up," Brady said, pointing to the rope coiled haphazardly over the edge of the Hill. "We can't just leave it, can we?" We hadn't been able to find the scaffold that Father Time had taken me down in the first time, and the wheel that the men from Personnel used to lower the whole scaffold was gone, but we were able to rig up a usable but shaky system of our own.

"Abe. Clock's ticking." Kite was jerking her thumb impatiently in the general direction of our destination.

"I know. I'm on my way." I stepped toward the path right behind our ghostly friend. I was already trying to figure out what I was going to do if I caught up with Bob again. I didn't know if I should confront him and disrupt his job or just observe him for a while to try to figure out what he was doing. I wasn't sure if I could allow myself to stand by and watch him do something like that again.

"Abe? Ropes?" Zane asked.

I couldn't believe they were talking about tidying the area. "All right. Fine. You guys stay here. Clean it up, and meet me at the tubes when I come back. There's a lot of explaining to do." I knew I had to go, but I needed some reassurance on another level. "Zane?"

He looked up from the ropes. "Yeah?"

"You know me, right?" I asked.

"What do you mean?"

"I mean, we've been friends for a while now, haven't we? You know who I am, right? I haven't changed or anything."

He shrugged his shoulders and nodded his head. “Sure, chief. We’ve been friends for a good long time. What’s the problem?”

“Nothing…” I turned and sprinted down the path to catch up with Kite, but I swear I could feel Zane’s eyes still fixed on me.

We were close to the center of town when the beam of the lighthouse swung our way. Its slow thick light illuminated our path with a beam that cut a deep red swath across the Hill.

“When did it start doing that?” I asked Kite.

“What?” she said.

“When did that light turn red?”

She stopped and looked into the beam that was pointed right at her and then she looked at me. I was concerned she might blind herself, albeit temporarily, by staring directly at it. “No idea what you’re talking about.”

“What? I noticed it once before, but it wasn’t quite that intense. You don’t see that?” I wanted to press her, but after talking to the Tooth Fairy, I was very conscious of sounding crazy to the people around me.

“Nope.”

I waited a minute. “I’m not crazy.” Saying it out loud had a reassuring feeling to me. I had to increase my pace to keep up with her. She seemed to want to float a little further ahead of me after that.

32

It wasn't a closet or an alley that I found myself in when I awoke this time. I was lying flat on my back on the cold, wet dirt of the Otherworld. I looked up and saw a canopy of green and yellow corn stalks creating the cover for me to materialize. It wasn't necessary, though, for it was dark all around. I could hear the tap, tap, tap of sprinkles of rain hitting the wide leaves of the stalks around me and the occasional rumble of thunder off in the distance as my body congealed. A flash of lightning lit up the sky, turning everything into a negative image of what it had been just a moment earlier.

When I felt up to it, I stood. A green sea of cornstalks waved in the strengthening breeze on all sides of me. Far beyond the waves to the left of me was a thick stand of trees and what appeared to be narrow road. The corn was uneven throughout the field—in some places it was over my head, in others it looked as if it might only come up to my waist. The entire field sloped slightly downward toward the road.

Even with the dots of rain and the occasional lightning, it was hard to tell if the storm was going to break full force, or if it might just blow past and menace a town miles away. With nothing but the corn to go on, I didn't want to hazard a guess as to where on the Otherworld I was. I could've been back in Iowa again, or Illinois, or Ohio. It could've just as easily been any one of dozens of other corn-producing countries. It was hard to say with so little to go on.

I scanned the field for some clue to where Bob was hiding himself or what he was up to. The desk attendants assured me that he had gone through moments before I arrived and that I would end up where he did. Apparently he'd managed to get a decent head start. I walked toward the road rather than deeper into the field behind me solely due to a lopsided mental coin toss.

As I trudged through the field, a part of me kept nagging to sit down and sort some things out. What did I *know*? What was going on? How did I know The Tooth Fairy and vice-versa? Had I really had the chance to look down her dress? Did I like it? Aside from all of that was the main question, the real question: did anybody really care that I'd done nothing to figure out why Ira was dead?

I kept walking.

Had I?

Coming up with the list of questions made my head hurt bad enough. I couldn't imagine actually piecing together some semblance of an answer to any of them at this point in time.

Plus, I felt like I had to know more about Bob before I looked for other answers. We were connected in some way, I felt it deep in my…my whatever I had. Gut? No matter how I joked about it or danced around the subject, we were family in some way, even if it was tangentially. He was a mirror, maybe? I was an Imaginary Friend, he was a Boogeyman, and we balanced something, somehow? I wanted answers about him and the Council, but I wanted balance as well. I wanted the chance to make something right, even if I wasn't having any luck with Ira.

The breeze picked up and sent a great ripple across the field, like a wave over a green ocean. The plants and the fresh rain made the field smell clean, freshly washed somehow. All around me, the corn swayed with a clamor of leaves brushing against leaves. A cool wind met the resistance of my face and I moved to a spot with lower corn so it could wash over the rest of me. The raindrops were cold and left frigid paths as they ran down my face to fall to the ground. They stung as they hit me, but I didn't flinch, never closed my eyes to them. I couldn't remember the last time I was able to enjoy such a thing.

From my new vantage point, I could see the field a little better than before. Even though all of the plants swayed in the wind, one nearby section caught my attention. It was not only swaying more than the others, but seemed to be going in a different direction. Rather than left and right, a small area seemed to be moving forward toward the road. I walked in that direction, skipping between plants and following rows in an effort to intercept the disturbance. As I did so, I noticed that even though that area was moving away from me, it was skipping over rows and plants so that it would be right in front of me, making it easier to catch up with. It was moving slower than I was, which was another added bonus for closing the gap quickly.

When this dark roaming mass came to a spot of low corn I saw Bob weaving in and out of the thin green and yellow rows. I could see just the back of him as he moved away from me, intent on something in front of him. He was slightly crouched and moving carefully. I wondered who he was chasing; after the rough way he treated the boy the first time we met, I tried to prepare myself for anything this time.

Since he was moving slowly, I picked up my pace. I dodged among the rows of stalks and made my way to a point that would intercept him. Along the way, the corn became taller than I was, and I lost him briefly. Although I passed through the same low area that I saw Bob in, the corn towered over my head by a full foot in most places. In these areas it grew dark and the cloudy skies did nothing to illuminate my way. I could still make out the stalks and the leaves and the pathway easily, and although the rain was a welcome sensation, I suddenly missed the sunshine I had come to enjoy on the few recent occasions on the Hill. The heat on my face was a sensation I could get used to, given the opportunity.

I heard a scream just ahead of me, followed by the heavy rustling of leaves. I picked up my pace and ran down the next row over. The sustained sound of stalks being pushed aside told me that Bob was running, no longer trying to be stealthy. The scream I heard certainly wasn't his, and suddenly, even over the din of scattering plants and heavy footfalls, I could make out the whimper and whines of his quarry. After a few seconds, I could see the plants still swaying in his wake. I closed in, pushing masses of stalks and leaves out of my way with both arms. I had to lower my head at times to keep my eyes clear enough to see even the ground. Every few stalks, I ran into ears of corn that slammed into me like rocks.

When I could see his back again, he was just one row to the left of me and moving quickly, though it struck me immediately that he was holding back. He seemed to be deliberately not running his fastest. Maybe it was his way of toying with the child that he had come to torment. *Let them get farther away and give them hope that they were going to escape before catching up with them and dashing their hopes.* Maybe it was all about the chase for Bob; he liked pursuit more than the capture.

I stayed one row over from Bob and ran up next to him. "What are you doing? This is crazy."

He stayed focused on what was ahead of him. "Working. I'm working. What are you doing?"

I looked ahead and could make out a flash of white but couldn't see who he was chasing. "I'm here to ask you some questions."

He laughed.

"What do you know about Ira's death? Did the Director tell you anything?" I stumbled and nearly fell on the gnarled roots of a large stalk but kept going.

"I didn't exist until after he died," he said, and sped up to take advantage of my momentary difficulty.

"That's not exactly what I asked you, now is it?" I called to him as I caught up. "Where are Ray and Thad hiding out? Is the Director keeping them somewhere?"

That got him to actually look at me. "Those idiots are probably dead by now, too. They're lucky they made it as long as they did." He looked forward again and smiled. I followed his eyes to see what he saw. Not far ahead I could make out the white T-shirt and long brown hair of a young girl scrambling to her feet and looking back at us. It was hard to make out all of the details of her appearance, but I could momentarily see her saucer-wide eyes. She turned and started running again.

"What do you mean, they're probably dead? Who the fuck killed them?" He was fixed on his target again—ignoring me. "What do you know about all this?"

"For crying out loud, you jackass. Look around you. All of them will be dead soon. And there's not a thing you can do about it." Bob seemed to enjoy the fact that the girl ahead of us was crying loudly as she ran. His smile widened into a grotesque show of long wide teeth. "Just like there's nothing you can do to stop what's about to happen now." He stuck both arms out to his sides and into the path of the cornstalks. His arms hit each one, making even more noise than he had been. It was like a giant baseball card in the spokes of an enormous bicycle. It was the sound of hundreds of birds taking wind against a hurricane.

The girl ahead screamed.

I ran after him, dodging the debris of the cornstalks he was displacing as he ran. It was strange to me that the strong, mature plants didn't even slow him down. He fed on the chaos he was creating. The noise spurred him on, and he ran just a little faster than before.

I could stop him; I could wipe that smug snarl from his face.

I lunged at him from behind and wrapped both arms around his waist. My weight worked with his own inertia and he took two or three wild steps to try to balance himself before he fell face first into the dirt. I had no idea what I could possibly do to him once I had him down, so I took a play from my partner and I sat on Bob. Unfortunately, Brady was much, much larger than Zane and had a distinct advantage in keeping him down. In my situation the roles were reversed, and while Bob wasn't that much larger than I was, it was enough to make a difference.

Bob stood up with me still on his back and began running with me hanging on. After a few big strides, he reached down and pried my hands off his waist and shook my grip loose. I rolled a couple of times off to his left, but I was up and running after him again before I stopped sliding. He hadn't gone far, but I couldn't see the girl anymore.

I ran my hardest in the row next to Bob's until we were nearly even with one another. He pumped his legs a little more when he saw me there. I reached out and pushed him as hard as I could. In all honesty, it wasn't that great of a shove, considering I was running and the row of corn was between us. It still managed to affect him. He stumbled off balance and drifted a few rows over, taking a couple of dozen plants out before regaining control.

I looked ahead and could see the girl directly ahead of me. I could only figure one way to help her out on such short notice: I would have to hold him off until she could make some sort of escape. I thought if I stayed back and delayed Bob, she could make it to the road and a wide open space. I knew Bob was bold, but I wasn't sure he would dare to stand out in the open like that, even during a dark, dreary rainstorm. I didn't know Bob well enough to know the extent of his powers here. Could he really hurt her, or just terrify her?

I was lost in the thought and the planning. When I looked up again, I saw the girl, her brown hair covering parts of her face, her eyes black with fear and focused on me. She was looking directly at me as she ran. She would look forward to avoid tripping and running into things, but kept looking back.

I turned to see how close Bob was, wondering how long I had to keep holding him off.

He wasn't there.

I scanned all around behind me and couldn't see him.

I turned back toward the girl as she ran into a low patch of corn less than twenty yards in front of me and I realized that she wasn't running from Bob. She was running from me.

I entered the low patch that she had just left and looked around again. Bob didn't emerge from behind me. I wondered how long I had been the only thing chasing her. I looked around to see if Bob had gotten in front of her, fearing he was waiting just up the path for her to run right into his arms. As I looked for him, I noticed how close we were to the edge of the field. It was just a few yards to the open two-lane road beyond. I was sure that it was there that she would find safety. The storm still hadn't started up with any kind of force. In the distance, I could see lightning strikes The rumbling of thunder took its time covering the space from there to us. The raindrops were coming more quickly, but the wind had calmed some, and they didn't hit me with as much force as they originally had.

The idea of the road as sanctuary dimmed in my mind a little. A sound came to me in competition for my attention over the thunder. It, too, was just a rumble at first, but it wound down to a grind before becoming a rumble again. Not far up the road, an enormous grain truck was straining through the gears to make it up to speed on the open country road. A farmer, maybe, hoping to make it somewhere before the storm front managed to unload its full force.

If the girl stopped when she made it out of the corn, she would be all right. I hoped there was a drainage ditch that would slow her down, stop her, or force her to look around and find the truck barreling down on her. It was noisy enough that maybe she had already heard it and planned to flag it down when she got to the side of the road. It didn't seem like she would be able to see it, though, as even in the low areas, the corn was still over her head. She wasn't slowing down, either. I was sure of that fact, because I was apparently still chasing her. I had it in my mind that Bob was waiting to harm her in some manner, and that I had to save her. With the truck coming I was even more sure that I had to catch up with her and help. I was confident that I could save her from anything, but with less than a dozen seconds to the edge, I had to push myself as hard as I could to catch her.

"Stop!" I yelled. This seemed to terrify her even more. Maybe Bob had never spoken to her.

"No! Get away from me!" The voice was tiny even for the frame it came from—breathless, exhausted, terrified. She was still running headlong toward the road, oblivious of the corn, the stalks, the leaves, and the enormous vehicle that was roaring down the wet pavement toward us. She was still looking back at me most of the time, not watching where she was going.

"I don't want to hurt you."

"That's what he said," she shouted back at me.

"I want to help you."

I got closer, and I was sure I could grab her. Instead, I ended up grabbing a large ear of corn that swung back at me as the plants tried to settle back into their rightful place in her wake. I fought through the swaying mess and tried to imagine the seconds we had left, since the stalks were over my head and I couldn't see the road.

I reached again. I was close enough to really see the girl up close. I saw things I hadn't in anyone else. She wasn't quite as young as I had perceived her to be; in truth, she was closer to her late teens than her early ones. She was short and had a slight frame, which made her seem much younger from a distance. Her eyes were wide with fear, that was understandable, but they were a light brown with flecks in the pupils that made them glisten even in the low light of the field. Her cheeks were narrow, though they were now covered with welts and thin lines of blood from where the leaves had hit her in the face and cut her. Small droplets of blood clung to her jawline. Her hair fell down over her face, and she had to keep turning her head quickly to whip it out of her line of sight.

It was the first time I really looked at an Otherworlder that wasn't Truman or one of my other assignments. The idea of them had always escaped me. They had always seemed like window dressing in a store, the props to a play. They were a part of my job. That's not to say that I looked at this poor woman and suddenly understood their world or condition. Quite the contrary. To suddenly realize what the Otherworlders were all about would have taken a quantum leap in reasoning that I was incapable of, though I gave myself credit for admitting their enigma.

The point was, at the time, I got some of it. Not about them. But about myself.

Like many jobs previously, I botched this one because I was too much in my head. I was thinking about it more than I needed to. My deep introspection had lasted just long enough that the girl broke through the corn ahead. She was out of the field and in the split second before the stalks closed behind her, I saw that my hopes were realized: there was some sort of wide drainage ditch between the field and the road that would force her to slow down before she got to the road itself. If my hunch was correct, as long as the truck didn't slow down, she would be fine.

That was about the time when two pieces of information fought for precedence in my mind. The first was a quote that came rushing back to me: "Real men don't need math." It was my excuse to Truman for why I didn't help him with his homework. I didn't really know math. I never did. I never needed to learn. So how could I possibly have calculated everything correctly?

The speed of the truck times the distance of the road, added to the velocity of the girl, minus the…what the hell were those things? Hypotenuses? Minus the hypotenuse of the area of the field. No. There needs to be a factor of time in there somewhere. The number of minutes it takes the girl to run from corn stalk 'A' to cornstalk 'B', divided by the hours it takes a train leaving Chicago, plus…

The second bit of knowledge that was that I had no idea where Bob had gone. The idea just appeared in my mind, that I should know where he was and what he was doing. That's when I noticed the truck coming up the road. It was inconceivable that he could be driving the truck. Wasn't it? There was no way that an Imaginary could manipulate a vehicle. We had no concept of how the things worked. There were no cars or trucks on our Hill, so we've never managed to get any sort of orientation to them. Most of my colleagues had expressed the same discomfort with motor vehicles, so how would it be possible for this single entity to be the exception?

Of course, he was an exception. He was something all-new, all-different. This year's model.

I stopped at the edge of the corn, becoming a spot of black still hidden in the camouflage of the densely packed greens and yellows.

Maybe he wasn't driving, but was manipulating the driver in some way. He tried to manipulate the boy, tried to get him to do something or other that he didn't want to, but could he be doing that *here*? I began to think I was seeing things that weren't there. I was making anomalies just to explain things that probably had a perfectly reasonable explanation.

I looked through a break in the leaves, watched the girl stumble and fall in the ditch, then pick herself up and scale the other side of it. I tried to imagine how the next seconds would play out—would she stop? Was she too terrified? The gears on the truck creaked again as the vehicle bounced on the road.

They saw one another. Didn't they?

It made sense to me suddenly that this was Bob's job now. This was *the* job now. Scaring people. That's what *Boogeymen* did. Whatever was happening, it was just one of my co-workers doing his job. What business was it of mine to stop that? The truck was huge and the headlights fell on me like daggers, forcing me to step back into the corn and out of sight. I heard the cry of tires braking on the nearby road and the complaint of the vehicle's engine winding down as I fell to the ground. I put myself down on the darkest spot of ground I could find.

In moments I could feel myself going, and none of the shouts and roaring engines mattered anymore. One last drop of rain worked itself down a stalk and several leaves before dropping off and landing on my cheek.

The cold trail it left lasted until I dissolved completely.

I woke up inside a return tube with no one to greet me, no one to help me out. I turned the crank and pushed open the door as soon as I could. In the room beyond, there were more empty tubes, some lab coats, and a wrench or two that the technicians and lab workers used to adjust things that weren't working. But no workers.

I walked down the lonely hall to the front desk, where Heins stood by himself. "Where's Helga?"

"She didn't come in for her shift." He spoke slower than usual.

I'd never walked in and not seen her face at that desk. "Is she all right?"

Heins shrugged.

"Do you know if I can get ahold of the Director or the Council if I need to visit the Otherworld again?"

"Hmmm?"

I couldn't tell if Heins was bored or sleepy, though I wondered if he ever slept. I'd seen him here just as regularly as Helga, and no one else ever seemed to grace those chairs.

" I might need to—" What? Why would I have to go back to the Otherworld? The whole cornfield incident was pretty awful. I wondered if I should go back and see if the girl was okay, but I had no idea who she was. "I might need to go over to the Otherworld again soon."

Before I could go on and ask again about the Director verifying the card, Heins pulled one out. "Where do you need to go?"

He knew the procedure, and I felt like I should correct him. I didn't want him to get in trouble for me, but the way he was staring off at the door, not even looking in my direction…

"Where do you want to go?"

I wondered how everyone was. Poor Zane, wandering around with that weirdo Brady. He had to be bouncing off the walls by now. I wanted to update them both and huddle for strategy. We were going nowhere, and I had no idea where we should have been going.

"Hey," Heins said. "I'm busy. Where do you want to go?"

33

It was awkward for me to come back to Truman for more advice. I wasn't having much luck with my investigation, though, and needed his help to find a direction. We'd had a good talk last time, but I had completely ignored things he was trying to tell me. I felt bad about that and wanted to be there for him.

"I'm sorry to just show up like this unannounced," I said with a smile. "I would call first, but—"

"No phone service out there yet, huh?" He laughed. "That's just fine. After all those years of making you show up when I wanted you to, I guess I'll live if you come by on your own once in a while." His demeanor had loosened up a bit since I saw him last. His body seemed more tense then; arms at his side, head down a little. Maybe that was it. Maybe it was something else, like the smile on his face.

"Look, I won't keep you long. I understand you had something you needed to talk to me about. I had a few questions that were on my mind that I wanted to run by you, too." I was babbling. Was I babbling? "But you go first."

"Oh. It's no big deal."

"No. I want to be there for you. After all, you passed along some of your hard-earned police expertise on to me; maybe I have some wisdom I can pass along to you."

"Well, thanks." He looked away from me for a moment and turned a little red. His smile got bigger as he did. "By the way, I don't know how to say this exactly, but I might have talked out of turn with you last time. See, I was so pleased to see you that I may have exaggerated my law enforcement credentials before."

"What do you mean 'exaggerated'?" I asked. It seemed that everyone had something they didn't want to tell me lately.

"I'm not a cop. I'm a security guard at the mall."

"You're what?"

"A security guard, at the mall. I tried out for the police force, though—didn't pass some of the tests." I looked at him and saw that he was in pretty good shape. "Most of the tests." Unless those cigarettes were affecting him, I didn't see what test he might have failed.

"Why didn't you tell me this? I was basing my investigation on things you told me. This could have been disastrous." Not that the situation wasn't revealing itself as a mess anyway.

He looked hurt. The large man that he had become faded back a little ways to the boy I used to know. "You sound mad. Why are you mad? It was supposed to be like a game. Like the good old days. Remember? Remember hide and seek?"

"Why did you lie?

"I never lied—exaggerated, maybe." That was true; he never actually said the words 'I am a policeman' to me. It was a lazy omission at best.

"It doesn't make any sense. You wanted to talk to me, needed my help with something, but then just want to play around? You're not a kid anymore."

"You don't need to yell," he said quietly.

I was raising my voice but couldn't help it. What he was saying didn't match what the others told me. "Look, I'm not yelling."

"You are. You are yelling." He was still very quiet. "I think you should go."

"Look…"

"Go!" He shouted. "Just go away."

It occurred to me that I didn't have to do as he said anymore. "I need help finding out who killed this guy. That's all I wanted."

"Yeah. And I could've used a Friend these last twenty-some years. Life's hard, I guess." He coughed, looked around, and walked toward the living room, where I could see the cloud from a still-lit cigarette was filling the room.

I could stay just as easily as go.

I left anyway.

34

"I was wondering when you'd get around to reporting to me," the Director said. In the initial meeting with the Council, I had been afraid he was the one I wouldn't be able to get away from, yet we'd barely crossed paths the whole time. "I thought you'd check in sooner. I am your supervisor, you know."

I hated the tone in his voice. He'd known infromation from the beginning that would have made things easier on me. We could have ended this before it got started. "I've been a busy person."

"Busy? And yet you have nothing to report to me?"

The lighting in his office was playing tricks on me—deepening the darkness under his eyes, exaggerating his size, making him more imposing. He grew larger in the shadows, inflated by my fear and his stature. I felt like I was back in his office getting yelled at and thrown around. In the moment, things Sarah said came crashing into my thoughts. *We see what we think we're going to see.* Or something like that.

"That seems strange," he said.

"Well, it's been an odd job to keep a handle on." At least I hadn't lost my power of understatement. "We've been going at it almost nonstop since I met with you and the Council." When was that? Yesterday? The day before? Time moved so quickly on the Otherworld, and seemed to inch along on the Hill. My jumping from one place to the other was fucking up my internal ticky-thing.

"But nothing to report to me?" He shook his head and leaned back in his oversized stone seat. "I was worried that you were going to fail me, and it looks like I might have been right," he said half-heartedly. There was no conviction in his words. There was none of the fire of that last meeting before Ira died. There was only this *boredom*—an almost relaxed tone of someone going through the motions. Maybe he figured all along that I'd fail, and he'd somehow be vindicated in his own mind. "I'll have to see if Elf division has an extra bed in their barracks."

"Please check on that, sir, in case I decide to give up the investigation. As it is, I'm still working and have some things to do. I didn't stop by to report to you. I was never told, or asked, to keep you up to date on the situation." If he could be bored, I could be insolent, I suppose. It felt really fucking good.

He raised an eyebrow, "Oh? Then why are you here? Did you miss me?" At least I seemed to pique his interest a little.

"I'm here to ask you questions, sir. I'm trying to get to everyone that might have some information on this."

The Director snorted. "And you think you need to ask *me* questions?"

"We obviously haven't closed our investigation. We don't know how Ira died, and everybody is still a suspect. Including you." I don't know whether I smiled or not. I know I tried not to, but it still felt like I was. "After all, you found him. They have a saying on the Otherworld, '*He who smelt it, dealt it*,' and you've been stinking for a while now." Did I just accuse my boss of smelling like shit? Yes, I did.

His eyebrow went down, and both of his eyes narrowed to slits. I could feel the intensity of his gaze burning into my mind. "I have no clue what you're babbling about, but please, ask whatever you'd like." His voice had dropped a couple of octaves.

"Thanks. I'll be brief." The shaking that had struck my arm on the way down the cliffside returned; it was slight and noticeable only to me. "Like I said, you found Ira, right? That's what you told us at the meeting the other day."

"Yes. That is what I said."

"He didn't show up for a job. You went looking for him. That's what you said."

He nodded.

"He had a job the night before that, too, right?"

Again he nodded affirmative. "He was a busy and productive member of our society. Unlike some of the others I could name." He looked at me like he'd slipped something clever into our conversation, something subversive.

"Look, sir. It's just you and me. There's none of this sly bullshit. We both know what you're saying. No need to dig at me every chance you get. Just tell me what happened with that last job that he actually showed up for. How did it go?"

He took a deep breath but he didn't answer.

"Well? What happened?" I asked.

"Look." He paused. "I don't want to speak ill of the guy. He's dead and gone. I'm trying to be respectful."

The Director, trying to show some feelings? Anyone else I would have believed, but I'd always known this one to say whatever the fuck he wanted to say. "I'm just looking for some answers here. If you don't have them, maybe there's someone who does. I figured you were the Imaginary to talk to. You know all the comings and goings, you know all the assignments. You know everyone's weaknesses and strengths. Seemed logical you'd have some information about the Imaginaries around you. Guess I was wrong." His smug smile didn't seem to be returning. "I suppose I can talk to some of the peons down at Personnel. Maybe they can look it up for me."

"He botched it, okay?"

"What?"

"He fucked it up. Are you deaf?" I couldn't read him now. It wasn't exactly smugness in his voice, but it didn't seem to be genuine sorrow or concern for his old friend Ira.

"He blew it? Blew it how? What went wrong?"

"I don't know. How would I know?" Indignant. That's what I heard. It angered him to feel forced to answer a question from someone as low as me. "You all think I'm omnipotent. You think I have some crystal ball to watch you as you do your jobs, but I don't. It's more like a child's Magic 8-Ball. The answers are brief. I get the end results, yes or no. Try again later."

"Was that a random or a special?"

"What?"

"Random or special?'

He appeared to process the question or the answer in his head for a moment, staring up at a spot on the ceiling. "Special," he said in an exasperated tone.

"Why?"

"Why? Same reason I had to send you on a few gimmies. He was screwing up assignments—he wasn't getting things done the way he used to. I thought he needed an easy one to get his confidence back. Maybe he needed a boost, so I sent him on what looked like a simple-as-shit assignment."

"So you picked this one yourself? You didn't tell someone in the office to pick an easy one for Ira and then trust they would do it?"

"No. I picked it with my own two hands. Shuffled through the cards one-by-one. Do you get what I do at all?" He shifted, turned himself away just a little. "I certainly don't get to play hopscotch or dominoes or whatever you do with those kids on the Otherworld." All the times I had to appear before him to explain things, I had no choice but to sit and listen to him. "Are we about done here?"

"Let's run through this real quick—" I guessed I was pushing my luck anyway; wrapping it up was probably a good idea. "He doesn't show up for a job, so Personnel notifies you," I said. He nodded as I hit each point, and soon his head bobs were exaggerated and wild. "Ira's a friend of yours, so you go check it out. You open his door. Find him laying there on the floor turning invisible. Right?"

Again, the Director nodded. "That's what I said before."

"What did you do next?"

"I went to talk to Morty, and Mother Nature, and…"

"Father Time. The Council. That *is* what you said. You went straight to the Council? You didn't send a messenger? You went in person?" I was running the Director through a gamut of emotions that I'd never seen played out on him. He was confused now. Maybe I was turning into a detective of some sort if I could make my boss actually feel emotions.

"Yes, I went in person."

"Immediately?"

"Immediately." He was emphatic.

"Do anything else?"

He finally stood up and walked around behind his chair. "Are we almost done here?"

I really hoped so. "Did you do anything else?"

"No. Why?"

"What happened to the job Ira didn't show up for?"

"What?"

"The job he didn't show up for. Did it not get done?"

"Yes, it got done. We can't leave a job undone."

"So, we only have a short window. Did you assign someone else to do it in Ira's place?"

"I…I don't remember. It was a crazy morning. I'm sure I sent a messenger to Personnel to do it."

"When? You said you didn't do anything else; when did you send the messenger?"

"I said it was crazy. I must've done it on my way to the Council. I don't know."

"You were helping Ira out by giving him easy ones. Was this a special or a random?"

"I told you, I don't remember anything about it."

"It was only a short time ago."

"I don't remember."

"Okay." I had a new favorite sport; annoying the Director. I didn't want to wear out my welcome entirely, though. "Don't worry about it. I'm sure they have some record of it at the Department, right? I'll just ask them to look it up."

I turned and walked toward the door, splashing in the water on his floor as I went. "Thanks for your help," I said. "Sir."

35

I left the Personnel Department and strode quickly back to my apartment, our makeshift headquarters. There, Brady and Zane sat at the kitchen table, staring at a small stack of cards. Neither moved when I came in. "Any problems?"

"Nope, everyone in Personnel was real cooperative," Zane said.

They'd followed my instructions perfectly and picked up the records for the two days' worth of assignments surrounding Ira's death while I was talking to the Director. I was excited that we had all acted as a team. It was the first time I could say that since we started. I wasn't sure exactly what I wanted to find on the cards, but I figured they might hold something that would get this investigation on track. I timed it for the boys to get the cards when I did just to make sure the Director didn't mess with them if he felt I was on to something he didn't like. It was the conversation with him that solidified that hunch.

"Did you guys look through them yet?" I asked.

"Yes. Twice," Brady spoke up. "Not a lot to sort through."

"Nothing there," Zane said.

Even though the codes about destination and completion were indecipherable to us, the timestamp and person's name were easily readable at the top. "You didn't find anything around the morning Ira died?" It seemed incredible that the morning's activity dropped to such a low level.

"There were some Imaginary Friends, a couple of ghosts, some other basic stuff like that, but not one Boogeyman went out. In fact, I don't have a record of one doing anything again until after Ira's funeral."

"Well…one," Brady said sheepishly.

"Well, he's not really one of us," Zane replied.

"What do you mean?" I asked them both.

"The Director went out once in that time period. Fairly early." Brady took the lead. "He was gone for quite a while, it looks like." He handed the ticket to me.

It was stamped with the Director's name at the top and a time of L0236 over R0420. He left around two thirty-six and returned at four twenty in the morning. Gone nearly two hours. "Did you see a ticket for Ira? A blank one?" I asked.

"Sure. We ignored it. We thought you were looking for everyone else's movements." Zane flipped through the tickets quickly with Brady leaning over his shoulder. After a couple of false stops, Zane pulled one out. "Here."

I took it. The heading had Ira's name, but no time stamps to indicate he did the job. I looked at the numbers and letters that made up the code on the rest of the ticket and, as usual, nothing made sense to me. But when I held it up next to the Director's ticket, something meshed in my mind: Except for the names, the two tickets were identical. I turned toward the light, held the two up, and layered them on top of each other; I could see through the cards, and every character on the cards lined up. "Hand me another card."

"Which one?" Brady asked.

"Doesn't matter. Any one."

They drew from the middle of the pile, and I put it next to Ira's card. Even though the code was still a mystery, I could tell they were different. The letters were in different places. The numbers were different. "Give me another." They did, and again, none of the codes on any of the cards lined up the same way again. I explained to my bewildered comrades what I'd discovered and showed them the cards. They took turns comparing them all and even pulled more from the pile to try to match up. None of the tickets even came close.

"So what do you think this means?" Zane tossed the cards back into the pile with a flick of his wrist.

The pieces were there, but I wasn't sure how they all fit. I cautiously told them what I felt were the most obvious points. "It looks like Ira died, the Director found him, and then the Director went and did the job Ira was supposed to do before he told anyone Ira was dead."

"Why?" Brady asked.

"I don't know, but he felt he needed to lie to me about it." I was optimistic that we might be on the brink of a breakthrough for the first time. "Let's get out there and see if we can ask the right people the right questions."

36

Ray trembled as he spoke. "You're here for me now?" He tried to focus on me, but his left eye twitched two, three, four times in rapid succession.

"I'm here to talk to you, and you don't have to yell," I said as calmly as I could.

"*No*! No! I'll talk as loud as I want to. I have friends nearby." He pointed to a random wall. "I have friends everywhere. And if they don't hear the sound of my voice every so often, they'll come tearing in here and deal with you! They'll make you suffer."

I knew he was lying, because he had no friends. As far as I could tell, his only real acquaintances were Ira and Thad. One of them was confirmed dead, and Thad was still missing or hiding. I had almost no fear of being interrupted and "dealt with" by a marauding gang of his friends. Besides, anyone managing to bust through the door would have to get through Zane and Brady first. The two of them would at least delay any assailants coming my way and make a big ruckus in the process. Friends of Ray's were the last thing on my mind.

I felt bad for ever doubting my friends. Zane had bounded into my apartment with word that the very Boogeyman we were seeking had shown up at the Wet Dream while he and Brady were questioning some of the regulars about recent events. They both said Ray kept his face hidden under a hood and sat in the dark booth in the back corner. After a quick drink, he said goodbye to his waitress and slipped out the back. Zane said no one else in the bar batted an eye, like he had been in every day since Ira's death, though the three of us couldn't locate him no matter what we'd tried. When he left, they followed him, and once they were sure they had his hiding place pinpointed, Zane came and got me while Brady kept watch. It was good to see the two of them finally succeed at something, although I was pretty skeptical when Zane showed me the place where Ray had been hiding: Ira's old apartment. I'd assumed it had been empty since his death, but I suppose checking it would have been wise. I would have gotten around to returning to the scene of the crime, given enough time; I mean, that's just what detectives do.

"Look, Ray, I'm just here to ask you a question or two about Ira."

"Right, *questions*." He leaned toward the wall as he said it. "I'm sure you just have *questions* for me." He was wide-eyed and certainly afraid of us. "You definitely aren't here to make me disappear like Ira or anything."

"Seriously, we just want to talk. You were one of the last ones to see him alive; you may have some information for us."

"Whatever."

"What other possible reason could I have for cornering you like this?"

He opened his mouth but was stifled by a sudden fit of twitching. He pressed his hand against his face in an effort to force it to stop. "Are you kidding me?" he finally said. "What reason did you have the last time you attacked me? Was that just work? Did you just have some questions then?" He pressed his hand into his face harder.

He was digging way back to the time I scared him on the camping trip with the kids. I wanted to apologize again but held back. It was a joke, after all, and a long time ago. "Look, I was having a little fun, and it just didn't turn out that way for you. Things are different now; I have a job to do. If we move past that, maybe we can get on with this and both go back to what we were doing."

We stood there staring at each other for a second or two more. He slowly pulled his hand away from his face and looked at it like he expected to see something there. He twitched again, but only slightly, not as bad as before. I wondered if this was some remnant of my attack on him, or if it was something brought on by what had happened to Ira—or what might have become of Thad. I felt an uncomfortable tension creeping up my back.

"I don't believe you," Ray yelled as he took a step closer to the nearest wall.

"At least tell me why you choose to hide out here. I mean, Ira's place? Isn't that kind of morbid?"

"What are you, kidding me? No one wants to come here. The place where the guy kicked off with no warning? I know the Imaginaries on the Hill. None of them want to come here. '*Why, what if something in his apartment killed him? Maybe it could kill us too*!' they're thinking. That's why no one wanted to associate with me or Thad after Ira died. '*They probably didn't have anything to do with his death, but just in case*...' But I didn't have anything to do with anything. None of this is my fault."

"Ray. Ray. Stop." His twitching and yelling were giving me a headache. It was like his whole body was one big spasm, and I had a hard time looking at him without feeling uncomfortable. "You don't need to keep yelling like that. The only people around are Brady and Zane, and they don't care what you're saying. Let's just calm down and have a nice casual conversation."

I reached out to pat him on the shoulder to reassure him my intentions were good, but he knocked my arm away before my hand got to him. "Don't touch me," he yelled over his shoulder. "Talk all you want, but just don't touch me."

My head throbbed from the noise and the strain of talking to my neurotic witness. I quickly grabbed him by his shirt and pushed him against the wall. "Stop yelling," I said. "You're giving me a headache." I didn't push him that hard, but it still made a thud that echoed in the room.

"Look, I'll tell you what you want. Just leave me alone." He turned away from me again, talking to his invisible army in the walls. "Someone help! Help me!"

I put one hand on the back of his head and slammed him against the wall to emphasize each word I spoke. "Stop...yelling...stop...yelling!" It was a process I repeated a few times while Ray struggled uselessly against me. It became a steady rhythm in my head. A tempo that fit with some great rally song that I had heard through an Otherworld radio long ago. There was a high school football game being broadcast and the score was close—within a point, I think. Suddenly, through the tiny speaker you could hear the fans stomping their feet on the metal stands and clapping their hands in unison. Stomping then clapping, stomping then clapping together. They were singing something at the same time, but it was lost behind the clapping and the stomping and the announcer's commentary.

"Abe! Abe!" There were voices beside me and hands on my arms. "Take it easy. Let him go!" It was Zane talking to me, trying to sound calm. My hands were still on Ray, and I was still pushing him into the wall until they startled me. "Just let him go, and we'll watch him while you get yourself under control."

I had no idea how long I had been hitting him against the wall, or what Ray had yelled in order to get them to come in, but they all looked terribly frightened. I took a firm hold on his shirt and flung him into a corner of the room. He fell to the floor and brought his arm up to shield his face. I noticed a rounded indentation in the wall where his head had impacted. I took a breath and tried to look composed so everyone would just calm down and let me do my job: asking questions.

I didn't remember being able to tower so far over Ray; we'd been roughly the same size as far as I could remember. And throwing him seemed like such an easy thing.

"You know about Ira. Tell me." Long sentences weren't forming just yet.

He didn't hesitate to speak, and his words came in a low tone. "You know what it's like on the Otherworld? It isn't easy over there anymore. We all were struggling. You had problems, right? We all had them."

He was right. The strikes I had against me and the talks I had to have with the Director about my failures all stemmed from troublesome jobs I had been on. "All right, I had a few problems."

"The kids aren't buying the same old song and dance anymore. They're more sophisticated, or desensitized, or tougher," he said as he lowered his arms.

"Desensitized?" Brady had placed himself between Ray and me so he could see us both.

"Yeah, it's a word that they use over there these days," Zane said to him. "I caught it on a news broadcast one night. It means, like, if I pull your hair once, it'll hurt and you'll be mad. But if I pull your hair repeatedly, it'll hurt less and less and after a while, you won't even notice I'm doing it."

"Oh." I could see the wheels turning in Brady's head, processing the information. "I don't get to see as much TV as you guys. I'm usually in the woods."

"Whatever. What does that have to do with Ira?" I asked.

"It has to do with all of us, not just Ira. You need to see some of the things we're competing with on the Otherworld. You think the stuff we use is clever, or scary? They've got bigger things to fear these days. A window shade flying up in the middle of the night? Some rattling chains in the attic? Shit. That's nothing. They're too busy guessing who they're talking to on the Internet at night."

"The inter-what?" Brady asked.

"I'll explain later," Zane said.

"These kids aren't scared of crunching leaves and creaking doors—they want someone to hold their hand while they walk through the metal detector at school."

"Yeah, great. Boo-hoo. The Otherworld's a scary place. What does that have to do with Ira or anything else?" My headache was subsiding, but I was still having a hard time concentrating and making sense of what was going on. It was like there was a little man marching around in my head in thick boots, stomping on lightbulbs and kicking the sides of my mind periodically.

"They laughed at him."

Zane, Brady and I all leaned in at that. "What?" I asked.

"That night at the bar, he told Thad and I about his last special on the Otherworld. He didn't want to talk about it, you know? He was all shaken up, said that the Director was on him to post some better results. So he's trying like crazy to impress the boss. Right? His mark that night is a girl, like eleven, twelve years old or something like that, and he thinks he's got it made—"

I knew that sensation. This whole thing was that sensation for me.

"So he gets there, and the girl is pacing back and forth in her backyard around midnight talking on her cell phone to her friends and giggling. It's a cloudy night—no stars, no moon—and she's illuminated by just a porch light. Ira's standing behind a row of bushes getting his game face on and waiting for the right time, just out of the reach of the light." He squinted as he told us the story, as if he were reading it from some far-off cue cards. It was the first time he'd managed to concentrate on anything other than yelling since I walked through the door. His shaking had subsided, though I could still see his tremors.

I wondered if the concentration was a show for us, designed to make us believe the things he said so we'd leave him alone. It seemed to me that he was concerned with telling the story right, that it had struck him in such a way that he knew it was important. My outburst and physicality with him seemed to stir something in him as well. He was genuinely afraid of me, but I couldn't really figure out why. Was it because I had managed to scare him and he couldn't shake that?

"He told us he waited there for ten or fifteen minutes for an opportunity. All he needed was just that right moment where she was most vulnerable." Zane and I nodded our heads. We knew the feeling. Ira was a master of it. "But Ira was confused; his timing was off or something. I mean, he expected to slip under the bed—a little noise, a little tug of the sheets, some yelling and he's out of there—but that wasn't it at all. There was this little girl outside in the middle of the night talking up a storm. He just wasn't prepared for it." Ray was shaking his head. "He said as he sat there listening to the inane half of the phone call, he forgot it all. Everything he was supposed to do and say abandoned him. It was like a blank page. It was all new to him."

"We've all had those moments," I said. "We doubt what we're doing, question our choices." I knew all about how a brain can go mushy.

"No it was more than that. You should have seen him when he told us this story." Ray shook his head, sure I didn't understand him. "He was shaking a little and he went all pale, paler than usual," Ray said. "He told us he didn't know what to do to get this girl scared. He panicked. All he could think to do is lean over, grab a branch and start shaking it."

Zane, Brady and I all cringed in unison, but Brady spoke up. "Uncoordinated branch shaking? That's so crude. Even I know you got to time something like that just right. That's some pretty basic stuff right there."

"I told you, he just blanked out. What was worse, he said he kept it up for a few seconds. No build-up to make the girl wonder what she heard or nothing." We were all shaking our heads by that time. "Just shook it for all it was worth."

"And the girl?" I asked.

"The girl heard it and turned toward it. Told her friend she thought she heard some little animal in the bushes. She said earlier in the evening that she had seen a rabbit nearby and figured that was all it was."

"Bet Ira hated that," Zane said.

"It wasn't that he hated it. It just flustered him more. He tried harder to scare her, even though his instincts hadn't come back to him. He started to move toward her, exposing himself to the light." Ray crouched himself down some to show us how Ira was positioned. "The girl giggled a little and told her friend on the phone, '*It is a bunny, there it is.*' Then she said the words that made Ira slink back into the darkness; '*Maybe I'll catch him and keep him for a pet.*' And then she laughed at him as he pulled back into the darkness."

It was terrible. It was possibly the worst reaction any of us could get. I'd botched jobs, but never to the point that I got the complete opposite reaction than the one I was going for. As far as I know, no one ever thought I was funny as an Imaginary. I could see how that would crush a Boogeyman's spirit, especially one like Ira.

"He heard '*Come back, little bunny*' as he faded into the black."

Zane shook his head and spoke up. "Ugh. That's devastating. I don't know how I would recover from that. Laughed at by a little girl."

"That's just it, though; I think one day you *will* have to react to something like that. I think we all will. Hopefully we can deal with it better than Ira did," Ray said.

"What do you mean?" I asked.

"Our audience is shrinking. Think about it, Abe. You haven't gone out to do any real work since this whole thing started. Zane's been helping you, so he hasn't done any Boogeyman stuff in that same span of time, either." He was coming out of his quiet contemplative state and getting more animated again. He pointed at himself. "I haven't had a job since Ira died, and I'm pretty sure

Thad hasn't either. Let's not forget Ira himself. He hasn't been getting a whole lot of work himself, now has he?"

The streets had been full of stragglers as I'd walked through town, and it certainly occurred to me that there were an awful lot of Imaginaries with excess idle time lately.

"When is the last time any of us had more than a day off without at least one job? Before this it was unheard of. And now?" He did a quick head count for everyone's benefit. "Let's see. One. Two. Three. Four? Wait. Five. Five, including Ira. Five of us that haven't had a real job in all this time? And we're not alone. There are plenty of others doing nothing out there."

"So? We're in some kind of slump, an Imaginary depression of some sort. We'll bounce back." Zane folded his arms and lifted his chin just a little. "I could use some time off anyway."

Ray's eyes got wider and his voice raised a bit. "Are you not following me here? The less we work, the more we're off of the minds of the Otherworlders. The more we're off of their minds, the less they believe in us, and the less they believe in us, the more we start to see a repeat of what happened to Ira."

"The Otherworlders killed Ira? Is that what you're telling us?" Zane asked. "No one on the Hill did it?"

"They've been killing us off slowly and discreetly for years. No one noticed, no one said anything."

Brady twisted his arm hair absently with shaky fingers, then crossed his arms to make himself stop. "You're just speculating, getting paranoid. Isn't all of this just a theory that we have no way of testing?" Brady asked. "I mean really, aren't you just telling me a twist on the bedtime stories that the Otherworlders tell about us? *You better watch out or the Boogeyman'll get you.*"

It *was* a theory. On our world, it was hard to prove things, no matter how much we wanted to, you know? Like killing each other. We saw how that worked out.

"Yeah. You're right. There's no lab where we can try it out." Ray hung his head so we couldn't see his face anymore. "But I did sit there and watch Thad disappear the same way Ira did."

We took notice of that. It was as close to something solid and verifiable as we had come in the whole conversation. We hadn't seen Thad in some length of time. It could be true.

"*Just faded away.*"

37

I'd waited in The Council's chambers for hours to talk to them about what I'd found and what I'd been told. The discussion with Ray would be something they'd need to know. I wondered if they'd care about my outburst and violence with him, so I decided I would glaze over it, just in case. It was chilly in the chambers, even though the sun was still as bright as it had been the last time over the castle. After a while, I heard them mumbling in the outer hall for a few minutes before they finally filed in.

It seemed that they had elected Mother Nature as the spokesman of the group. Whatever news was coming my way would sound better coming from her. I don't know if they thought I could be persuaded by a woman, or if she was just naturally the head of that particular committee. It was obvious from her stern demeanor that she wasn't here to listen to me talk about the investigation; she was here with her own agenda. "I think you've discovered something about yourself, and you're discovering what you were."

"It isn't something you're becoming. It's something you're going *back* to being," Father Time said.

"What? I don't understand. Becoming?" I had nothing to go back to; what did they think I was becoming, some little kid's friend again? "I don't understand. I was an Imaginary Friend, then you recruited me to do this detective thing. What do you think I'm reverting *back* to?"

"You didn't start as an Imaginary Friend. You—"

"What?" I'd heard them wrong. Or they were joking. I was sure of that. I just didn't know why.

Death held his hands up in a placating gesture. "This is going to be a little difficult to understand at first, but I'm sure it will make sense when you let us explain."

"Yes. Let us tell you this. It'll be easier to grasp if you take a moment to listen." Father Time smiled as he spoke, but it was an uneasy smile.

"What do you mean I wasn't an Imaginary Friend? I remember it all...for crying out loud, I just talked to the adult version of the kid I used to belong to. How exactly do you explain that?"

"It's *hard* to explain," Mother Nature said.

"Try."

Death leaned back on two legs of his chair and began to bounce a deep blue racquetball like he had when I had first entered the room. He threw it at the floor, it bounced into the nearby wall, and then it would sail in a high lazy arc back to his hand.

Throw...floor...wall...arc...catch.

Throw...bounce...bounce...arc...catch.

"You did spend time with that kid, but you weren't his Friend. You were never his Friend," Mother Nature said. She looked toward Death out of the corner of her eye.

"Yeah, look, take it easy. None of this is your fault. You were an experiment. Sometimes it takes a while to work out all of the kinks," Death dropped in casually.

Throw...bounce...bounce...arc...catch.

"Not my fault? What's not my fault? What have I done that's not my fault?"

It was Mother Nature's turn to take over again, and she stood with her hands clasped in front of her. Apparently this was going to be a delicate conversation. "The whole thing is really just the Otherworld's fault. They brought us all here to serve at their whim and then they discarded us when they didn't need us anymore. Unfortunately for us, they didn't limit our lifespan in any way. None of us knew how long we'd be here. There are a few that seem like they're going to live forever."

"Yeah, there's been nothing we could do about it, either. We've always been at their mercy. It's been a real one-way street." Father Time pounded the table, his anger a contrast to his normally quiet demeanor, a contrast to the man who traveled down the side of the Hill with me. "We were frustrated for the longest time by it."

"Frustrated, but we came to accept it. Until recently," Death said as he loosed the ball with more force. Throwbouncebouncearc...catch. "Recently, you changed some things for us."

"Mort. One thing at a time please," Mother Nature said.

"Yeah, Mort." I said. He stopped bouncing the ball but he didn't look at me. He huffed through his nose and folded his arms.

"The things we were doing as a matter of course just weren't working anymore. No one believed the sun was a God riding a chariot across the sky anymore. No one thought I controlled the weather, or Father Time controlled the length of a day. Death was just a symbol, a way to emphasize a point." Mother Nature's soothing voice made almost any news bearable. "There were fewer and fewer believers and less and less need for us. What's worse, there weren't any newcomers joining our ranks. No one was coming up with fresh Imaginaries to believe in. Sure there were new Imaginary Friends, but there wasn't anything else, really. No new Gods, no new Easter Bunnies, or any such things."

I thought about when I was waiting for Thad and Ray to go to the Personnel Department and no one came by for assignments. "How did this happen so fast? We were doing so well."

Death stood up and walked away from the table. He produced two more racquetballs and started juggling them. "It's simple, really, chum. We grew stagnant. We forgot the first rule of show business: always keep them wanting more. We hit them with our big guns right off and had nothing to follow up with. They've seen it all. No one asked to see the act anymore. Take the Boogeymen, for example." He pulled a fourth ball out of his robe and began juggling all of them. I noticed he had his sleeves hemmed up so they didn't hamper what he was doing. "You guys were going great guns with the whole grabbing ankles and flipping blinds thing. Scared 'em good for a while. But it got old. Who's afraid of that now, though? Scratching on the windows? Please. It's like a magician doing the rabbit out of a hat trick every time. They love it the first half-dozen times or so, but eventually they want to see something sawed in half." I hadn't been paying attention very closely to his words, but I was hypnotized by the juggling. It wasn't until he stopped that I realized he was holding four bright yellow tennis balls rather than the racquetballs he started with. "Eventually, you gotta wow them again. And that was the problem. We had nothing that would make them sit up and take notice. Nothing up our sleeves, so to speak."

It was after I noticed the balls had changed that I realized he'd said "you guys." "*You guys were going great guns with the whole grabbing ankles and flipping blinds thing.*"

"All right, so it was pretty tame stuff, but there was near-constant audience turnover. Kids grew up, and new kids came along who hadn't seen it all before. We relied on a fresh audience every so many years to keep the mystery alive. Plus, the ones who had seen it tended to prime the ones who hadn't. Big brothers and sisters loved to scare the crap out of their siblings with scary stories," Death said.

Father Time seemed emboldened by the group effort of explaining things and spoke up again, "Yes, yes, yes. That was the way we did business. The problem is, the Otherworld changed, prepared them more quickly. They let them grow up faster than in the old days. The kids who hadn't seen everything yet could easily see it at any minute and they knew it. In the old days, things lingered longer. They lurked just out of sight."

"So we had to come up with something different. Something they hadn't seen before. Something that could linger. Stick with them and worm its way into their safe places," Mother Nature said. "Namely, you."

Death laughed, "You were way ahead of your time in that department, Abe. Let me tell you, you lingered."

"You were created like a Boogeyman with a little more kick. An Uber-Boogeyman, if you will. You were made to spread more mayhem than the ones who came before you. We wanted you to make more noise and do what the others hadn't. We wanted you to take your time with your subjects and really work them, rather than go for the quick in-and-out." Mother Nature seemed to be enjoying her role as spokesman.

"We had hoped you could do more damage that way. Get one kid good, and he would suddenly become your greatest asset. Your target would become your ally and spread the word," Father Time said.

"I don't understand what you're talking about. I know who I am. I know what I do." I looked around at them and decided I didn't want to know what they were talking about. They'd led me down some path into a dark woods, and now they wanted to start cutting down the trees. "I'm leaving."

"You were really good at it."

"I know who I am. None of you are going to change that."

I exited the room and wandered the halls to the courtyard. None of the guards were about. No one hanging around. It was quiet everywhere. I crossed the bridge and stopped to watch an empty rowboat twist in the water. I had had Imaginary Friends. A number of them. That's where I started, that's what I did. I wasn't a monster.

I drifted through the town, unintentionally ending up on my favorite stool at the Wet Dream. The crowds were thicker, the mood a little more dour. I threw the umbrella out of my drink and took a gulp.

Next to me, Zane's friend Delia sidled up to me and waved for the bartender to bring her a drink. She nodded at me as she waited. "You've been scarce the last few days."

"I have."

She got her drink and took a sip, then turned and looked at me. I was afraid she expected me to carry the conversation from there.

"What's new?" She asked.

I thought about that one. "I think everything is new. Or not. I think it might all be old, but just new to me."

"You lost me."

"I think I'm an Imaginary Friend, but I may not be," I said. "I may be some kind of monster, and I may be really good at being a monster, but I don't remember being a monster." I took a quick swig of my drink. "I'm also a detective. Maybe a good one. Maybe not. I chased a girl through a cornfield."

She paused. "Wow. Usually when someone asks what's new, they're looking for a response like 'not much' or something like that."

I looked at her, thinking about when I met her right here in the bar. "How's the Tooth Fairy business?"

It was Delia's turn to take a drink. "Still an Associate Tooth Fairy. Working my way up."

"Ever meet her?" I said. "The Tooth Fairy herself?" I didn't wait for a response. "I have. I think."

"She's pretty special, I hear. If you've met her, then you must be special, too." Delia looked impressed by the idea that I had met her boss. "I don't honestly know anyone who remembers even seeing her."

Did you hear she's crazy? I almost asked. Before I could go on, Zane burst into the bar.

"I've been looking all over for you. You have to come quickly. It's Brady," Zane said.

We ran down the streets toward my apartment, ducking through crowds that stood like zombies in the streets. They barely noted our passage, barely moved to avoid our advance. Zane told me what he could, but he was alarmed and stammered over his words. We headed to my apartment, where they'd gone to wait for me and plot our next move. Delia trailed us from the bar, and Kite appeared in the hallway. She danced in the air outside my door, alarmed and frightened.

I pushed inside and found what I'd feared most: Brady was on the floor and fading. He was still moving and mumbling, but I could see the floor through his body. He hadn't become completely opaque, but it was happening. "What in the Hill happened?" I knelt down and managed to grab his huge hand in mine. "How?"

The hairy beast coughed. "The Otherworld is becoming a cold place for things like us."

"I don't believe that. Hold on, you'll be fine." My hand passed through his like it was smoke. I couldn't get a grip on him.

"You have to start believing that." Brady's voice was a whisper. "They don't care about us anymore." He faded more until he was barely an outline. He stopped moving, but his big yellow eyes remained fixed on me.

38

They were preparing a memorial for Brady before he disappeared completely. So many Imaginaries got involved, it was crazy. But they had little else to do, so they went in with both feet. They decorated, threw streamers and whatnot. It was gaudy, but it kept people from thinking about the whole thing too much.

I stayed away from the crowds and went to Mother Nature as quickly as I could.

I had to wait for the secretary to let me in, and I nodded to the beast under her desk before entering.

When I came in, Mother Nature was sitting at her desk, looking at a paper and practicing the things she'd say at the service.

I sat down and stared at her. Waiting. Watching her lips move as she rehearsed.

Finally, she couldn't ignore me and dropped the paper with a flourish. She looked at me just as intensely as I was staring at her. "You don't look like you used to. When you were an Imaginary Friend, you were softer. Your face was less angular and jagged."

My hands went to my face, looking for points and barbs. I hadn't changed. Not as far as I could tell.

"Yes, we sent you in like Truman's Imaginary Friend, but you were more of an Imaginary Enemy. No, an Invisible Enemy, because you came to him as a friend, then turned on him without him seeing it. You did nice things together for a while. So, some of those memories are real. You gained his trust, got familiar. But you slowly worked in the other stuff," Mother Nature said. "You were good; we were surprised when he got away from you as early as he did. Still, he managed to spread some good stuff to his friends thanks to you. That made things easier on all of us. Let me tell you, you were devious. Messing him up in school? Brilliant."

"This is crazy. An Invisible Enemy? I didn't do that on purpose. I only had his skills at math. I couldn't do it any better than he could."

"He didn't know that, poor boy. He looked up to you. You could have told him you didn't know squat and saved him some embarrassment." She had her hands held in front of her with the fingertips touching.

"Look, we on the Council want you to understand everything. We want you to be comfortable with who...*what* you are and what you used to be. You remember things the way you remember them because you had a breakdown of sorts after the job with Truman."

"You went monkey-crackers is more like it," Death called from the doorway. I didn't know how long he'd been standing there.

"Mort, please. You're not helping here." Mother Nature looked like she was going to slap his wrist but restrained herself and turned back to me. "Abe, something happened that wasn't your fault, and you couldn't handle it."

"So that's why the Tooth Fairy knew me. You guys stuffed me in a cave?" I *was* nuts. I had been sure it was just the Tooth Fairy messing with me.

Death shook his head sadly. "Remember what he did to Ray? Poor man. He has never been quite right since then. Developed a twitch. It was kind of unnerving to see a Boogeyman of that caliber unravel."

"Ugh. And what use has he been after that, really? Couldn't sneak up on people...not with that twitch..." Mother Nature repeatedly winked her left eye as she spoke.

Death leaned in, talking low and secretive-like. "I heard he tried to scare some brat once, and his eye twitched so much that the kid asked him if he was all right."

"People? You want to reel it in a notch? Okay. So I startled Ray a little. It was all in fun, and besides, it was an accident. The Director said so." If I was going to be slandered and attacked, I wasn't going to give them an easy target. I was just having fun with the man. I apologized. I certainly didn't willingly scar him for life.

"Ah, yes...yes...yes. The Director. I guess the two of you have a little different definition of fun than the rest of us." Mother Nature stood up and walked around her wooden desk. She brought the smell of lilacs with her. Thick, like spring had come again. "Yes. There are some things you should know about your friend the Director."

If any of what they were saying was true, obviously something had changed. I was perfectly fine. "First of all, he's not my friend. And second, if I was so out of control, what happened? How did I get to what I am today?" I *was* pretty sure I was perfectly fine.

The two of them spoke as one: "*Therapy.*"

39

Death, Mother Nature, and I gathered after the service, under the cover of darkness, out of sight. We went to get Father Time. He had fallen asleep during the service, and some of the Personnel goons had carried him home. He snored like a bulldog with asthma, and it took us a few tries to get him to wake. After he brushed his teeth and dressed—did I mention he sleeps in the nude? He does—he happily came with us to explore. Apparently the catnap had given him a second wind.

We talked very little on the walk over to the drop area, but what they said swirled around me like the mists we were about to descend into.

It was one comment by Death that stuck with me. I'm not sure if he knew its importance when he said it. He looked at the scaffold, which was set up much in the way it had been when Father Time had taken me for the ride. "You know, the first time we took you down here, you were so out of control that we had to lash you to the bottom to keep you still. You were kicking and punching the goons as they tried to get you on the thing. Then you were pushing and shoving and shaking it so bad we thought we'd all go over the side. We put you somewhere where you couldn't do us any discomfort. Lashed you face down and spread eagle underneath. You still managed to make it a rough trip for us, though."

Kite, Delia and Zane were waiting to help lower us down the Hill. They were joined by Thor, of all people, who only sniffed the air by way of greeting. He seemed upset that he'd been excluded from whatever it was he thought we were doing, but he lowered us anyway.

Like the other times, it was a silent trip, but it seemed like it went by quicker. No one spoke the whole way down, though I was tempted to ask questions over and over again until the answers became the ones I wanted. Maybe it would've been better if I just followed Zane and Brady's lead and only asked everyone I saw just one question, the same one, until someone told me what I wanted to hear. Then, the next day I could ask them another.

The cave was dark ahead of us. I was used to things starting in darkness, but this time was different. It wasn't just the physical absence of light, it was the absence of everything. Light, memory, recognition.

Understanding.

"The idea was just to evaluate how you did as the first subject and proceed accordingly. We wanted to make decisions about future Boogeymen based almost exclusively on how you did with Truman." Mother Nature lit a torch she had carried off the lift. She did it in one fluid motion involving no matches or accelerants, but there it was, with barely a snap of a finger—a one-foot flame on a stick.

"You just didn't want to stop. You had to go back out…*had* to. 'Work to do' you kept mumbling," she said, but she never looked back. She kept leading us deeper down the straight, narrow tunnel. It was almost like she were talking to herself and we were along for the ride. I was behind her, warm in the glow of her light. Father Time was behind me, with Death bringing up the rear.

"Yeah." Death spoke up for the first time since we started down the side. "That's about the time you began turning against us. We went to the Director and told him something had to be done."

I tried to turn around to talk to them, but the path was so treacherous that it became hard to proceed if I wasn't looking down at the ground. "The Director? But he's been on me since I became an Imaginary Friend, calling me a screw-up and everything."

I could hear the heavy foot falls and occasional slips and missteps of the two behind me. Father Time spoke up. "The Director? The Director hated to take you out of the game. He saw you as the coming thing. He was positive that we were all going to have to become more like you in order to survive. Aggressive. Loud. He thought we'd turned you into a wuss after we took you out of the cave."

"Just for the record, everything you remember from the time you became an average, everyday Imaginary Friend on is real. Therapy just erased your memories of what happened before it," Mother Nature said.

I believed her comment was supposed to be comforting and warm, but it wasn't. If they were all lying to me, they were doing a great job of coming up with a detailed backstory.

"It's just ahead." Mother Nature stepped carefully as she spoke, but moved ahead quickly.

The passage gradually widened. The floors and walls were smoother as we drew near. Before we reached the room, the hall became wide enough for us all to walk side by side. Mother Nature and I were in the middle, with Death on my left and Time on the other side of him. One of them patted me on the back a few times.

Father Time took another torch off the wall and lit it from Mother Nature's before continuing ahead. The rest of us stopped in what I could tell was a larger room before I got all the way into it. Our footsteps had a larger sound here. Beautiful acoustics.

Time walked through the middle of the room, lighting candles on tables and stands throughout. I listened to his shuffled steps, amplified in the room. I listened to the high hiss of the candles coming to life under his torch's touch. I could feel how easy it would be to lay on the ground and absorb everything that came my way. Maybe that was why they chose this place for me. Or maybe this was where I learned to appreciate sounds and music. I wanted to close my eyes and enjoy the environment, but the things I glimpsed in the flickering firelight kept me glancing around.

The walls were covered with pieces of paper. Squares of parchment were stuck haphazardly, covering every speck of space from floor to ceiling. In the center of the room there were piles of notebooks surrounding a simple wooden chair and table. I took Mother Nature's torch from her and hurried to the wall on my left. The torch provided plenty of light to show me the things drawn on the pages. There were lightning bolts and cloudy skies on one, bats and spiders on another. At first, every one of them was different and directionless. Some of them had random scribbles and lines on them but they advanced a little as I moved down the wall. There were shapes—circles and squares, triangles and x's. "Where did all of these come from?" I whispered to them, though I couldn't take my eyes off the pictures to look back. I was so enthralled that they could have left the room, and I wouldn't have noticed. I didn't even expect any sort of answer; I was just talking to be polite.

"You made them during your therapy." Death looked uncomfortable without something in his hands, like a smoker without a cigarette. "We thought maybe music would soothe you, or give you a calming diversion, so we borrowed some instruments from a God or two. We brought them in from time to time, but you didn't really take to them like you took to drawing. You always had to have a notepad."

After a few more steps I nearly fell. I had lost my footing on something on the floor. I bent down and realized there were pencils of varying length laying amid the notebooks and loose leaves of paper on the ground. I continued on, more careful where I stepped. I attempted to look at every picture but tried not to dwell on any of them.

The artistry continued to progress, getting better and more elaborate. There were stick-figure men and women holding hands. The women were represented with a s-shaped bob around their heads for long hair and the men had hats that looked like an upside-down u on a line. Some of the stick figures had houses and children and dogs and cars in their picture with them. Some had nothing but a great round sun with jagged lines around it in the corner of their world.

About midway around the room, I came to the wide arch of a doorway. "That leads to your bedroom. Not much in it, I'm afraid. A bed, that's about it." Time said. "Oh! And a closet. For your…traveling. Though we never let you use it during your therapy."

I recognized the images, though not that I'd drawn them. It was like I was walking through a museum and seeing my favorite paintings after a lifetime of only seeing them in catalogs.

"After you finished with Truman, there was a backlash from the other Imaginaries. They saw you as a monster. '*An abomination to the Hill*', I think Apollo called you. They wanted nothing to do with something as radical as you. They wanted to keep the status quo. Things had waned for everyone, but they naively thought it would turn around," Mother Nature said with a sigh.

"So in order to keep everyone else happy, you stuffed me down a hole." It was a statement, not a question. They'd done what they thought was right, at my expense.

"Yes, to keep everyone happy, but there was more to it than that. In you we had created a monster much bigger than the one we had intended to make," Death said.

"He's right. You were out of control. You were attacking everyone around you in one way or another. You never rested. Here…there…it didn't matter to you. You were just waiting for someone to drop their guard and wander into your line of sight so you could go to town on them. Mentally, physically—we never knew what was coming. It was like you were still trying your Boogeyman stuff here on the Hill," Father Time said.

"Remember what he did to Ray?" Death said.

Mother Nature shushed him, and I let it go. The memory that I had of playfully scaring him during that camping trip was far more sinister than I believed it to be. It was obviously me lashing out, just as they said.

Past the doorway, the pictures became more realistic—easier to interpret. There was one of a large hairy man with pigtails and a glass in his hand which I saw as an early attempt at a hairy biped. "Wait. I just met Brady. If you're right, why would I draw him?"

"You've known him since you got here. He'd been assigned to keep you on track from day one," Mother Nature said.

Brady was responsible for my career path on the Hill? That Imaginary could barely walk without tipping over.

Death could see my pained expression. "Kind of helps to explain how things went so poorly, doesn't it?"

Mother Nature punched him squarely on the arm. "Mort, that's enough."

Intermittently in my artwork there were obvious attempts at the Tooth Fairy. I'd drawn her with great care to always show her smiling. I guess it was part of the image, because when I thought of her, I thought of teeth. Whenever I came across a picture of her, I noticed two or three pictures of teeth and smiles stuck up around it. When I thought of the Tooth Fairy, I thought of smiles.

There was a scene of a row of buildings that was easily recognizable as the main street of the Hill, complete with the Wet Dream shimmering in the cold and lonely dusk. Toward the end, there was a series of drawings of ships at sea. There were rowboats filled with faceless oarsmen fighting a strong tide, schooners navigating a placid ocean, and pirate ships full sail against the wind.

There was one last row of pictures as I came back around to where the Council stood watching me. They were highly detailed pictures of Sarah. They were perfect. If it weren't the Hill, I might've thought they were photographs. In some she smiled, in others she was serious. There were hair-up pictures and hair-down pictures. Running, waving, knee-hugging, rock-climbing and even one of her sleeping were all pasted up in a neat line. I smiled to see her and wanted to tear them down to take with me and share with her. There was a lot I needed to talk to her about. I hadn't seen her in days, hadn't had the time. She'd be worried about me, I was sure.

"That's one that puzzled us. Other than Mother Nature, no other women came down to see you. So we couldn't figure out who that was.

We wracked our brains trying to put it together. As you got better and made progress, you started drawing her. The better you got, the more you drew of her. You were so close to being able to get on with being a regular old Boogeyman, but we wanted to know her connection to you. But you wouldn't tell us." Time was shaking his head at me as if he were still baffled by the puzzle.

Death stepped forward and thumbed through some of the notebooks on the table. "Of course, at first we thought they were drawings of your toothy friend. But we put a stop to that little affair long before you started your drawings of the mystery woman. Besides…" He stopped flipping the pages and picked up the book to show me a page. "They don't look much alike, do they?" The picture he held up was obviously of the Tooth Fairly in her puffy skirt and tiara. She looked nothing like the pictures directly behind me of Sarah.

"And you changed me from a Boogeyman to an Imaginary Friend through art therapy? That sounds far-fetched."

The light footfalls on the floor preceded Father Time. "There was more to it than that. We—the three of us—are the only ones on the Hill that can create something from nothing. We did our best to dream up a new you. We've created new things before, so we concentrated on making a whole new you."

"You wished for the old me to go away?"

They looked at each other for a good answer. Mother Nature was the only one to respond. "A lot of Imaginaries on the Hill wished you'd go away."

"And that was enough?" I knew it was, because there I was.

"Not to change you forever." Mother Nature touched a drawing of Sarah and examined it closely, avoiding eye contact.

I needed to leave. I was investigating a dead man, and here were people admitting they'd tried to end my life. "That closet? It works now?" I wanted to find some kind of glue to hold these strange puzzle pieces together. None of this was familiar, but I still felt too closed off within the cave. My life revolved around working out of closets and a cave made me claustrophobic.

"Well, yes. You weren't allowed to use it then, that's all," Mother Nature said.

"I want to go back up to the Hill."

"Look, Abe, you're handling all of this very well. Maybe you should take a few moments, or a day, to really process this." Death's tone was more concerned than it had been. He had been patronizing and ho-hum before, and I hadn't heard his voice so quiet since meeting him. He seemed uncomfortable talking to me here. Behind him, Father Time was shuffling though a stack of yellow cards that he'd pulled from an unseen pocket of his white robe.

I couldn't stay in the room a minute more, as the walls suddenly felt close and I was afraid that if I stayed longer, they'd lock me up in that room again and never let me out. I pushed toward the closet, and the closest thing to freedom I could think of.

As I opened the closet door and stepped in, I saw Father Time step forward with the paper that would send me topside. "Here. This is a sort of generic job card." As I closed the door and became enveloped in blackness, I heard one of them call to me. "We'll talk again soon, *right*?"

40

I shuffled out of the Personnel building and at the bottom of the stairs, Sarah stood with her hands clasped behind her back. "I was just about to come looking for you," she said.

"Looking for me?"

"I checked all your old haunts and couldn't find you. I checked the Dream, your apartment…well, that's it, really, but no one had seen you. I thought I'd come see if Personnel knew if you were on a job or something." She stepped forward and hugged me tightly. "So glad I caught up with you."

"Me too," I said. "Some crazy stuff going on, or I would have tracked you down sooner." I forced myself not to dump all of that crazy stuff on her right away. "Walk with me?"

"Sure."

It was good to take a break with Sarah again. We walked down an empty pathway to the outside of town. The city streets were more crowded today, mostly with people milling about, and we agreed to find some quiet place to talk. I wanted to spill it for her, make her tell me what to do. She could do that, I knew she could, but in this situation, I found there were certain things I couldn't bring myself to tell her, even if those details could've brought clarity to my life. The Tooth Fairy was one of the things I kept to myself. "There are so many things to piece together, and the more I look at them, the more they change, you know?" I said as I spewed out the story of the last few days. I guess giving her those pieces would've helped her understand, but I couldn't do it.

"Imaginaries or Otherworlders, we all see what we expect to see, Abe. That's the principle that we've operated on from the beginning," Sarah said. "If someone hears a strange sound, the next thing he sees is going to look like the Boogeyman. If a kid wants an Imaginary Friend, that kid's going to see the Friend he wants. They all fool themselves for one reason or another. Maybe it's out of hope, or fear, or desire. We do it, too." Her calm, knowing demeanor was a welcome change from the frenzy that had surrounded me since Ira's death. She was the opposite of the Council. She was a soothing brook.

"You're saying if I'm looking for a horrible creature walking around the Hill, I'm going to see a horrible creature, not what's really there. Right?" I asked. I thought of seeing my reflection in the water of the Director's office and how I didn't recognize myself. Was that my true reflection in a time of weakness, or did I want to see someone pathetic? Did this little ideal work only on others, or could we fool ourselves *about* ourselves?

"Yes, of course. It can be very powerful when we look the hardest."

"Bob." In a moment, I knew I wouldn't be spending a leisurely afternoon with Sarah. Each time I had encountered Bob I had been expecting a monster, and I had found one. I never stopped and looked at him carefully. I had never seen him for him.

"Excuse me?" She was startled by what must have seemed to her like a sudden change of topic.

"I just can't figure out the whole thing with Bob. Is he an enemy that I should be avoiding or fighting with, or is he someone that I need to come to some sort of agreement with and learn to accept?"

"If what you're saying is true, you have a right to be suspicious." Her hand was on my shoulder as she talked. "The Director hasn't given you any reason to trust him or anything associated with him. Bob himself goes about things in a way that concerns you. You should be suspicious. It would be strange not to be."

She was as perceptive as ever when it came to the things I tried to keep bottled up. "Why would I be afraid of him? I think we're supposed to be the same kind of Imaginaries. We're supposed to be part of the same team."

"You've seen him do things that frighten you, and you've been made aware that you were once the same way. I think it's good that you don't want to go back to that, but I think it's that fear that's keeping you from seeing the whole picture."

"Yeah," I said. It dawned on me then. She didn't have to keep talking. I think Bob himself tried to tell me, but I didn't have time to listen. Or the patience.

"You need to—" she began.

"To see him as he really is." I understood, even if she didn't. Things were obvious when I looked at them as a whole rather than as bits and pieces. "I think I already do." I hated to leave her, hated to keep things from her, but it was for her own good. If I could make some of this right I would tell her everything. "I'm really sorry, but I think I need to go."

"Go? You just got here. They can't expect you to work all of the time." Her disappointment was half-buried in her joking tone.

"I swear, I need to take care of this and I'll come right back to you."

"Swear?"

"Swear."

"All right," she said, resigned.

I nodded and gave her a hug. "See you soon."

I didn't take the time to look back, afraid a look might convince me to stay. I moved down Mythos street, turned onto Howard, and raced to the next. I took a few bounding steps down Water Boulevard and turned left toward the bridge. Sarah was far behind me by now. Ahead, a voice called my name from the fog that had grown thick in my path.

"Abe?"

In a moment, the fog separated, and the small form of a friend pulled herself free. "You've got a job," Kite said, waving a ticket in her hand.

"A job?" I asked. The word seemed foreign to me, though it hadn't been all that longs since I had been getting a couple each day.

"Yeah. I went with the guys down to Personnel to see if anyone would decipher the card for us. One of them asked me to deliver this to you."

"What kind of job? Is it a special or something? I thought they took me out of rotation while I did this other thing." They wanted me to work a regular job while they demanded I pretend to be a cop? There were others out there that were better suited and ready to get off their asses, weren't there? "Who gave it to you?"

"One of the desk secretaries. Before you ask, I can't tell them apart."

I looked at the ticket and tried to make sense out of the jumble of letters and numbers there, with no luck. All I could make out for sure was the name at the top. A-B. "All right, I'll head down there." Maybe a job was just what I needed to clear my head. If it was a new Imaginary Friend job, I might even have time to sit around and sort things out. But what if this were some continuation of the conversation I'd just had with the Council? Were they throwing me into the Boogeyman rotation? "Was Zane still there when you left?"

"Yes, I think so."

"All right. If you run into him, tell them I had to work. I'll catch up with them when I get back."

"Sure," she said. "I'm going that way now." She floated off and disappeared in the fog of the Hill.

On my way toward the Personnel Department, I was surprised to see so many Imaginaries still milling about in the streets with nothing to do. I was being called in, but all of these entities had plenty of free time on their hands? There wasn't any reason for a Boogeyman or an Imaginary Friend to be busy when other types weren't. I squeezed by the crowds and turned up the empty walk to the Department. There was no one waiting here to go on jobs—a vast difference from everywhere else.

I pushed open the doors and headed for the front desk to ask if they knew anything about why I was going out on a job. Neither of them was there, though. In their places stood two familiar faces, well, familiar heads: Bald and Balder. I hadn't seen them since they took me to meet the Council that first time. "I didn't know you guys worked in here." I couldn't recall seeing anyone other than the usual two standing behind the desk since I started.

Bald spoke up sheepishly, "We have to keep busy."

Balder coughed. "They move us around a lot."

"Where are the ones who usually work here?"

"Stepped out," Bald said.

"Break," Balder added. "Did you get your assignment?"

"Yeah. Kite gave it to me." I held the ticket up.

"Good," they said in unison.

"Suppose I should get going." They nodded to me as I walked toward the tubes.

I listened to my steps echo off the walls of the empty hall as I pushed open the door to the first chamber. I looked back to see if Bald and Balder were watching, but I couldn't see them. I stared at the job ticket in my hand. Nothing but gibberish with my name at the top. Somehow I hoped it would all rearrange itself into something I could figure out. I looked back again.

No Bald.

No Balder.

I reached into my pocket and pulled out another slip. It was the one that had been issued for Ira's last job but never used. The markings on it were very different from that of the ticket I had just been given, so I wasn't being sent wherever the Director had gone in Ira's place. I looked from card to card, weighed them in my hands, though it was obvious that they were only paper with writing and would feel the same.

I slid the new card into my shirt and stuck the dead Boogeyman's into the slot.

41

There was noise around me. The sound of leaves crunching under feet rose above the rest as someone passed close to me. Doors shut and opened at random as voices, male and female, mumbled just out of earshot. Voices not far off in the distance, talking about "searching" and "evidence"—words I had heard before.

I was on cold, hard ground and could feel my body displacing blades of wet grass as it turned from formless darkness to a solid.

My reluctance to open my eyes was reinforced by the reappearance of bright beams of red and blue that blanketed my eyelids. Wherever I was, it was the same place the Director had gone in place of Ira. Maybe he even found a way to kill Ira to get here.

I looked from side to side as I waited for the ability to put myself in motion. I was in a garden that had fallen into disrepair. There were broken sticks with faded labels stuck to them attempting to identify the plants that once grew there. A low section of fence to the left was missing a number of pickets. Unused bundles of wire sat nearby, rusting. A house with peach-colored siding stood just on the other side of the fence. Bushes and weeds stood tall on all sides of me, though they were thin and sickly enough that I could see what was happening just beyond them to my right.

A feet away, a well-manicured lawn was covered with a swarm of police cars, all blaring radios and running their engines. The lights on top of their roofs flashed red and blue haphazardly, completely out of sync with each other. Vans and ordinary-looking sedans sat among the marked police cars with their own versions of the lights stuck on their dashboards or attached to their bumpers. Men and women were everywhere. They were standing alone, in groups, in pairs. Some of them were silent, contemplative, but a few were laughing, somehow unaffected by whatever was quieting the others. Out by the street, several uniformed officers stood by a yellow tape stretched between the trees. Just past them, several ordinary people were trying to stretch themselves to become big enough to see something of what the police didn't want them to see. Next to them, a man pointed a large camera with a brilliant light on top at a smartly dressed young woman talking evenly and matter-of-factly with yet another man in uniform.

In the middle of the driveway, one particular patrol car was the focus of a lot of attention. Some policemen came and went while one stood at the rear of the vehicle by the back door. When one of the men came to the car, he'd open the back door and lean in, apparently talking to someone. I could see their faces move and jaws open, but couldn't understand what they were saying. They were talking too low and speaking into the muting cavern of the car itself. One thing I *could* tell, though, was they were exceedingly interested in that dark silhouette in the back of the car.

My head was finally together enough to allow me to move, though I was dizzy and disoriented. I felt I was well enough to roll over onto my stomach and move forward a bit. There were trees ahead, but they were a fair distance away, across a wide-open lawn that was currently flooded with not only red and blue lights, but the glaring white of several beams of headlights. But if I *could* make it, the trees were thick and wide enough to conceal me from all but the most intense scrutiny. They created a deep shadow on my side of the trunk that would offer someone like me natural cover.

I didn't know if it was worth it to take such a risk. I wasn't there on an official assignment. Whatever Ira was supposed to do was long gone. It would've been impossible to get past all of those people without more than one of them seeing me. Other Imaginaries work with group sightings—Bigfoot, Aliens, and Lake Monsters, for example, but Imaginary Friends and Boogeymen, have always been a one-on-one kind of thing. More than that ruins the effect; two people can reassure and comfort one another. They can find some solace in the fact they're not alone and that they both saw an anomalous presence. If one person sees something out of the ordinary, he has to fight self-doubt as well as the scorn of everyone he tells.

"Aren't you going to get a better look?" A woman's whisper behind me took me by surprise. Someone had seen me and spoken to me without blowing my cover. Even more amazingly, she had done so without a fear of the shadow lying in the garden. I quickly rolled onto my back and searched for the source. I looked both ways along the fence and didn't find it. I scanned the weeds beside me on either side and came up empty as well. A nearby window was open, and the curtains were shaking more than they should have in the light breeze of the night. I watched as they slowly parted, and a familiar tiara-decorated head appeared between the curtain and the window. Looking back into the room behind her, the Tooth Fairy slowly turned around, smiled a shiny smile at me, and waved her hand like a puppy wagging its tail.

I waved back, though less exuberantly. I think I also smiled. "What are you doing here?" I asked.

She stopped waving and raised her other hand to show me what appeared to be a pretty large molar. She pointed at it. "I'm working, silly. They let me work, remember?" She checked behind her again.

"Oh." I'd gathered from my little investigation that coincidence was a rare commodity when it came to the Hill. Maybe she knew that already, too.

"And here I thought you might've snuck out to see me do my job. Is it 'Take-your-Imaginary-To-Work' day again already? I always forget to mark my calendar," she said. Her smile got so big, I was afraid it would envelop her whole face, and I wouldn't be able to see the sparkle of her eyes. "Besides, you're not supposed to be here, are you?"

It took me a second. I wasn't, was I? At least I wasn't sent here, I came of my own will. "Uh. I guess not." Still, it wasn't a coincidence, was it? I knew this was the place that Ira was going, where the Director went in Ira's place.

She nodded toward the cars. "Why not just go check it out? With all of the commotion, who's going to notice you?" She had a point. It was a busy place, and there seemed to be little or no focus on my section of the yard. Whatever brought them to that place had been found before I showed up. They were focused on the inside of the little blue house on the narrow street, rather than its outside. "I don't know. There's a lot of people…"

"Give ya a quarter."

"What?"

She held up a shiny coin. "I'll give you a quarter to do it."

I looked at her beaming face, and then at the maze of women and men on the grass. It was crazy. Absolutely crazy. But part of me thought I could do it. "It's impossible."

The Tooth Fairly held up a fist, and when she opened it, there was more than one coin. "Two quarters."

I didn't need money for anything, really, but the idea of amusing her made me immeasurably happy. "You're on," I said. Her face was disappearing behind that smile again, and I was suddenly sure I could do anything with her behind me.

I surveyed the scene and began predicting, anticipating where the Otherworlders would go, how they would turn. I thought I would have to adjust to compensate for adults rather than the children that made up my usual playmates, but I found it just wasn't so. It was easy. I played a guessing game as to what would happen: one guy would sit, one would say something into a walkie-talkie, another would fold her arms in boredom. It all happened exactly the way I saw it in my mind, down to the last flinch, the last sigh. It was as if they had heard me announce their movements and point them in their directions: a perfect orchestra following an unseen conductor. I predicted each twitch of each person exactly, my natural instincts unfailingly accurate. I made my way toward the tree, moving and stopping as I felt the need. I was like the very ground beneath their feet. They never looked at me or even glanced my way.

It was beautiful.

By the time I reached the car, I could tell it was Truman in the back seat, sitting quietly with his hands in his lap. The door was open a crack on the opposite side of him, and I slipped in with ease. He stared out the window to his left and didn't look at me, but I could tell he knew I was there. I was like a mirror to him, sitting on the opposite side of the car and looking out the opposite window. I wondered why the people all walked with such purpose around us. "I don't suppose there's some sort of party going on?" I half-asked, knowing the answer.

He was slow to respond. "No," he said.

I had taken a big risk in joining him. There were so many adults around who could've easily seen me and ruined our secret. Yet he still hadn't formed any substantive words for me. It looked like whatever question he'd wanted to ask me originally was well past answering. And whatever answers I was looking for in that car weren't forthcoming.

"Maybe we should just get out of here." I hoped some face-to-face contact would rouse him to action. He still didn't look at me, but I talked to the back of his head for a minute anyway. "Come on. Let's just jump in the front seat and we'll hit the road. Me and you." I grabbed at his arm to pull him along, but I wasn't able to get him to move.

"I can't. She's...I didn't want to. I swear." There seemed to be a tear forming in his eye, and I was ashamed for him. I thought he had outgrown that sort of thing—crying about ridiculous matters. I wondered who it was, what had happened, and how he had been caught, but it didn't matter. I put the idea in my own head that he had turned himself in for some crime, some misdemeanor. It made me feel a little better, sitting there in the car with him. The idea that he was man enough to take responsibility for his actions gave me hope that some of the ideals I'd tried to instill in him when he was a child weren't all false memories. In the end, though, what I thought of him and said to him no longer had an impact. I could hear more people moving close, saw their shadows in the lights from the cars, and decided to leave.

I stopped with my hand on the door. "You and I were friends, once. Right?"

"We were friends once I understood what you were trying to teach me."

42

When I got out of the return tube, they were waiting. The Director stood in the hall, with Bob just behind him and a couple of Personnel goons a few steps back. "You should have just taken the assignment, Abe."

I pulled the unused card from my pocket and held it up. "Really, where did that card take me? Straight into a cave?"

"Something like that." It was exactly like that, I was sure. Transport me to an empty cave and forget me.

"Don't you think someone would notice? I've been in contact with the Council constantly."

"It would have taken a while, and by the time they noticed you were gone and dug you up, it would've been too late. They're a bunch of doddering old fools who don't know they're on the way out." He tipped his head toward the group behind him. "This is the new Council: me, Bob, and some others that will support me." That brought proud looks from all of them. "You've seen all of those Imaginaries standing in the streets with nothing to do. Do you think they're really going to keep following those three with things going so wrong?"

"You helped them go wrong."

"So did you, and much to my incredible surprise, you figured out enough about what was going on here to mess things up for me. Hiding you in a hole would give me enough time to get a few more new recruits going through the new program, and that would be all I need."

"I've already told others."

"Your dimwit partners? They've been dealt with already, and they're just waiting for you to get tossed into the hole with them. They were never a threat. And…" He pulled his stack of blue master key cards from his pocket and sifted through them until he found one that wasn't blue. It was a standard assignment card like any other, but he held it up toward me. "I took your only piece of solid evidence away from them."

The Director shook violently from head to toe, interrupting his tirade. "Is it extremely cold in here all of a sudden?" He looked around at his cronies for confirmation, but they all shrugged.

While he was turned, a familiar face materialized in front of the Director: Kite. In a brief moment, before the Director could even turn around, Kite had managed to levitate a number of the cards from the middle of the stack, causing them to spill out onto the floor near me. The Director realized what was going on and swatted at the nearby ghost, succeeding only in accidentally throwing more cards on the floor. Kite winked at me and disappeared just as the Personnel goons started advancing on her.

I didn't wait for everyone to digest what just happened. I fell to the floor and grabbed as many of the blue cards as I could. When the Director instinctively did the same, I took what I had and stepped back to the tube. Bob tried to step over the Director to grab me but slipped on cards. The ensuing pileup held off the goons long enough for me to stick a card in the slot at random and step into the tube. I sealed the door behind me and kicked myself for not pulling the card back out before I got in. As water filled the tube, I decided there was no sense in fretting over it. I could always put another card in at the next stop, and go somewhere else.

43

I opened the door, and my heart sank. The room I walked into was cut in half by bars. I thought somehow I had walked directly into a trap and they had me. But the place looked familiar. The bed, the lamp, the pile of change?

I was in the Tooth Fairy's room.

I looked around for her with no luck. It wasn't that big of a place, but I called for her anyway. "Tooth Fairy?" I had to come up with a nickname for her. "Toothy?" I called. That sucked. I'd have to work on it.

No one responded.

As much as I wanted to see her, I couldn't wait around. There was no telling when the Director's people would catch up with me. I examined the cards. The Director didn't have anything written on his; they were just plain blue cards with no hint of their destinations. I didn't want to give them time to catch up, so I picked another at random, stuck it in the slot next to the closet, pulled the card back out, and stepped into the darkness.

44

I felt around in the darkness for the door release and stepped out. I had to put my hand to my eyes to shield them from the sunshine that greeted me. The only place bathed in sunshine on the Hill was around the castle, so I had a vague idea where I'd ended up. When my eyes adjusted, I found myself high up in the cliffs along the river. I was on a small outcropping of rock that barely had room for me and the tube. It offered a wonderful view of the valley below and the river that wound through it. Somewhere, I heard what sounded like the rush of a waterfall, but I was afraid to move much in order to find it. The rest of the Hill was visible in the fog just beyond the shore. I couldn't figure out why anyone would put a transport tube here unless they really enjoyed the view. Even then, it was hard for anyone to get comfortable with so little room to move.

I decided to leave. As much as I enjoyed the respite, they could burst through the door at any time, and then where would any of us stand?

A noise caught my attention; it sounded like a laugh, or several laughs. It was definitely female voices. I bent down and looked through a group of trees that obscured the view on the left. Through the branches and leaves, I could make out figures in the water. The trees swayed and the women moved and I saw a long tail flop out of the water.

Mermaids.

I thought about yelling to them for help, but what could they do? They were no good on land, and by the time they sent help up for me, it would be too late. The river and waterfall would probably drown out my yells anyway.

I pulled a new card from the stack and stuck it into the slot, then carefully put the old one into a safe pocket away from the others.

45

I made it to a few more destinations, though they all were dead ends. A room of blackness, another with light so bright that it blinded me. I found a locked and barred closet. None of them offered me any way out of my precarious position. I never saw a soul who could assist me, or one who would want to.

Ultimately, they caught up with me in Elliott's room.

I materialized in the cold, blue water, and when I realized where I was, I tried to scramble to get out, but I hadn't fully solidified. I floated there like a drip of motor oil on the surface of a puddle. I didn't see Elliott and panicked that he might be lurking down below me, waiting for me to offer myself as a tasty morsel to the only monster that really existed. It was a nerve-wracking two minutes, feeling his presence, not seeing him. When I could flutter my feet and fingers, I made my way to the edge, and flopped out of the pool onto the side. From there, I rolled myself to the wall, hoping to keep myself from Elliot's clutches. Nothing happened. The ripples from my exit subsided and the surface became calm. When I could, I stood and headed around to the double doors, but before I even made it halfway there, the doors burst open and the Director and his entourage entered.

"How did you get here?" I was puzzled how he'd made it in a different fashion than I had.

"The Leprechaun has a closet in his room," the Director said. "He would've told you that eventually if we hadn't arrived. He can never keep a secret when someone stares at him long enough." All of his men chuckled. Maybe they knew Father Time told me not to do that. I'm sure Time gave the Council a full report.

"Come on, Abe. Just make this easy on all of us. You survived solitary life in a cave before, and you'll make it through this time, too. It's no big deal," Bob said. What he didn't mention was whether I'd be allowed to leave this time or not. That seemed like the most important detail to me.

"He's right. Why drag out the inevitable?" the Director said. I didn't want to admit to myself he was right, and I backed up, trying to move further from them, but once I walked around to the far side of the pool I would be out of space. There were only two ways out—those doors—and the odds of a secret trapdoor suddenly appearing were not looking good. The other option was swimming through the pool with Elliott, and I wasn't ready to test my friendship with that beast just yet.

They split up; a goon and Bob went one way, the Director and another goon came at me from the other. Neither group was in any hurry. They leisurely splashed toward me through the water that overflowed from the pool.

"It wasn't anything I planned. It was just the perfect coincidence. I was monitoring Ira's work anyway, so when they told me he didn't make it for an assignment, I started looking for him." He looked happy to be spilling this to me with his goons and Bob looking on. Their expressions remained blank and I had to assume they already knew all of it. "As I'm leaving the Department, I pick up his card so I can hand it to him while I'm chewing him out for being late. I look at it while I'm walking."

"You know all of the codes?" I asked

"I invented the codes. Of course I know them," he said. "I see what the card says and I can't believe my luck. I've been looking for a way to get you back to your old ways and I'm suddenly holding a card in my hands for your old friend Truman." The laugh that followed was like the bark of a lone dog in the night. The echo of it in the chamber brought it back to me more times than I cared to hear it. "So I go to Ira's place and at first I'm thinking I'll coach him a little, get him to give Truman the full treatment. Then I thought I would tag along with him and double-team the guy—really send him around the corner," the Director said. "But when I got there, poor Ira was already on the ground, fading."

"Why don't I believe that?" I looked around for something to defend myself with, but knowing the results of Zane's various experiments, I was well aware that I couldn't injure any of them. With the right weapon, though, I might be able to knock them off balance. Unfortunately, the floors around me appeared spotless.

"Believe me or don't, doesn't matter. He was already shuffling off when I got there."

"Why didn't the card come to me? Shouldn't it have been a special, since I originally dealt with Truman?" He was my charge, no matter how things went bad. I should have been the one to take that call. Maybe I could have prevented whatever followed. "I was his friend."

"When you cracked up and started taking things too far, we severed your connection to him. Any call he made was up for grabs. We were surprised, though, that you still held on a little. It was unusual the way you managed to keep your connection to him open, despite our best efforts at erasing it. You weren't notified by anyone in Personnel when he wanted to talk to you, yet you still knew. Still responded."

"I don't remember any contact."

"Red. Whenever he tried to contact you, you saw the color red." He shrugged. "No idea why, you just did. I heard you wanted red pencils during your therapy. He tried to contact you a couple of times right after the accident."

"The lighthouse?"

"The what?" He looked annoyed.

"The lighthouse in the center of the Hill?"

All four of them looked at each other for a second and I moved on. Did they not see it?

"All the times I saw the color red you went to talk to Truman?" I said. "There were so many. What else you did do to him? What else did you make him do?" I tried to count the number of times in the last several days I had seen a red light and gave up. It had become natural for me to see it and I had nearly ignored it most of the time.

"I don't have that kind of time. He was ignored a little. Sometimes I went, but eventually I sent Bob in my place." He hiked his thumb to where Bob stood, flanked by the goon. "Truman didn't care who showed up as long as someone paid attention to him. As long as someone fed his needs and gave him a voice to listen to."

"He still wanted to talk to me, though." It was a small consolation.

"Of course he did, we never pretended to be you. We made it clear from the beginning who we were." As the Director talked, I could see Bob shifting his weight from foot to foot. Unlike the rest of the entourage, who kept their grim looks directed at me, he shifted his gaze around the room when I looked to him.

"And that was?"

"Friends of yours. That's all. Just friends." His smile made me shiver. The idea that they were going around calling me a friend was unappealing. "He was happy to have more friends."

"So was the whole 'policeman' thing your idea, then?"

"I couldn't help myself. I saw him wearing the uniform when I took Ira's job and thought it would be too funny to see you bumble around like you were important, the same way he did. Walking around with his chest puffed out when he wasn't even allowed to carry a gun, just a can of mace, a stick, and a radio. He had to sew his official patch on himself."

"So you lied to the Council and told them I should do this because Truman did, when really neither of us were doing the job? He was mall security and I was just supposed to flail about until I found out who I really was?"

"Something like that." He was walking more slowly now, drawing out his story, letting me dangle a little before they grabbed me.

I was cornered at the far end of the pool. With two of them on each side, I had no chance of pushing my way through. Swimming across the pool was an option, but Elliott was unpredictable. Besides, they could run around the pool faster than I could swim it, putting me right back where I started. I hoped that if I kept them talking, they would continue walking slowly, thus giving me more thinking time. "So, Thor, how did you let yourself get talked into this?"

Everyone stopped moving. I liked that reaction. Bob looked especially stunned. Did they all think I was so stupid that I wouldn't eventually figure out Thor was missing when Bob always seemed to be around? I wasn't the quickest, but I did have some sense.

Bob looked to the Director with wide eyes. "You swore no one would ever know," he shouted across the expanse of water.

"Don't raise your voice to me. I gave you this chance and you ran with it." The Director looked at Bob with narrowed eyes and bared teeth. "Don't disappoint me now like some people."

"You *wanted* to do this?" I asked.

The Director spoke up before Bob could answer. "Wanted to? He volunteered for it. Needed to make a new name for himself, he said. His chest was as bloated as yours with your little responsibilities."

"I thought all of the Gods declined the offer to be reassigned. They didn't want to sully their images by becoming common Imaginaries, or something like that."

"They were fools," Bob's voice boomed throughout the enormous room like a barrage of thunder. "Afraid of having a new chance at infamy, and comfortable with living off of their old, dusty names."

"You didn't have that problem, though, did you? You were always worried that you were being forgotten. You were so insecure, you had to pester everyone who came back from the Otherworld for news about yourself." I remembered the feeling of dread every time I saw him coming because I knew what would follow.

"And there never was any news, was there, Bob? They'd already forgotten about you altogether." The Director and his goon started walking toward me again, though he kept his eyes mostly on Bob and pointed a long gnarly finger at him. "So we fixed that. Got you a respectable job. The Gods belong to history; you'll have a name in the future."

"*But he figured it out. He recognized me.*" He was pleading to the Director. Some of the annoying neediness that he had been notorious for was seeping back into his voice. "You said that wasn't supposed to happen."

"Look, Thor, or Bob, or whatever you want to be known as now," I said. "No one on the Otherworld would ever know who you are or were. If you're scaring them, they won't care either. I'm willing to bet that the vast majority of the people on the Hill wouldn't have a clue, either. Maybe a few, but only a few. I suppose if I could put it together, others can too." I was torn between making a workable escape plan and gaining Bob's trust. The two weren't necessarily mutually exclusive in my mind. "Is this why no one on the Hill recognized me when I switched between a Boogeyman and an Imaginary friend?"

"You were a completely different Imaginary. The change in profession does bring about some cosmetic differences," The Director said. "You didn't immediately recognize Thor as Bob, did you?"

Everyone was moving again, Bob was slow to start, but fell in behind the goon. Both moved slowly, the goon unused to leading, Bob reluctant to follow someone after his exchange with the Director. They had come far more than halfway and would reach me in another couple of minutes, even at their slow pace. In the middle of all of us, the water churned for a moment and then was calm. "No. Not at first."

"He looked pretty fierce, didn't he?" The Director's progress was slowed as he paused to examine the statues that lined his side of the pool, so I cautiously took steps toward him to stay evenly between the two parties. "Think about it, Abe—who is everyone going to want to follow in the coming days?" He stepped onto the pedestal with the statue of Father Time. "This guy? Every year he goes out with the latest New Year's Baby and acts like it's a lark. Like it's a spur of the moment thing and he's just giving the people what they want. He's as much a slave to the Otherworld as every other Imaginary. He can't resist what he was made for. He can't sit at home on the couch when the ball drops on New Year's Eve." He patted the statue on the back a few times, creating a wet cracking sound. "They call, he answers."

I was still shuffling my way toward the Director and his goon while Bob and his goon advanced on me. They were still quite slow, intrigued by their boss's show. "Maybe Father Time gained some wisdom in his years. Maybe he does it because he enjoys his New Year's duty." I hadn't had that feeling explicitly spelled out for me in the last few days, but I did get the idea of obligation. He felt the Otherworlders would be let down if he himself didn't show up, but I never believed he didn't have a choice.

"You can interpret that guy how you please." The Director leapt to the ground and then climbed onto the statue of Mother Nature. "But trust me on this one." He slapped the statue's face a couple of times, roughly. "Her indifference to the Imaginary condition is a real turn-off for the average working stiff. She's never shown a bit of interest in anyone's life but her own. Sure, she'll listen and smile if there's a crowd, but when the public face comes off, and you're just one-on-one, she could care less. You ran into that when you spoke with her alone. Didn't you? A seriously cold fish, wouldn't you say?"

"I caught her in the middle of a stressful situation," I said. I made sure to steal a glace to Bob so I knew where he was. Out of the corner of my eye, I saw the wide, dark shape of Elliott slicing through the water at the bottom of the pool, but in a moment he was gone again.

"She's been under stress since the day she first appeared, my friend. Trust me, I've known her longer." He stroked the statue's stony hair while he talked. "If it wasn't one thing, it was another.

"And of course, we can't leave out our good friend Death." He hung on to Mother Nature's statue but pointed to the next. I couldn't tell if he was trying to break them or if they were just wonderful props in his little demonstration. "What is it with him and all of the sports gear? Doesn't he have work to do instead of roaming a golf course or a tennis court?"

"If you had his job, wouldn't you need a distraction, too?" I asked.

"And that brings us to your flaw, my friend." That word again: *friend*. "You have an excuse for everything and everyone. When you failed, it was everyone else's fault but yours. It was a nightlight, a rake, the sudden appearance of an adult. Never your own incompetence," he said. "And now here you are, covering for everyone else, too."

I remained silent and looked out over the water for a dark shape.

"Ah, nothing to add to that? Surprising." He dropped down from one statue and walked past Death's athletically posed likeness. "Maybe you're learning after all. I hope for…" He stopped mid-sentence as he stepped toward the last, empty pedestal. "Where's my statue?" Suddenly, nothing else seemed to matter to him. "Where is my statue?" The words were more pronounced as anger rose in his voice. He spun around looking and quickly focused in on the pieces of the head and torso scattered against the wall. He stumbled over to the debris and knelt. He touched a piece gently—a shard of his head—as though it were a child he didn't want to wake. In an instant, he snatched it up and held it close to his eyes, making a mirror of the face, minus a broken nose. He walked back toward where the statue had once stood holding up the piece.

In the whole room, he was the only one moving. The rest of his people stopped to watch what the Director would do next. His sudden outburst made the dark room crackle with energy. It was a hatred that he hadn't found a way to focus yet. All of his men looked momentarily unsure of what to do next, and I was just as confused. Bubbles popping on the surface of the water were the only indication that time hadn't stopped altogether.

"Who is responsible?" he asked. "Who did this?" No one wanted to venture a guess for fear that the gathering wrath would be turned toward them. Though I said nothing, the Director's eyes still fell on me. "You were down here with Time," he said. He carefully cupped the piece of his statue's head in both of his hands and stepped onto the pedestal. "You were down here with Father Time and the two of you destroyed it in a fit of jealousy." The words were amplified in the huge room, echoing, accusing me again and again.

Knowing what happened the last time I was in that room, I felt like I should give him a friendly warning. "Look, sir. I really think—"

"Shut up," he said in a low voice. "That was always your problem: thinking. Well, you'll have plenty of time to think back in your little hole in the ground."

"No, I just think you should get down from there."

The Director looked to his men. "Let's go. I want this over with."

The men looked at each other and took tentative steps toward me. Bob was the slowest to comply.

Just then, the water seemed to jump toward the Director in an arc from the pool. It took a moment to see that it wasn't just water rising, but a great volume of liquid being shed off Elliott as his head and neck broke the surface and came back down at the stunned Director. He didn't move to avoid the creature, nor did he say anything, although it appeared his mouth was opening. His hands were still out in front of him holding a piece of his statue's face.

In a second, the great creature's neck began to slowly disappear into the water, and in the space where the Director had been standing, there was nothing. An obvious lump bulged in Elliott's throat, slowly making its way down toward the enormous body.

I looked around at the remaining Imaginaries in the room, the two goons and Bob. All were transfixed by the form before them. I wondered what was going through their minds as they looked at this great creature that had swallowed their leader right before them. It had really happened so fast that I'm not even sure they all were clear what happened.

I smiled inwardly because I thought I knew what was going to happen. I imagined how mad the Director was going to be when Elliott started choking and spit him out against the wall, like he'd done with the statue. The idea of the Director dazed and covered in Elliott phlegm was the best sight I could have to keep me company if I were going to be exiled in a cave for a good long time.

Elliott kept sliding backward, though, until only his massive head was propped on the edge of the pool. He groggily turned toward me and I prepared for him to clear his throat and tell me his motives, his story. It was that feeling I had before; he was just looking for someone to understand. *Sometimes monsters are just monsters, my ass.*

Nothing.

Maybe he had the Director stuck in his throat, but he didn't talk.

In another second he sunk back under the water without so much as a wink or a nod. The moment the last bubble from Elliott's wake popped, both goons ran for the doors and were gone. Bob continued to stare. I understood the turmoil he felt. My first encounter with Elliott had been frightening enough, and I'd only seen him spit out a statue.

Elliott's sleek form cut through the water with surprising speed. The pool was vast enough that he could build up a head of steam and still maneuver easily. He was graceful despite his massive frame. I made sure to stay away from the edge of the pool; I wasn't dipping my feet this time, not after that, anyway. I leaned against a column and relaxed as much as I could, waiting for Bob to register a reaction.

The Council showed up minutes later, but all they found were three monsters enjoying a cool day at the pool.

46

The Council took a softer approach when we met again. We sat on the bridge, the four of us, with our bare feet dangling over the side. We were too high up to reach the water, but it still felt good.

Some splashing toward the other side of the river drew our attention. Two mermaids had broken the surface and lingered by the shore. They laughed together and swam in a straight line on the surface. Both had long red hair that trailed on the surface long after they had submerged. Their wakes fanned out across the river behind them.

"You were experiencing a slump of your own, weren't you, Abe? Like the one that Ira was having before his demise."

My last job as an Imaginary Friend had been a disaster. A few others before that weren't exactly by-the-book. The Director had been on me constantly to do things better. "Yeah, I had a few problems. That doesn't prove anything."

"But the Director loved using you as an excuse. If you failed, he could say we needed to be more extreme to get through to the Otherworlders. If you succeeded, he could strut around and tout the wondrous job his new little toy was doing. Your successes were all proof of what he had been saying."

"I don't understand why any of this matters, now." I swung my feet in short fits back and forth. "I'm better, I'm productive. I can become an Imaginary Friend, now that I know what I was."

"Things are changing, Abe. Always changing. Changing faster than we ever anticipated. We made some mistakes with you, but we are going to need to be more aggressive in our efforts to deal with the Otherworld. It's like Mort said with his magic analogy—we need to have new material." Mother Nature nodded toward the riverbank where Bob sat staring at the waves. "That's what led to Bob being brought onboard. The Director thought this crisis of Imagination was the perfect time to take a major chunk of power for himself. He saw a dawning of the era of the Boogeyman. His idea to convert most of the Imaginaries into these...these walking harbingers of...*darkness* wasn't entirely without merit. We've lost ground in all of our key demographics."

Though I already knew it, it still hurt to hear that what I used to be was so horrible to some people. I was glad someone had brought me away from it. Yet, I could feel some of what I used to be trying to come back. I hoped it was the good parts of the old me. I believed I made someone happy somewhere in my history.

"It hasn't quite come to that yet," Death said. "I know I tend to have a reputation for the darker side of things, but really, I'm all about fair play. I have my doubts about how healthy it would be to unleash swarms of…of…Super-Boogeymen on the world. Until now, we've been about doing some good, too. Teaching lessons and whatnot, instead of just being pants-wettingly terrifying. Nothing's gotten that bad, of that I'm sure." In a fluid motion, he pulled two short sticks from his right sleeve. He fixed them together to make one long stick and then pulled some string and a cork from inside the robe. He tied the string to the end of the stick and the cork to the other. Where he produced the small hook from, I couldn't be sure, but he tied it just inches below the cork and cast his line out into the water near where we had seen the mermaids swimming earlier. He sat there quietly as he watched the cork rise to meet the waves.

Bob had come to stand within earshot of us, so I yelled to him. "How did he convince you to do it?"

"See...Here's the way he explained it to me. We give Imaginaries work as Boogeymen for a while, drum up business, and get people on the Otherworld to believe in something again. You know, scare 'em. Terrify the shit out of them. Once they're frightened enough, they start believing in all sorts of crazy things again. It makes all kinds of sense, right? Make the whole lot of them superstitious again." He looked like he wanted to be in a meeting room so he could show us charts and figures about how effective frightening was. Maybe there was a board necessary to show rising and declining trends in the things people believed. "Once that happens, we can make them believe anything. Everyone works after that and they can go back to what they do best. Everybody wins. Everybody's happy."

"Everybody's happy?" I asked. "Even following that logic, isn't the Otherworld going to be crawling with mean and nasty shit for a long time? Aren't we going to make it a pretty miserable place to live?" I was all for doing my job, but too many conductors make for a very disjointed symphony.

"It's headed there already. Look at the horrors kids get exposed to these days. It's inevitable; what's the harm in accelerating it some? Make them immune to it, the same way they became unaffected by us. We're helping. The

Otherworld was pretty miserable before and they survived," Bob said. "And with our help, I might add. This can only be good for us—ensure our survival for years to come."

"We'll survive one way or another. We always do." Except for the unfortunate few, like Ira and Brady. "But taking them back hundreds of years to prolong our existences?" Death was a strong ally, even with a makeshift fishing pole in his hands.

"Oh please, what are you worried about? None of you are in danger. Death, Time, Nature? Where are you guys going? Nobody's forgetting any of you. It's the rest of us poor bastards that have to be concerned."

"The name Thor wasn't exactly in any danger either," I said. Bob looked offended, even hurt, at the prospect that the Director might have lied to him.

Death was distracted by his line, but still managed to participate in the conversation. "People have enough to be afraid of, that's why the whole 'Boogeyman'll get you' thing wasn't holding water. We need new ideas, just not ones as extreme as the Director's."

"Speaking of which, we didn't always agree with his methods, but we agree that he was a necessary part of the world in which we live," Mother Nature said. "Since we have no idea if he's coming back, we need to have someone fill his position." She and the rest of the Council looked at me expectantly.

"Are you guys offering me another job? I mean, the last one didn't exactly work out."

"Didn't it?" Death wagged the fishing pole and smiled.

"Well, not the way I was led to believe it was supposed to work out."

"Yes, you have the talent for it. You have a varied background that would help you make wise decisions to affect policy. You could be an important voice for all the other Imaginaries." Father Time nodded his head as he warmed to Mother Nature's suggestion.

"I don't know anything about the administrative stuff."

Death lifted his line out of the water to examine the empty hook closely. "Not that hard of a job anyway."

I wasn't getting roped into something else new without a backup. "How about a partnership?" I asked. I could use someone to help with any math that came up. "Between Bob and me, we've got just about every Imaginary experience covered. I think we'd make a good team."

Bob's face lit up. "I think it could work."

I didn't think about how pathetic he was when he was Thor, or how terribly he frightened me as Bob. I only considered how similar we had become: neither of us liked who we used to be, and we didn't look forward to what we had to become. He wasn't satisfied with his legacy and saw the Bob persona as a way to start over and create a destiny he could control, though his discomfort with the methods he had to use wasn't something he was prepared for. Both of us had a clean start and could move in whatever direction we wanted, though I hoped that working together would steer us in the same direction.

Maybe the Council remembered what an annoyance Thor used to be, and they were glad they wouldn't have to deal with him themselves, but they agreed quickly. It was possible they were hoping I'd be a buffer between him and them. Thor's neediness would stick to me and not them. "I don't see why not, if the two of you don't mind sharing an office." Father Time immediately stuck his hand out to seal the deal by shaking on it.

"Not a problem," Bob said.

I remembered the vast expanse of the Director's office from sliding across it on my face. It would need some design work, but it would be large enough for two. "You should know I want everyone to be able to do what they were imagined for. No transfers to Elf division, or other demeaning demotions. Everyone does their own thing. If a giant, flippered Scottish beast wants to be a giant, flippered Scottish beast, then so be it."

Death was again engrossed in his fishing rod. "Whatever. We'll work it out."

"Welcome, then," Mother Nature said. "We look forward to working with you both." She held out her hand and I shook it before I did the same to the others. "We'll start the paperwork in the morning."

There were matters that we needed to discuss to get things working properly again, but no one seemed in the mood for in-depth analysis. Still, small gestures never hurt. "I need a favor that may go a long way to helping people keep their wits about them as we work on keeping them busy. Two, actually."

"Two? That's a little greedy, wouldn't you say?" Father Time was half-joking, I think. We'd already made the deal; haggling over details seemed petty. I think they hated not knowing what I was going to do next. It showed on their faces. They'd orchestrated everything I did from the time Ira died, so it felt good to be unpredictable.

47

Things had to be explained to Sarah. Discussed and sorted through. There was so much that she needed to hear from me. She was there for me at the most important time of my existence. I could see now, though, that I had to let her go. She needed to get out and see what was going to happen next in her life and I was holding her back. I was the only thing keeping her stuck here. I would go to her and everything would be taken care of. As down and exhausted as I was feeling, I still made the walk back home.

Along the way, I passed growing groups of Imaginaries milling about outside the Personnel Department and the streets beyond. I considered stopping to tell them it was going to be all right; things were coming together again. Some of them turned to look at me, nudged the Imaginary next to them. They followed my progress, but didn't speak to me, and as more realized who I was, they stopped talking altogether. I sorted through words in my head but couldn't come up with enough to explain what was happening to us. I plodded along with heavy feet and spoke to them without stopping. "I'm all right." I nodded to them. "You all will be too. Just give us some time to sort things out." A few looked ready to cheer when I started speaking, but they stopped as I continued on my way without another word. I should have just kept my mouth shut.

At the door to my apartment, I nearly knocked before opening it. Things felt different, and they were about to change a little more. I was learning how to be what I wanted, not what the Director or the Council felt best. I wondered whether I was changing into someone new, or if I was actually slowly reverting back to the thing I used to be before they tried to fix me.

Everything was still in its old familiar place. Furniture arranged just so. Comfortable quilt draped over the back of the couch and pillows placed at either end. Shades drawn. Lights low. I trudged to the bedroom and opened the door slightly. It was darkest here. There was still a blanket over the window.

She was sitting at the end of the bed. Her feet were flat on the floor and her arms were resting neatly on her knees. "It's time, isn't it?" she asked.

I knew what I was going to say. Even though I hadn't rehearsed it. I could have, *should have*, practiced it on the walk from the tubes. I had come home to end this, but I didn't want to answer her out loud. It would be an admission that things were changing. It would also be an admission that things people were saying were right; I had been everything they said and more. Even though I had seen enough to convince me, doing this would prove it once and for all. I'd be the crazy weird one, the extreme failure, the different one.

I stopped when my shadow fell on her. The darkness made things oddly easier for me to handle. I took a step back to the doorway and let the dim light come through. "I'm afraid so." I had to look at the floor rather than her face. I felt like I was lying to her, or had lied to her and was just now caught. "Look, you know I couldn't have done this without you. I'd probably still be in a cave looking for my marbles if it weren't for you helping me cope."

"No. Please. Don't try to thank me. It's insulting." She folded her arms and turned away just enough to hide half of her face. "You know I really didn't do anything at all. It was you."

There were frenzied footsteps in the hallway, followed by an insistent pounding on my front door. "Abe! Hey, Abe? Are you in there?" It was Zane. Probably came to kill me. He was the worst assassin in the history of assassins, but he sounded none the worse for wear. "Hey! Abe?"

"What?" I called over my shoulder without taking my eyes off of her.

"Hey, you're home. You're not going to believe this, but it's snowing outside!" He was yelling to be heard through the door, though he didn't need to. He sounded giddy.

"Yeah!" It was Delia. "We stole a bunch of shields from the Roman Gods. Bob set it up—stole 'em from the big castle for us! We're going to use them to go sledding by the river!" Another giddy Imaginary.

"You have to come!" Zane yelled.

"We're going. It's snowing for crying out loud. *Snow*-ing! We'll leave you a sled. Meet us there!" I could hear Delia thump down the hall before she finished her sentence.

Sarah stood up and came to me. "Abe. Your friends are here," she said. "Grab your sled. You don't want to keep them waiting." She touched my arm the way friends do when they don't have anything else to offer. "Please, don't make a big deal about this. Let it go."

I patted her arm and walked toward the front door. I only saw the dimmest outline of her in the low light of the apartment. I opened the front door and picked up the shield that lay in front of it. I didn't want to look back, but it was a reflex, an instinct. I looked back at the bedroom, but when the bright light of the hallway illuminated it, there was no one there. It had been a long time coming, I supposed. It was time to go it alone, for better or worse.

I walked down the hall with the shield weighing heavy in my hands. At the door that led outside, I looked out at the sudden wonderland of white my town had become. There were large light flakes languidly making their way to the already-covered ground. The Council had kept its word. The streets and walks, the grass and buildings were all wearing a light coat of flurries. In the center of town, others had already taken to Zane and Delia's idea and were sledding down whatever incline they could on anything they could find. They used shields, salad bowls, trays, and when all else failed, they used nothing and just went down on their rear ends.

Out of the corner of my eye I saw something move. I had been so enthralled with the weather that I hadn't looked around me when I stepped out the door. Thor was standing just five or six feet to my right. He definitely looked like Thor, at least. Red hair, the works. There were hints of Bob, but not much. His face was pointing up and his eyes were closed loosely. His mouth was open as wide as it could be. He swayed just a little. I thought about trying to sneak away before he opened his eyes so I wouldn't have to have a conversation with him. It seemed like he had done a few nice things for us, though, and the spirit of the new day encouraged me to be cordial. Besides, I was almost positive he had seen me already. "What're you doing?"

"Catching snowflakes," he said.

"Really?"

"Aye."

"Fun?"

"Soothing."

I shook my head knowingly even though he couldn't see me. He was the calmest I had seen him. It was another wonderful note in an unusual afternoon.

"So, you're going to be Thor now?"

"What's to say I can't be both?"

It sounded a little greedy to me, trying to have it all, but at least he was making decisions. And if he ended up with the good traits of both, it wouldn't be a bad thing.

"How long do you think a change of seasons will keep everyone happy?" he asked.

"The novelty will wear off, but it'll give us time to figure things out. It's better than what we had, isn't it?"

"Prettier, at least."

"Definitely prettier," I said. It was nice to have a conversation with him that I didn't feel desperate to get away from. "You know, they have Thursdays on the Otherworld."

He lowered his head to look at me as a snowflake landed on his cheek. "Pardon?"

"Every week they have a day called Thursday. I don't know how it happened, but it was derived from 'Thor's day' long ago."

"I'd forgotten. They still do that?"

"Every single week. Let the others have their stupid planets and cars. You get your name mentioned constantly. It's on every calendar throughout most of the known Otherworld."

"Hmmm…" Thor went blank for a moment, then smiled and tilted his head back again. "Thank you."

"No problem. See you around the office," I said and walked on.

A blanket of activity covered the Hill. Imaginaries swarmed up and then sped down the slope where I thought there'd been a lighthouse, but there was nothing. The thing I'd looked to every day was nothing but another figment of my own imagination. It was gone now, lost in the haze of memories that someone had molded for me.

Out on the incline, there were Gods and Yeti and big-headed Aliens. Lines formed to hurtle down at a speed that would be dangerous to fragile Otherworlders. At the bottom of the slope were others who welcomed those that made it all the way down and jeered the ones who crashed midway. I saw a throng of sleds go down with multiple Imaginaries on each one. The New Year's Babies. Not sure they should've been let out, but it was a new day.

No one seemed to mind that they weren't working.

A small group of Imaginaries came rushing past me with their capes bundled around them. One noticed me and stopped. "Hey! It's him." The rest of them stopped and looked. It was embarrassing. Had I done anything, really? I had once been the nastiest thing on the Hill and could possibly slip back to that state if I wasn't careful. Whatever version of things they had heard, these

Imaginaries didn't seem to mind my dark background, not now, anyway. A small goblin stepped closer than the rest. "Hey." He reached into his cloak and pulled something out. "Would you sign this?" He handed me a pad of wrinkled paper and the nub of a worn-down chewed-on pencil.

I took my time and carefully blocked out each letter: A-B-E. I considered my work for a moment and, satisfied, I started to give it back to him. I had been looking for paper all this time and here it was in my hands, too late to help. I paused to ask him where he got it or how I could get one, just in case the need ever arose again. He abruptly leaned forward and took his pad in one quick swipe. He looked at the signature, such as it was, and leaned back to show his friends, who all said "Ooooo" and giggled. They turned and ran toward the fun. At least I'd managed to steal his pencil. That was something.

The goblin stopped after a few steps and looked at the paper again. He tore off the sheet I wrote on and folded it neatly, then stuffed it in his pocket. With a flick of his wrist the rest of the pad soared through the air and hit me square in the chest. I reached up and grabbed it before it fell. "Keep it," he said. "My wife makes them out of river reeds. I've got tons of them." He took off to catch up with his friends. I waved even though he was no longer looking at me.

Something else hit me right after that, in the side of the head this time–something cold and wet. I cleaned off my face and saw the Tooth Fairy standing nearby, wrapped up in a hat and scarf. With both hands she packed snow and ice into a ball to throw at me. I was thrilled to see her, standing on the Hill with the rest of the Imaginaries. The Council had kept both promises. I wanted to run to her, take hold of her, and bask in her warmth. I also wanted to make sure the white chunks in her snowball were definitely ice and not something else small, white and hard.

She was still smiling that wonderful smile.

In spite of the weather, the gray sky seemed a little brighter. As the flakes fell upon my head like grace notes, I hummed an Otherworld tune to myself. *Something about being all right.*

It was snowing on the Hill.

It never snowed on the Hill.

Acknowledgements

Thank you to the great readers in my family who always pushed me to explore new authors and ideas.

Thank you to the friends throughout the years who encouraged me to be a weirdo whenever possible.

This book would not have been possible without:

- Caffeine
- Music
- Time
- Patience
- Amazing Teachers

About the Author

Each night Matt Betts fills a bathtub full of pop culture and then soaks in it, absorbing it through every pore. It's not pretty. The Ohio native is the author of the speculative poetry collections *Underwater Fistfight* and *See No Evil, Say No Evil*, as well as the novels *Odd Men Out* and *Indelible Ink*. He lives in Columbus with his wife and their two boys.

www.ingramcontent.com/pod-product-compliance
Ingram Content Group UK Ltd.
Pitfield, Milton Keynes, MK11 3LW, UK
UKHW041637190726
13854UKWH00006B/2548

9 781947 879041